Quantum Bridge

By Aaron C. Gord

Layout by Aaron Gord

Aaron Gord
Please feel free to email me at Drognoraa@gmail.com

Printed in the United States of America

First Printing: 2010

This book is dedicated to my wonderful wife and partner, Suzanne.

With her smile, her laugh, and most importantly, her heart, my soul has learned to sing.

Quantum Bridge
Table of Contents

1- "Loss"
2- "The Abyss"
3- "Replay"
4- "Torment"
5- "Darkness"
6- "The Storm"
7- "Outside"
8- "The Spill"
9- "Discovery"
10- "Memory"
11- "Awakening"
12- "Old Friends"
13- "Back Home"
14- "Walls"
15- "Morning"
16- "Learning To Fly"
17- "Out Of Bounds"
18- "Splashdown"
19- "The Cliffs"
20- "A New World"
21- "Captivity"
22- "Searching"
23- "Bound"
24- "Life Hutch"
25- "A New Lease"
26- "Reality Check"
27- "Realization"
28- "Greetings"
29- "Loading Up"
30- "Revelation"
31- "Traveling Buddies"
32- "Coming Clean"
33- "Into The Void"
34- "Last Hope"

35- "The Battle"
36- "Sleep"
37- "The Longest Day"
38- "Parents"
39- "Hero"
40- "Dark Findings"
41- "Goodbye"
42- "New Friends"
43- "Colorado"
44- "Waking The Dead"
45- "Outlander"
46- "Fixer Upper"
47- "Escape"
48- "Into The Frey"
49- "Hitched"
50- "Battle Lines"
51- "Exit Stage Left"
52- "The Meeting"
53- "Desert Dealings"
54- "Reunited"
55- "Sarah"
56- "Your Wish"
57- "Dinner"

"Loss"

John watched as the car pulled slowly away from the curb, knowing his life would never be the same. He stood very still, letting the chill from an autumn breeze penetrate the bare skin of his hands. The car crested a small hill at the end of the street and disappeared from view. Along with it went John's last hope for a normal life. At least that's how he saw it. Everything he had worked for, prayed for, was gone forever.

John's breath slid slowly out of his lungs. He hadn't realized he'd been holding it, clenching it inside his chest for the last minute or so. He turned and headed back toward his empty home. "I guess I won't need a place this big anymore," he said, thinking aloud.

Passing by the rose bushes that lined the steps brought back a flood of memories. His chin began to tremble. Tilting his head back, he stared skyward as tears began to stream down his cheeks. He groped for the handrail and tugged himself up the first step and then the next, his legs protesting with each new exertion. They had said it would be months before he could walk normally again. The cold metal of the railing bit into his hand. His legs wobbled precariously as he struggled to master them. He'd lost control of everything else in his life, and now even his dignity was in jeopardy. His knees gave way as he sank onto the concrete steps, still clenching the railing.

The tears came in earnest.

"The Abyss"

Days passed without number. Neighbors came and went without notice, each one making a trip to the kitchen to drop off a dish of this or that and then offering an uncomfortable "Hello" or "Hi, John" as they stepped quickly past his decaying body on the way back to the door. They couldn't even look him in the eye now. Not that he'd have noticed in his abysmal state. He hadn't bathed for at least a week and hadn't eaten in roughly the same amount of time. Reruns of *Gilligan's Island* and *The Price is Right* became his only friends. At least they offered some escape from his thoughts.

John wondered if he would ever be able to return to the world of the living. He wondered if he wanted to come back to life at all.

"Replay"

The car slid sideways for the briefest of moments before plunging completely off the side of the road. Sarah didn't even have time to scream as they bounced across the ditch and into the dark, snow-covered field. A single thought raced through John's mind as he wrestled with the steering wheel, trying in vain to regain control of the vehicle.

"We'll be alright. We'll be alright."

A split second later, they slammed into the unseen boulder. Maybe it was best that Sarah never saw it coming.

"Torment"

A clinking sound shook John out of a fitful sleep. The remote control had slipped from his lap and landed with a *thunk* on the carpeted floor. John twisted his body around on the couch, trying to reach it without getting up, something he had gotten quite good at over the last few weeks. The problem was that he usually got a cramp somewhere while doing it. *There's nothing worse than getting a cramp when you barely have the will to live anyway,* he thought.

Several grunts later, he managed to reach his hand onto the carpet and started feeling around for the remote.

"If I have to live through another episode of *Happy Days*, I'm definitely going to kill myself," John said aloud. Runt, nestled at the foot of the couch, responded with a series of chirps that sounded surprisingly like "Me too." Runt didn't meow like a normal cat. Of course, there was very little that *was* normal about the large orange ball of fur Sarah had picked up from the pound a few months ago.

John felt around under the couch until he discovered something solid. Unfortunately, it was just the heel of a slipper he'd sloughed off weeks ago. Casually tossing it across the room, he went back to fishing around the floor. This time he came up with a plate, which had something encrusted on its surface.

At least it isn't sticky, he thought.

Finally, he got hold of something that seemed about the right shape. He had to stretch his arm to its limit to reach it, and sure enough, he got a cramp in between his shoulder blades. It was one of those cramps you couldn't get rid of - you just have to suffer through them.

Groaning in pain, John pulled the object up and found that he'd retrieved an old kitchen knife. He let out a heavy sigh and sank back onto the couch, trying to reach the cramp between his shoulders. The task proving nearly impossible, he gave in.

"How could there be so many things lying around on the floor but not the damned remote?" he seethed through his teeth.

Giving up on the cramp, he started to examine the kitchen knife. It was one of those Ginsu knives with the highly publicized, perpetually sharp blade. John ran his thumb across its edge and to his surprise, found it to be quite sharp. A thin red line appeared along the tip of this thumb. He watched, expressionless, as a little droplet of blood welled up at the edge of the cut. It grew to the size of a BB and then ran slowly down over the fingerprint and into the small crevices in his skin, coming to a halt in the middle of his palm. He hadn't even felt the cut. *The knife must be incredibly sharp*, he thought.

Runt watched from the foot of the couch as if sensing something was wrong. John stared at him for a moment, then placed the edge of the blade against his left wrist. The light from the chandelier flashed off the blade as he turned it this way and that, imaging what angle would be best and least painful. This would certainly be a way out for him. No more hurting, no more suffering. Of course, it would make a hell of a mess of the couch and the front room. And who would find him? It would probably be Mrs. Weggly. That would be all she needed. After all the help she'd given him, this would be how he would repay her. That old woman had lost everyone who had ever mattered to her, but she still kept going. Sarah had had an attitude like that too.

More tears now.......

"Darkness"

The picture frame had been one of her favorites — a wrought iron outer rim attached to a metal frame with words of hope and love inscribed. "I always remember, Memories, Times together" – these and other sayings surrounded a picture of Sarah. She was smiling in that way she had, just a little crooked but charming nonetheless.

It had been a beautiful autumn day late in the season, and they had gone for a long hike to see the fall colors at a local state park. John had taken his camera with him to get some shots for the paper. Sarah was in rare form, being silly and tossing leaves and twigs at him. They'd tangled a few times, wrestling around on the dry grass alongside the trail. She was always so playful, he remembered, so full of life and so in love with him. He had asked her to marry him that day and had snapped a quick photo of her reaction—a look of bewilderment quickly replaced by pure joy. That's the image John caught, that perfect moment now frozen in time.

It was one of her most cherished photographs. She looked for days to find just the right frame for it. Sarah always made everything so special. John never knew that a photograph or a frame could mean so much to someone until he met Sarah. She had a heart like no other, and he was amazed by her ability to find something wonderful in everyday moments – the words to a song, the warmth of sunlight streaming through an open window on a Sunday morning. She was so firmly rooted in the present, not thinking two years or even two days ahead. Sarah had said, "I don't know what tomorrow holds, and I don't want to know, I just want to live right now, this instant."

Living with Sarah had been a fantastic experience. John had always planned for and worried about what was to come, wondering if he should switch jobs, wondering if he was wasting his life. He was always concerned about getting to places on time, about what people thought of him. She had been like a breath of fresh air right when he needed it most, a bright ray of sunshine piercing his ever-darkening clouds. Yes, that photograph had captured the essence of Sarah, not just the smile or the spark in her green eyes, but the very soul itself.

John slid his fingers along the edge of the frame and stared out the window. A dark storm front was just starting to appear on the horizon. They were calling for a blizzard of historic proportions. He remembered only a few months ago Sarah quoting the Farmer's Almanac, which was predicting a severe winter. None of this seemed to matter now.

He set the picture down slowly and pulled himself up from the chair, the sudden weight on his broken legs sent a wave of pain through him great enough to make him clench his teeth. He'd forgotten that he wasn't supposed to sit for more than an hour at a time; the bones wouldn't heal properly unless he kept some weight on them. He reached for the walker that he had become so familiar with over the past weeks and eased himself forward, allowing his arms to carry some of the load. The doctor had said not to rely on it too heavily, but in his current mental state, John had little strength to put into his recovery. He could walk without the metal contraption, but the effort was too much to ask of him. He slid the legs of the walker before him with each painful step. At least the hardwood floors made his shuffling easier. It was ironic that they'd been thinking of carpeting the whole house just a month or two ago.

John worked his way into the kitchen and flipped the switch for the overhead light. The fluorescent bulb sputtered to life with an audible hum. The wood floor creaked as he moved across it. When he reached the refrigerator door, John realized that it hadn't taken him much effort. Perhaps his body was healing even without his help or his will.

The refrigerator was stuffed full of plates and dishes; each one still neatly covered in plastic wrap. Though he'd been unable to eat for days, the food was now starting to look better to him. The mind may be suffering, but the body goes on. The persistent rumble in his stomach convinced him that it was time to give in. He wasn't going just to fade away, regardless of how much he wanted to do so. Since the accident, he'd gotten weaker with each passing day. The accident had claimed his wife Sarah and his unborn child, but it hadn't taken him, no matter how much he wished it had.

Runt wandered into the kitchen while John stared blankly into the refrigerator. He let out a handful of chirps and clicks to get John's attention. John didn't think he'd ever heard Runt make a "normal" sound. Unfortunately for Runt, he'd been a bit remiss in taking care of him since the accident. He looked down as Runt circled his legs and pawed at the walker.

"You must be starving," John said, realizing how much time had passed since the last time he'd fed the cat. Runt responded by poking his head into the fridge, pushing his nose into one of the covered plates.

"You hungry for that, little guy?" John asked, reaching for a plate filled with roasted chicken. Neighbors had been bringing food by all week. Mrs. Weggly from next door had been helping out by rotating the untouched plates to positions in front of the newer ones. She had a little system going so that John would know what would spoil first. She had told him, "No sense in getting Salmonella on top of everything else." She had been a great help in the last many days, keeping the place up when John didn't have the ability to help out.

Mrs. Weggly had lost her husband over ten years ago and had lived alone ever since. Now in her seventies, she was spry as ever, planting, gardening, and playing bridge with her friends. John wondered how she had lived through the loss of her husband. They had never had any children and had done everything together. But she seemed to get along very well. Maybe she was more firmly rooted in each day than he was. That was a virtue he was never able to pick up from Sarah. Maybe Mrs. Weggly hadn't given as much of herself to her relationship as John had to his. Whatever the case, John was glad to have her there, even if he wasn't able to tell her so.

Runt's squeaking voice brought John back to the moment. Those big black staring eyes reminded him that somebody still needed his attention.

The plate felt cold as he carried it. He wasn't able to use his walker and hold the dish at the same time. Carefully putting one foot in front of the other, he made his way across the kitchen and set the plate on the counter top. The smell of cooked chicken filled the air as he peeled back the plastic. Within seconds, Runt began making a barking noise, a strange sound to hear coming from a cat. He circled around John's legs, bumping time and again into his casts. A week ago, this would have sent him through the roof with pain, but now it was just a mild discomfort.

Healing, John thought, *Must be healing up.*

John retrieved a paper plate from the large stack Mrs. Weggly had left and placed several chunks of chicken on it. Runt, wild with anticipation, jumped onto the counter (where he knew he was not allowed to be) and began wolfing down the chicken in massive gulps. Small bits of bird flesh flew from his mouth in a fashion resembling the African lions of the veldt.

"I guess you're not terribly far removed from your cousins, are ya, little tiger?" John said while watching the spectacle. As if in response, Runt looked up from his quarry, piping loudly.

"O.K., O.K., I'll leave you alone then!" John chuckled. As Runt went back to eating, John grabbed a few pieces of chicken for himself and eased into a chair at the kitchen table.

Sinking his teeth into the first bite, he realized just how hungry he was. He began stuffing in the meat in his mouth as though he were starving.

"Another good sign, I suppose," he mumbled to himself between bites. He was ravenous, finishing the chicken in a few mouthfuls. Swallowing the last bite, he looked over and found Runt finishing off his last scraps and licking the plate.

The effort to waddle back to the refrigerator didn't seem so bad this time now that he had a reason to do so. Opening the door again and again, removing plate after plate of food, and sampling his way through each one made John feel alive. It was as though he'd never eaten before. Runt was glad to help out with whatever scraps John was willing to throw down to him, gobbling up everything from roast beef to pumpkin pie. The two sat for an hour nosing through nearly all of the plates.

"I'm sure this will surprise Mrs. Weggly, eh Runt?" John

sputtered over a mouthful of green bean casserole.

After the feast, John and Runt headed into the family room to lie down for a nap. Bellies stretched almost to bursting; the two curled up on the couch. Runt mashed himself against John's stomach. He was always ready for a nap. They slept for hours.

A deep, dreamless sleep.

A healing sleep.

"The Storm"

A howling wind roused John. Runt awoke at nearly the same time and began licking his chops, making a loud smacking sound. He pawed at his face, no doubt still detecting remnants from the afternoon's feast. The howling wind sent a shiver through John. In response, he snuggled deeper into the folds of the soft leather couch. It had gotten dark outside, and he wondered how long he'd been asleep. A glance at the clock over the fireplace showed just after three P.M.

"Why's it so dark out, Runtster?" John asked the cat. Runt stared blankly at him as cats are known to do when posed with a question. Fumbling for the remote that he'd finally found buried in between the cushions, he turned on the T.V. and tuned to a local weather channel. The weatherman was dancing excitedly back and forth from one map to the next, pointing out large fuzzy sections moving ever closer with each sweep of the radar.

"Uh oh," John said to Runt. "Looks like a big one."

The meteorologist was hurriedly calling out snowfall depths all over the area. John turned up the volume and settled in to hear the report. "Four to six inches already in Jackson, and we're expecting at least a foot by nightfall," the weatherman crowed. The screen flashed to a wider viewpoint. From the looks of it, the storm might last for days. A good part of the country stood to be blanketed by it. Another screen popped up showing the ultimate snowfall expectations of the meteorological crew. "...Looks like we can count on another several feet of the white stuff before this is all over," squawked the weatherman. John hated it when they called snow "the white stuff." It was one of those clichés that everyone overused.

"What's wrong with snow, Runt? Hmmm? What's wrong with just saying snow?" Runt, unimpressed by John's smug expression, jumped off the couch and headed toward the kitchen.

"Well if you're gonna act like that, just see if I invite YOU to the next feed!" John shouted after him. Runt didn't even turn around.

"Outside"

The next few days passed quickly and with them came the promised winter storm. Even though John hated to admit it, the weather folks had been right. A two-foot thick blanket of snow covered the entire area. John and Runt had continued their eating spree, and both were much better off for it. John had begun making regular trips to the bathroom once again and was starting to thicken up a little. Runt, for his part, had put on a pound or two as well.

John sat digging the blunt end of a ballpoint pen under the edge of one of his casts while Runt batted at his fingers.

"I'm not playing, Runt, I'm itching! God, you have no idea how much I'm itching!" The doctors had told him that the itching was a good sign – it meant that he was healing properly. All he knew was that it was driving him crazy.

After digging at the cast for a bit, John got to his feet and shuffled to the front door. He pressed his nose against one of the glass plates and was temporarily blinded by the bright white light reflecting off the deep snow outside. Swinging the door open, he sucked in a long breath of cold air. It was invigorating. Gazing through eyes reduced to slits by the brightness, John observed a world transformed. The snow covered everything, the neighbor's cars, and mailboxes, even the houses. The whole area looked like something from a fairy tale.

Across the street, Mrs. Weggly stepped out onto her porch.

"Hello, Mrs. Weggly!" John yelled across to her. She looked over, craning her neck and covering her eyes with one hand.

"Hello, John!" She called back. "Feeling better?"

John peered around him again, letting the wondrous landscape soak in for a moment more, then said, "Much better, Mrs. Weggly, much better!"

She smiled and nodded her head. "I'll try to bring you something to eat in a bit as soon as I get dug out!"

"Oh, don't bother, there's still plenty in the fridge," John said, waving her away.

Turning around, he headed back inside, wondering how anyone would be able to dig a path through snow that deep anyway. He had visions of Mrs. Weggely digging a trench taller than her, flinging shovel after shovel of snow out over her head. The idea made him laugh out loud. That was a sound he hadn't heard for a long time.

"The Spill."

The sound of the phone ringing sent John shuffling back inside. "Now, where is that damn thing?" He hadn't had a call in weeks and had no idea where he had left the phone. Hobbling around the room, he began tossing old newspapers and unread mail off end tables and chairs. It was amazing how much junk had accumulated in the last couple of months. It was also amazing how much better his legs were doing considering his condition. He'd been eating pretty well for the last few days. *Perhaps that's what's made the difference*, he thought.

The ringing continued for what seemed like a lifetime while John scrambled around, cursing and throwing random objects about the kitchen before making his way into the family room. "It's got to be here somewhere!" he exclaimed, perplexed by how hard it was to find a device that was so incessantly calling out to be found. John stood still, concentrating with all the strength he could muster.

"Ah ha! I have you now, you rat!" he bellowed, hopping back toward the kitchen. Rounding the corner, he spotted the phone hanging on the wall in its cradle exactly where he had left it.

"Damn, you idiot!" he huffed, cursing himself. Both legs tinged a bit in pain as he thumped across the floor, arms stretched out before him, looking like the mummy from one of those old black and white movies. His eyes narrowed as he approached the object, which continued to sing shrilly. He wondered, "How long can that thing ring?" Apparently, the answering machine was turned off, or it certainly would have picked up by now.

He was almost within reach of the phone when he stepped in something squishy. A thick liquid seeped through his sock instantly, squeezing up between his toes.

"Runnnnt!!!!" John started to scream, but his outburst was cut short. As his foot slid out from underneath him, he lurched sideways toward the basement door. The portal was latched and closed tight. He slammed into it hard, and to his surprise rent the bolt right out of the wooden frame. The door swung in toward the basement as he pitched headlong down the stairs. Halfway through his tumble, John caught a glimpse of Runt standing in the basement doorway watching his decent.

I'll kill that damn cat! was all he could think. *If I live through this, I swear I'll kill him*!

"Discovery"

A pounding on the front door brought John back to consciousness. He was lying flat on his back on the basement floor just a few feet from the stairway. His breathing felt heavy, and he wondered if he'd suffered some internal injuries from the fall.

The world around him came slowly into a focus as he opened his eyes. The ceiling swayed and twisted until he had to close them again to keep from feeling sick. He lay very still, trying to figure out just how much damage had been done to his body. He wiggled his shoulders a bit and flexed each one up and down off the stone floor. Other than feeling very stiff, they seemed OK. His arms were fine. Turning his legs over and back without any undue pain showed that his extremities seemed all right, but the crushing weight he felt on his chest worried him. Hazarding another bout with the spinning world, he gently opened his eyes. Things had slowed down a little, and his focus was sharper. Tilting his head forward, John tried to get a look at the rest of his body. An orangeish, blurry lump was protruding from his chest.

"Oh my God.... Oh my God," He panted.

His mind raced while trying to imagine what he may have hit or landed on while falling down the stairs. Or was this matter protruding from his chest some crushed vital organ that would soon fail and send him to the afterlife?

John had gathered a deep breath to call out for help when something strange happened. A raspy tongue raked softly up his chin. He lifted his head and found himself gazing into Runt's green eyes. The cat was perched on John's chest and had scooted up so close to his face that he could smell the chicken scraps on his feline breath. From this close, Runt's features were distorted, as though John were looking at him through a wide-angle lens. And though his name was Runt, he was by no means small. In fact, the name was a misnomer. The cat was easily 20 pounds and looked more like a sausage than a house cat.

The pounding on the front door was now interspersed with a frantic call. "John! John! You OK?" John recognized the voice, but couldn't quite place it.

"Well, this is just great!" he thought. After all, he'd lived through in the last month, and he was going to die from a fall down the stairs. And even worse, it would be with help only seconds away at the front door.

Runt let out an entire sentence of chirps and squeaks then turned to look back up the stairs as if to tell John that someone was at the door. An entire gambit of emotions ran through John's mind. The first was a desire to murder Runt in cold blood. But that was quickly replaced by the relief of realizing he wasn't going to die, not immediately at least.

Grabbing Runt under his front legs, John lifted the chunky cat off his chest and plopped him down on the floor beside him. By this time the pounding on the front door had turned into a panicked drum roll.

John rolled onto his side and pushed himself into a sitting position. His head swam with the effort, and he could feel his heartbeat thudding in the back of his head. Reaching around, he found a large bump protruding from the base of his skull.

"That's gonna hurt for a while," he slurred under his breath. He had no sooner than gotten to his knees when the pounding on the front door stopped. But the noise didn't stop for long. Seconds later, there came a loud thump followed almost immediately by another, and then finally by a crashing, splintering sound. John, who had managed to grab the basement stairway's handrail, fell back onto his hands and knees and finally, with his head swimming, fell prostrate to the basement floor.

"Memory"

Sarah walked a few steps ahead of John, but even after all these years together, he had an idea of what that meant. She was lost in her own thoughts. He had known Sarah to get that way sometimes. After having a bad day or when something was weighing heavy on her mind, she would just drift off, even if she was in a room crowded with other people.

"So, how was work today, Sweetie?" John asked. No answer. "Did you talk to your boss about that position you put in for?" he tried again. And again, there was no response.

She walked with her arms folded across her chest, head hung low, just far enough ahead to keep John from reaching her, far enough to keep him from touching her shoulder, her hair. It was obvious she wasn't looking for consolation. John always struggled with how to deal with her when she was in one of these moods. She would just clam up, saying nothing. Luckily, it didn't happen very often. They usually had a wonderful knack for communication. But occasionally, when too many lines got crossed, things would break down. Even then, however, they were still talking, just not with words. Body language would be enough. Unfortunately for John, the issue that caused the breakdown was many times of his own doing. Something stupid that he'd said or done without thinking had hurt her feelings. The real issue would come out soon enough. But for right now, he would just have to wait until she felt ready to talk about it.

They walked on a while longer in mutual silence. The last of the snow had finally melted, and tiny buds were just starting to appear on the trees and bushes along the trail. John gazed at them with excitement. *I really need to come back here and get some shots of these for the paper,* he couldn't help thinking. Even though he knew Sarah was upset about something, it was hard not to take note of the explosion of life all around him. Spring was one of his favorite times of the year. But something just wasn't right about their walk today. Nothing that John could put his finger on, but something felt amiss.

Sarah marched on, maintaining her sullen pace, occasionally glancing down in front of her. John began to wonder if she was holding something. They would sometimes bring Runt along on their hikes. He was one of those cats that just loved to be held. He'd nestle up into your neck and purr like a small outboard motor. And he never had any desire to leap from your arms and chase after a bird or a bug. He was perfectly happy just to be along for the ride.

John decided that he needed to make a move. The two had just reached an outcropping of rock that they both really loved and from where you could overlook much of the town. On a cloudless day, you could see nearly to the lake, and there was always a gentle breeze blowing, bringing with it all the scents of the forest.

"Sarah?" John said, reaching out for her. "Can you tell me what's wrong?" he asked. She took a few more steps out onto the tip of the outcropping then stopped. John halted several steps behind her, still holding out his hand. He watched her there, hair gently swaying in the evening air like waves rippling on the surface of the ocean. Sarah loved the water. Standing in the tide as it washed over her bare feet, she said it felt like going home.

John waited silently as she peered down for a moment, then started to turn. Time seemed to slow in that instant as she bent her face toward him. He followed her gaze as it traveled away from his face to the object cradled in her arms. John looked on at first in bewilderment, then in wonder. Sarah cradled a newborn baby girl close to her chest. He knew that it was their child. His eyes widened, jaw hanging slack as the breath was drawn out of his lungs. Sarah looked up at him and smiled a gentle, caring smile. The same smile she would use when she'd tell him that she loved him. John met her gaze and, trembling, began to reach out his hand toward her once again. In an instant, the vision dissolved before his eyes. Sarah began to glow like a torch in the darkness. Tears sprang from John's eyes as she rose from the earth and ascended toward the heavens like an angel. She became a beacon in the night sky, rising higher and higher until finally, she disappeared in a bright flash. John dropped to his knees.

"NOOO!" he screamed, his arms reaching out into the darkness above him.

"NOOO!" he wailed again, this time trailing off into a desperate, trembling sob.

"Awakening"

"John! John! Wake up!" Chuck exclaimed while violently shaking John's limp body. John launched himself into a sitting position on the couch, his eyes searching widely around the room.

"Sarah! Sarah!" he called out.

Chuck grabbed him by the shoulders and held him firm.

"She's gone, John, she's gone! You were having a dream, man, you were just dreaming!" Chuck roared while squeezing John's shoulders harder.

"I found you at the bottom of the basement steps. You'd hit your head or something, you've been out for hours," he added.

John's breathing came in gasps as he tried to take in his surroundings. Everything seemed unfamiliar to him. The dream had been so real. His face was wet with tears. Those at least had been real. Wiping his eyes with the back of his sleeve, he sniffed hard, trying to clear up his running nose. Chuck released his grip and leaned back, eyeing him cautiously in case he had another spell. John could see the concern in his friend's eyes and tried to master his emotions, at least for Chuck's sake.

"I'm O.K., I'm O.K.," he said between pants. "Damn, Chuck. It was so real."

The two spent a much-needed moment in silence. Chuck stood up and wandered around the room, examining the knick-knacks on the mantle while John composed himself. He wiped his face with the front of his shirt and blew his nose into a dirty sock that had been lying at the end of the couch. The filthy state of John's house didn't bother Chuck at all since he lived in a pigsty himself. It had been a running joke between the two of them that every time John would visit, Chuck's place seemed worse. And every time he'd visit, John thought it couldn't get any worse. But it always did.

Chuck was a bachelor. Not so much because he wanted to be, but because he had never found the right girl. He'd had a handful of relationships but had always come out on the losing end. John thought that Chuck would make a great partner for someone someday, but he was certainly a diamond in the rough—a rather rough diamond, at that.

"So, what the hell you been up to, John?" Chuck blurted out suddenly. Apparently, he'd decided this crying business had gone on long enough. John was happy to have the awkward silence broken as well.

"Well, let's see.... I lost my wife, YOU IDIOT!" John yelled. "What the hell have YOU been up to?"

Chuck sniffed, gazed around the room for a moment then replied, "Nothin'." Another brief moment of silence passed as John rolled himself off the couch and stood to face Chuck. The pounding at the back of his head returned, but he endured it by gritting his teeth. In a moment, the worst of it had passed, and he let out a deep sigh.

Chuck meandered his way around the room and was now standing just a few feet inside the foyer with his back to the front door. The two stared across the room at each other, momentarily speechless. John tilted his head to the side, trying to get a better look at the door that stood six or so feet behind Chuck. A sliver of light was creeping in along the jam. The whole thing looked rather whopper-jawed. The hardware at the hinges had been pulled clean out of the wooden frame and lay scattered about the floor.

John wrinkled his brow and stretched his neck out questioningly toward Chuck who was standing there with a dim-witted look on his face. With his hands jammed into his blue jeans and wearing a red and white sweatshirt, he appeared much like a medium-sized human rocket-pop. John's eyes widened as he watched the crack in the jam grow larger and larger until at last the door, slowly at first, then with ever increasing speed, fell inward. It slapped against the floor just behind Chuck's feet with a loud *Thwump!* Chuck just stood there as if nothing had happened. John stared at him through half-closed eyelids, the corner of his mouth twisting up into a wry smirk. "Ya hungry?" he drawled.

After patching the door back to its hinges, the two walked into the kitchen. Chuck eyed the dirty plates and utensils strewn about the table and countertops with an approving eye.

"Damn, John, looks like my place."

Chuck cleaned off a spot at the table while John ambled around the kitchen. John offered a rather dirty looking pot in Chuck's direction. "Coffee?"

"Sure," Chuck said while eyeing the vessel's coffee-stained exterior. Maybe this level of uncleanliness was a little too much, even for him.

"You seem to be getting around pretty well," he added.

John hadn't noticed until now, but his legs really were coming along nicely. The itching under his casts had subsided, and he was moving about without any help from his walker. It was still a bit of a shuffling motion, but nonetheless, he was mobile. There wasn't much pain, either. Or maybe the ache from the lump on the back of his head was just blocking out everything else.

John filled the percolator with water and tossed a few tablespoons of ground beans into the filter basket.

"Now that's not some of that frou-frou coffee, is it?" Chuck asked, raising his nose ever so slightly.

"I don't drink crap," John said, flatly back to him.

A smile stretched across Chuck's face wide enough to swallow his own head. Watching John stagger around the filthy kitchen wearing an old, dirty pink housecoat, casts on both legs, and holding a ratty looking coffee maker in his hand while talking aloofly about "not drinking crap" struck him as funny.

"What?" John spat, noticing Chuck's silly expression.

"Oh how the mighty have fallen," Chuck returned, still smiling.

John didn't say a word. He just turned his back, plopped the coffee maker down on the counter, and plugged it in.

Soon the house was filled with the scent of fresh brewed

Highlander Grog. John grabbed a cheese ball out of the refrigerator and pulled a box of crackers from the cupboard, bringing them both to the table. Tossing a bag of plastic silverware down in front of Chuck, he quipped, "Eat up!"

Chuck didn't miss a beat. He was used to eating less than healthy meals. Grabbing a plastic knife, he ripped into a sleeve of crackers and started gobbling them down. John poured two cups of coffee into large green plastic glasses.

"They're the only things that are clean," he said as he offered the steaming brew to Chuck.

"So, it looks like your legs are coming along O.K.," Chuck said in between bites of a cracker smothered in cheese ball.

"Yeah, seems like it. They barely even hurt at all," John said, stirring creamer into his glass.

"How long's it been since we talked last, John?"

"I don't know, probably at least a couple of months. You were out of town on that job when everything happened here," John said, looking down into his glass.

"That's right. Must have been two, two and a half months, I'd guess. Well, I'm really sorry about everything, man. I wish I'd have known and could have been available. No one got in touch with me, or I might have been able to get back earlier."

"There's nothing you could have done anyway, Chuck. I was such a mess with the arrangements and my legs and all that, I probably wouldn't have even known you were here."

"Still," Chuck offered, "I still wish I could have been here."

An awkward silence hung between them for a moment. John knew Chuck was not one to get emotional or show how he was feeling too easily. He'd been brought up that way. His father was one of those "Real men don't cry" guys, and unfortunately, some of that had rubbed off on him. Luckily, his Mom was just the opposite, so Chuck turned out as an interesting genetic mix of the two – at times he was all staunch and manly, but he could let a little bit of the squishiness show through when it really mattered. It seemed to be a pretty good combination in the end.

"So, how the hell did you get here?" John asked, breaking the silence. "The snows gotta be two feet deep out there."

"Well, actually," Chuck started, leaning back and crossing one leg over the other in an authoritative, experienced sort of way, "you can get through just about anything if you have the right equipment."

John took the bait.

"And what type of equipment might that be?" he asked, shaking his head back and forth.

Chuck winked at him and said, "Well, let's go take a look-see."

Chuck was one of those "new car every year" types, and it seemed that lately, each new vehicle was more expensive and more exotic than the last. Chuck's job and lack of any monetary drains such as a family or even a house payment allowed him to indulge in some pretty pricey toys. The two wandered back through the front room and tugged on their winter coats. Chuck had a silly grin on his face before he even opened the front door.

John was sitting on a short bench in the foyer, pulling his boots on over his casts when Chuck cracked the broken front door open. A cold but refreshing blast of air swirled in from outside. John couldn't help but feel invigorated as the icy air slid down into his lungs. A smile broke across his face in anticipation as he looked up from his task to see a bright yellow Hummer parked in a snowdrift outside.

"I did have to get little bigger tires, though," Chuck admitted.

To John's eyes, they appeared huge. The monster was sitting right next to his snowed in Honda. Other than the fact that they both had four wheels, they couldn't have been more different.

"Chuck, those tires are taller than my car!" John exclaimed, unable to take his eyes off the behemoth. "It's gigantic!" he blurted out again. "What kind of gas mileage does it get?"

Chuck shook his head and said, "You just have to take the fun out of everything, don't ya, John Boy."

Chuck knew how much John hated to be called John Boy. It was a name that he got called in school when he was younger.

But John could hardly be angry. Sometimes your closest friends are the ones you let get away with the most.

"I have to get my camera for this one," John said, stepping over to the mantle where he kept one of his many camera bags. "This one's great for walkabouts, or *driveabouts* as it may be." He chuckled.

The two stepped onto the porch. John looked a fright, still wearing his pink robe underneath the heavy winter jacket. His boots hung open around his ankles, too small to snap tight around his casts. Chuck looked him up and down for a second and then said, "I guess we'll just have to keep you in the car then."

John raised his eyebrows and shook his head side to side. "What? What are you talking about?"

But by the time he finished his sentence, Chuck was already down the steps of the porch. John followed at a slightly more gingerly pace, still feeling a little unsure about the newfound stability of his mending legs.

The truck was enormous. John had to admit that something deep down inside of him found it incredibly cool. He started having fantasies of showing up at work in the monster truck, maybe even using it to run over the boss's little red Miata.

"It would probably crush it flat," he said, eyes staring blankly off into the distance.

"What's that?" Chuck called back from his digging.

"Nothing, nothing at all," John said as he started toward the truck again.

Chuck hauled himself up into the cab and unlocked the passenger door. John grabbed the door handle that stood almost at his eye level and pulled the door open slowly. The thing was built like a tank. Now, with the door open, John could see the height he would have to scale to get into the seat.

"A-hmmm!" he snorted while poking a gloved hand out to Chuck.

"Oh, sorry, mi lady," Chuck said as he reached across and grabbed hold of John's hand.

He gave him a pull and hauled him into the front seat. Again,

John was surprised at how little pain he had while stepping into the truck.

His eyes wandered over the dashboard. It was functional, but still attractive, in a tough sort of way. Chuck stuck the key in the ignition, turned it, and the creature came to life with a rumble.

"V8," Chuck said, leering at John.

"But, of course, what else is there?" John responded with mock enthusiasm.

Chuck slipped the gear shift into reverse and goosed the gas pedal. The truck lurched backward, dislodging itself from the snowdrift instantly. He backed it around until it was pointing toward the street.

"You sure you're on the driveway?" John asked.

Once again, Chuck just smiled. Popping the shifter into drive, he stomped on the gas. For its size, the Hummer moved pretty well. It leapt forward through the snow as easily as if it were out on the open road.

Out on the street, the snow was not nearly as deep. The plows had been through at least once, so the going was much easier. Nevertheless, there were no other cars on the road. This was strictly monster truck territory.

"Wanna go any place in particular?" Chuck asked.

"Nah, just cruise around a bit. I'd love to see how many people are snowed in," John said. "Maybe I can get a few shots of them waving from their windows begging to be helped."

"You're actually quite sadistic, aren't you, John?" Chuck asked. John just smiled in response.

The vehicle was amazing. The giant tires and four-wheel-drive made quick work of the snowy roads. John, who at first had been a bit worried about getting stuck, quickly realized that it would take something more than a couple of feet of snow to stop this machine.

The two drove toward downtown. John lived on the outskirts of a relatively small village; just over three thousand people lived in or close to Jackson.

Watching the snow-covered countryside pass by from the passenger seat reminded John of why he had come to live here in the first place. He had been lucky enough to get the job as Photographer slash Reporter slash Editor for the local paper. It seemed at times that he pretty much had to run the place by himself. He didn't mind, though. For the first time in his life, he felt at home. The corporate world had been rough. Too much politics and too little actual work getting done. Lots of busy, de-humanizing tasks that went essentially nowhere, but made a few fat cats look good.

When he and Sarah had decided to make their break from the real world and come to Jackson, it was the best thing they could have done. They both loved the small town feeling, getting to know their neighbors, and just plain slowing down. John remembered how, after just that first week in town, he felt like he could breathe again. Sure, there were schedules to keep in Jackson as well, but he also had a sense of purpose. The work he did here made sense to him. That was something he could never have said about his job in the city. They hadn't had to move far from their home in the sprawling urban center to get away, either. A mere forty miles was enough.

The two rounded the corner into town. John began pointing out the various buildings and establishments that Jackson had to offer.

"That's the paper," John said, pointing toward an old brick two-story building. "If you look up there on the corner you can see my office." He pointed at the upper right corner of the building where an old computer monitor could be seen through the window.

"Doesn't look too bad to me," Chuck said. "At least you get some natural light throughout the day. I have to stay down in a pit for the most part. You never know where they're gonna stick me."

Chuck worked as a consultant for a major high tech support company. They were always sending him out to work on this job or that, usually fixing system problems that no one else could figure out. The idea of doing that kind of work made

John shudder. It was nearly the same type of stuff he had done before he decided to ditch it all and become a photographer. He had come home from work one day exhausted and upset and told Sarah that he wanted to change his life. "Sure," she said, surprising him. "If you think it will make you happy, then let's do it," she said, reaching out for his hand. He remembered how much her concern for his happiness had meant to him.

"John," Chuck said, reaching over and poking him on the shoulder, snapping him back to the present.

"Hmm? What's up?" John said.

"You just kind of disappeared there for a minute."

"Sorry, just remembering some stuff about when we first moved here."

"That was a good time for you wasn't it, John?"

"Sure was… It sure was," John said, trailing off again.

The two drove on for another few minutes in relative silence. The roads weren't nearly as bad here as they had been by John's house. Chuck started looking for drifts and chunks of snow in the road to smash into or run through, bringing a smile back to John's face.

"You're really just some kind of maniac, aren't you?" he said.

Chuck's only answer was to veer into yet another snowdrift.

"You'd better be careful. When all the snow melts and they find that there are no mailboxes left on this road, you know who they're going to come looking for?" John warned.

"Not me!" Chuck said, grinning. "I don't live here!"

They drove on for a while longer, busting snow drifts whenever possible. John stared out the window for the most part while Chuck turned down this road, then the next, looking for more adventurous terrain. The time they spent in the car was somehow good for John. Even though they weren't speaking much, just being with another human was having a healing effect on him.

They journeyed on until Chuck began to approach a rather treacherous looking fork in the road, the kind of bend that could get you into trouble if you weren't paying close attention.

Chuck slowed down to a crawl and asked John, "Which way you wanna go from here? Or do you wanna go back and find something *real* to eat for lunch? I think I saw a McDonald's back there in town."

After several seconds with no reply, Chuck looked over at John. He was staring intently at the "Y" in the road in front of them.

"John, you OK?" he asked.

John sat very still and silent. Chuck knew there was something going on.

"This is where it happened," he whispered at last.

Before thinking, Chuck asked, "What happened? What are you talking about?" But just as quickly, he understood.

Chuck pulled the truck over to the side of the road, sensing that this seemed like the right thing to do. John was staring down both legs of the road in front of him.

"If we had just turned left that night. If we'd just turned left and gone to her parents, none of this would have happened."

The silence was palpable. The two sat staring out the front window of the truck as plumes of white exhaust wafted about in the cold February air.

"Isn't it amazing the difference a second can make, Chuck, even a split second?" John said without lifting his gaze from the road outside.

"You ever hear what happened that night? Did you see it in the paper or anything? Probably not, since you don't live around here. It was one of those crisp winter evenings. Kind of like today, but without all the snow. There was a bit of ice though, just enough anyway." A painful smile turned up the corner of John's mouth.

Chuck shifted the truck into park, listening to his friend's story.

"Sarah and I were heading to Lafayette for dinner and a movie. She wanted to go to her parents for dinner, but I wasn't really up for a visit. I liked to have her all to myself as much as I could, especially on the weekends. That was our time.

You know what I mean? When the two of us could just hang out together and not have to worry about what was going on at work or getting up early."

John continued speaking, his words spilling out in a monotone voice, trancelike. Chuck didn't interrupt with the usual "Hmms" or "Uh huh's" that someone would normally use when listening to a story. He knew this recounting was more for John's sake than his own.

"We took off just before 5:30. Figured we could still make the matinee and then get dinner afterward. Sarah was wearing that frilly scarf that I'd bought her for last Christmas. She really loved that silly thing. She just had to go back and buy the matching hat and gloves at the after Christmas sale. She wore that getup everywhere if it was even remotely cold." John smiled.

"We were headed down this road that night, just like you and I are now. We came to this very same fork, and I started to turn right. Sarah was telling me a joke that she'd heard at work. She was turned sideways in the passenger seat and was waving her hands around, poking her gloved fingers in the air this way and that as she told the story. I was laughing out loud as we rounded the bend. I was driving too fast, caught up in the moment, I guess. I wasn't paying close enough attention to the road. It happened so quickly. We hit a little patch of ice and started to skid. I remember Sarah stopped talking all of a sudden as the tires lost their grip." John swallowed hard, a lump forming in his throat.

"The car slid off the road like it was on butter. We were probably going like forty or fifty miles an hour. Somehow it didn't seem like we would really get hurt. I remember thinking that we'd just get bounced around a bit. It's strange what goes through your mind when something like that happens. You know, you really don't have any idea how fragile you are until something like that happens." John paused for a second, staring unblinkingly out the front window, then reached for the door handle.

Cracking the door open, he slid out of the seat and down onto the snow packed road. Chuck clicked on the hazard lights and stepped out of the car to follow him. The two made their way to the ditch on the left side of the road just down from the fork on the right. Chuck followed a dozen paces behind John, giving him some space. About sixty feet down from the bend, John stepped off the road and into the ditch. He began trudging through the knee-deep snow, poking this way and that with his feet. Chuck stood back, letting the scene unfold. Finally, John found what he'd been looking for. He bent over and thrust his hands into the snow, pushing handfuls to the left and right. A few seconds later, Chuck saw the edge of a large boulder appear. He walked over and started helping John undercover the rock. It was immense, easily three feet tall and a half dozen feet long.

"This thing must weigh tons," Chuck said aloud.

John's response was slow in coming.

"We hit this boulder as we slid off the road, Chuck. Now you tell me, what the hell's the chance of that happening? The one damn thing alongside the road for miles, and we hit it!" John roared as he waved his hands, indicating the entire length of the thoroughfare.

"Anywhere else, Chuck, anywhere else and we'd have just slid off into the field. Anywhere else! How's that for dumb luck?" John shouted, his chin quivering with anger.

He sat down on the rock, his breath heaving. "Sarah went right through the windshield. She didn't have her seat belt on because she was sitting crooked in her seat. So when we hit the rock, she went right through the glass." John panted and struggled to master himself. Chuck knew he needed to get this out. He'd heard that people who'd been through traumatic events often relived them again and again until they could make some kind of sense of the tragedy. Chuck just hoped his friend would be lucky enough to be able to get over his hurt someday.

John stood up and pointed twenty or thirty feet out into the field behind the rock. "She landed out there. I didn't know where she was because I was out for a second, or it could have been a minute, I don't know. But when I came to, I couldn't see her anywhere. The car's headlights were busted out, and my glasses were gone, and Sarah wasn't there. For a minute, I thought maybe she'd just crawled out of the wreck. I tried the doors, but they were both jammed shut. I suddenly realized that she'd gone through the windshield. I pushed myself out of the driver's side window and tried to stand up. That's when I found out my legs were broken. I hadn't felt anything before, and I didn't care. All I could think about was Sarah. I called out for her again and again. But she never called back. It was so dark, Chuck. There was only a little moonlight to search by. I crawled around on my hands and knees searching for her, calling her name.

The emotion in John's voice sent a chill through Chuck, and he struggled to keep his own composure. John staggered out into the field, snow crunching under his boots with each step. When he got to the spot where he'd been pointing, he stopped, staring down into the snow. Chuck followed just a few steps behind, watching his friend dissolve before his eyes. "It was right here, I found her here. She was laying on her stomach right here," John said, dropping to his knees and plunging his hands into the icy snow. He kept them there for a time, his eyes darting back and forth over the snowy ground. Chuck could only imagine the terrifying scene he was replaying in his head. He stepped forward and dropped down next to John, but his friend seemed to take no notice.

"I rolled her over onto her back. I kept shaking her and yelling her name, but she was gone!" John sobbed, looking suddenly up at his friend. "Not even a goodbye, Chuck, no last words, no last *I love you* like in the movies, just gone. All of our dreams, all our hopes, gone in an instant!"

John dropped his head and wept openly. Chuck had rarely seen him cry, even when they were kids, and one of them had gotten hurt. He knew John was suffering as never before. Chuck put his arm around his best friend's shoulder. He said nothing, holding back his own tears; he knew there was nothing of any worth he could say.

"Back Home"

Later that evening, the two sat at John's dinner table snacking on the remainder of the cheese ball and crackers. Chuck, who was in between jobs, decided he should stay with John for a bit to help him out until he got back on his feet, literally and figuratively.

"You don't have to do this, Chuck," John said. "I'm getting around just about as good as ever now."

"Ah, come on, I don't have anything to do for at least another two weeks, and it would be fun to get reacquainted for a while. After all, I haven't been around for a couple of months now. And after that last job I could use a break myself," Chuck said. "Now, are you gonna help me get my clothes and stuff or not?" Chuck asked, pointing over his shoulder toward the truck.

"Chuck, you don't have any clothes in the truck," John answered incredulously.

"Oh, that's right," Chuck said, his eyes blinking rapidly. "Let's run to town and get some supplies! 'sides, I'm tired of eating this nasty cheese ball!"

John shrugged his shoulders. He knew Chuck well enough to know that when he was in one of these moods, it was best just to go along with it.

"Well, can we at least wait until morning?" John pleaded.

"Sure. Do you think we can make this cheese ball last that long, though?" Chuck queried. "Or maybe we can order a pizza!" he said, raising his eyebrows.

Chuck could have lived off pizza alone, and in reality, he probably did. John remembered the last time he'd been over to Chuck's house. He had dozens of empty or half empty pizza boxes lying around. You had to move them just to find a place to sit down.

"I'm guessing the pizza guys won't be delivering tonight, what with the snow and all. Last I checked the average pizza boy couldn't afford a Hummer to use as a delivery vehicle." John said.

"You're probably right," Chuck said. Standing up, he started rifling through the cupboards and the pantry, looking for something else to eat.

"Chuck?" John said, "I'm sure you won't starve to death before morning."

With all seriousness, Chuck answered, "I wouldn't be so sure about that, John."

"Walls"

Watching from his bedroom window at the back of his grandparent's house, Eric seethed. The kid living next door was heading out with his friends once again while he sat home alone.

To be so full of resentment at the tender age of seven didn't bode well for Eric's mental health. After the death of his parents, he'd closed himself off to the rest of the world. Unwilling to make any new friends for fear of suddenly losing them, he stayed locked away in his room most of the time, coming out only for school or meals with his grandparents.

School. That was another sore subject for Eric. His strange behavior didn't go unnoticed by the local schoolyard bullies. Sensing weakness, they immediately targeted him as someone they could push around. Verbal abuse quickly escalated to shoving matches. At first, Eric would back down, allowing the delinquents to have their fun, but soon the harassment became too much for him to bear. That's when he started fighting back, not with his words, but with his fists. For a time, it seemed to help, and the bullies moved on to easier prey as bullies are known to do.

Two years passed with Eric just getting by. Emotionally, he remained cut off from everyone around him. Even his grandparents couldn't reach him as his test scores slid even lower than they had been before.

The kids at school began to hit their growth spurts, and it became evident that Eric, already shorter than most, was going to be a late bloomer. The bullies returned from summer vacation, now several inches taller than him, and in greater numbers than before. They traveled in packs like wild dogs, always more secure when surrounded by their own kind.

Eric's isolation escalated with each day's beating and abuse. Try as he might to defend himself, the odds were against him. He was the school's whipping boy. Suffering in silence, his distrust of people solidified into a hardened shell, and it had drawn the once bright spark from his eyes.

It was a small school, less than a hundred children spread across six grades, most of them relieved to let Eric take the brunt of the bullies' attention. He continued to be the scapegoat for his entire fourth grade school year.

The summer months passed far too quickly as he turned the pages of his small desk calendar each day. He dreaded the approaching fall months when he would have to return to school to face the bastards again. He'd never give up though, no matter how badly they beat him down. Somewhere inside, he'd been given an indomitable spirit. Regardless of his emotional condition, he would always fight back.

The first day of fifth grade looked as though it would turn out to be a replay of the fourth. Passing through the hallways was like the parting of the Red Sea, the other children making way for him as though they would somehow be marked for abuse if they stood too close to Eric. They made him feel like an outcast. But for some reason, as he rolled into his fifth-grade homeroom, the idea of being an outcast no longer bothered him. In fact, he was starting to feel pretty good about himself. At some point during the last summer, he'd decided that he was O.K. just the way he was. A handful of the more perceptive children noticed the difference in him as well, a quiet confidence that had not been there before. Of course, the bullies saw nothing new, only an object on which to take out their own misguided aggression.

The harassment started immediately. The first recess sent Eric slinking into a corner to spend time by himself while the other children ran out to the grassy playground. He'd have preferred staying inside, perhaps in the library where he could read, but the teacher forced him outside so he could be with the other kids. She told him it was important to develop his social skills.

"*She's obviously never been beaten up on the playground,*" Eric thought to himself while waiting in the corner for the inevitable attack. Sure enough, he didn't have to wait long.

One of the members of *The Crew*, as they liked to call themselves, pointed him out to the rest of his hoodlum gang.

Within moments, they were headed toward him, the whole group wearing smug smiles as they moved in for the kill.

Then something strange happened, something that would change Eric's life forever. Two new kids unwittingly, obviously unaware of the pecking order, crossed the path of the approaching gang, causing the leader of the pack to check his stride.

Both of the new guys were from out of town. Eric knew little about them other than that they had been hanging around together for the last many months. And that their families had moved in on the same street only a few houses apart. Apparently, they had become fast friends.

"Hey you dumbasses!" the lead brute called out while giving one the new kids a quick shove.

What happened next would go down in the history books, as every child in the school witnessed a changing of the guard that day.

The new kid turned around and without saying a word, popped the big bully square in the face. The thug stumbled backward, lost his footing, and landed hard on his butt. He sat still for a moment, groping at his bloody nose, taken off guard by the idea that anyone would dare challenge him. Then he balled up his fists as a look of absolute rage twisted his young face. Two other members of *The Crew* stepped out from the crowd. Now they were a gang of six.

It looked like the makings of a slaughter as the two new boys faced off defiantly against the thugs. And then the fight was on.

The new kids stood back to back, fending off blows from all directions. They weren't doing too bad of a job until the big guy stood up and jumped headlong into the fray.

Bum rushing one of the boys, he knocked him to the ground and began pounding away with both fists. Two of his cronies held the boy down while he did the dirty work. The other new kid was holding his own against the other three delinquents but was unable to come to his friend's aid. Eric saw the look in his eyes as he fought, outnumbered and overburdened. In that scene, he saw himself.

The boy shot a glance in Eric's direction as the battle raged on, and that was all it took. Something snapped inside Eric. Years of pent up frustrations turned to fire as he charged out from the corner straight for the oversized bully who was still thumping away on the pinned down new kid. Crashing headlong into him, he drove his full weight into the boy's back. The force of the blow sent the thug tumbling sideways, taking one of his friends with him. Like a jaguar onto its prey, Eric was on top of him in an instant, raining down blows on his adversary's face and chest. He struck with such lightning speed that the boy couldn't even get his arms up to defend himself. The new kid on the ground, whose name Eric would later find out was Chuck, rolled to one side, twisting free from the guy who was sitting on his legs. Leaping to his feet, he began swinging punches wildly.

The three punks going after John turned and watched in horror, their fearless leader getting whipped before their eyes. John took advantage of their distraction by slugging one of them in the back of the head. Not the noblest of blows, but effective nonetheless, especially when you're outnumbered. The boy dropped like a stone, knocked out cold by the hit to his skull. The other two turned back to John just in time for one of them to receive an uppercut to the jaw, sending him to the ground next to his unconscious friend. The last punk put up his fists momentarily, then turned and ran like hell. John leapt over to Chuck, who was thumping away at another thug who was quickly losing heart. The remaining punks knew the tide had turned and scrambled away in different directions, yelling obscenities over their shoulders as they ran.

Chuck and John had to pull Eric off the leader of the gang, as he showed no signs of letting up on the thrashing he was delivering to his arch nemesis.

"He's done, man! He's finished!" John said as he and Chuck dragged Eric off the leader. "He's had enough!"

Eric stood up straight, his body rigid, a wild look in his eye.

"You never touch me again!" he spat at the leader who was

slowly rolling onto his hands and knees, blood draining freely from a busted lip and cut above his eye.

The thugs never did bother Eric again, and he became fast friends with the two boys who had stood beside him in the fight. They didn't seem to mind that he was a little difficult to get to know. All they knew was that he had given them a hand when they needed it most. And that was enough to make him O.K. in their books.

Eric never caught on with most of the people he ran into in his life, always remaining a bit of a fringe member of society. But those two boys, John and Chuck, who he met as a child would stay with him through thick and thin, and for a longer period of time than anyone else in his life – they stuck with him well into his adulthood.

"Morning"

Sure enough, Chuck made it through the night without wasting away, but he was up bright and early, ready to head into town nearly at the crack of dawn.

Chuck yelled up the stairs, "You ready yet, John? Geez! I see how small-town life works! Sounds like an excuse for never being anywhere on time to me."

"Well, some of us have BROKEN LEGS!" John shouted back.

"Can't use that excuse forever, Johnny!" Chuck said, grabbing his coat. "Now let's move before I expire!"

John made his way down the stairs, taking them at a pretty normal pace, not one at a time like he had been doing for the last month. *Coming along nicely*, he thought to himself. *I'll need to see about getting these damn casts off pretty soon.*

The two were getting bundled up when the phone rang. John made his way through the clutter while Chuck groaned, "Just let it ring, I'm starving!"

John eyed him with disbelief. "Man! You'd think you'd never been hungry before!"

John checked the caller I.D. and smiled. "Well, haven't seen that name in a while."

"Who is it?" Chuck asked.

John raised a finger for silence while clicking on the speakerphone.

"Well, fancy hearing from you, Mr. Eric!" John said, smiling.

"How're things going, John? How you holding up?" Eric asked.

"I'm doing alright, I've got an old friend of yours staying with me right now," John said, eyeing Chuck.

"I hope it's not a female friend, John!" Eric laughed.

Chuck's mouth dropped open. "Bad taste, you pinhead!" he yelled.

Eric laughed loudly on the other end of the line. "Ha, I had a feeling you'd be there, Chuck hole! Who else would be bothering John when he least needs pestering?"

"How's the weather been over there, man?" John interrupted.

Eric Livingston lived about thirty miles west of Jackson in an old farmhouse situated on ten acres. He made his living buying up old odds and ends and selling them through an online auction service. Everyone had told him he was crazy for trying it, but he'd always said, "I don't want to sit in a stinking office all day unless it's my own!" And as it turns out, he was doing quite well with his small business. He'd even built a pole barn just to help house his auction wares.

"Well, amazingly it looks like the bulk of that storm missed us over here. I'd guess there's not more than an inch or two of snow on the ground," Eric said.

"We're coming over to pick you up for breakfast!" Chuck blurted out from across the room.

"Sounds good to me, I haven't eaten anything good in days. They don't deliver pizza out this far, ya know."

"God. Another one," John said. "It's a wonder the two of you aren't married."

"What?" both Chuck and Eric responded simultaneously.

John laughed so hard that he nearly started crying, but in a good way for once.

After a short drive, John and Chuck rounded the corner onto Farm Road. The street was aptly named since it cut through nothing but vast crop fields interspersed here and there with little white farmhouses.

"Man, they all look the same," Chuck said, then broke into song with a verse from "Thank God I'm a Country Boy."

The two reached their destination, an old, two-story farmhouse. It was painted bright yellow, which contrasted horribly with the sky blue of the pole barn that stood beside it. Eric had constructed a breezeway to connect the two buildings. It was painted yet another gut-wrenching color.

Chuck was appalled. "Oh my God, who in the hell would paint something like that? Is he color blind?"

John just smiled. It was always fun to get Chuck and Eric together. They were both eccentrics, but each thought the other much worse off.

Chuck brought the truck to a halt and turned off the ignition. The two stepped out of the vehicle and surveyed the area around them. Eric had only bought the place six months ago, and the last time John had been there, the house had yet to be painted. The old white paint had been flaking off the siding so badly that the house had started to look like a Dalmatian.

The wind whistled across the barren acreage, whipping along little bits of snow. Chuck started toward the house while John waited for just a second longer. He closed his eyes and listened to the sound of the blowing snow. It made a sound like sand being dropped onto a metal plate, a rushing tinkling of sorts. He opened his eyes to find that Chuck, ten paces in front of him, had turned around and was watching him suspiciously.

"I'm fine, just keep moving," John said, starting again for the front door. Chuck turned back toward the house just in time to see Eric step outside.

He was wearing a ratty old jacket covered in yellow and blue paint stains.

"I cannot, no, will not believe what I'm seeing here!" Chuck yelled to Eric.

Eric stopped in his tracks and held his arms out to the sides, and while spinning slowly, he said, "You like?"

"No, I don't like," Chuck replied. Then, turning to John, he added, "John, I'm not going into town with him dressed like that."

John could only grin at the exchange. Eric was enjoying getting Chuck's goat as well.

"So how's the auction business going, Eric?" John said, intervening once again.

"Great! I've already got most of the barn filled with stuff. In fact, I'm gonna have to start sorting through it to see what's what," he said, pointing at the large blue building. "You wanna see?" he added.

"Sure! I'd love to see what kind of junk you've been selling," John said.

Eric opened the door that led into the little breezeway he'd constructed.

"You wouldn't believe the things people will buy," he said, pulling twice on the latch to get it unhooked. "You'd never guess there's a market for most of this stuff."

Chuck and John followed Eric into the barn. Eric flipped a switch just inside the door, and several overhead lights flickered to life, revealing tables covered with just about anything one could imagine. Old pots and pans, electronics, car parts, even old shoes filled the vast interior of the barn. One of the back corners had items piled up as if they'd just been dumped off the back of a truck.

John and Chuck looked around in amazement. There were easily thousands, if not tens of thousands of items littering the place.

"How do you know where anything is?" John asked, awestruck.

"Well," Eric said while pulling a tarp off a big pile of electronic doodads, "I usually just start with one pile and try to sell everything in it. But I try to separate out some of the *high-cost* items," he said while making a waving motion over the table covered in electronics.

"How much did you pay for all this stuff?" Chuck asked. "Did it all come from one place?"

"Most of the items on this table came from an auction where a business was closing. You can get laptop PC's, printers, and monitors for pennies on the dollar!" Eric said excitedly.

"You sound like one of those commercials for cheap carpet," Chuck piped.

"But really." Eric stopped and surveyed the items on the table. "I think I have about a thousand bucks in all this stuff. And I bet you I'll gross five, maybe six thousand when I sell it all."

Chuck and John looked at each other, eyebrows raised.

"Maybe he ain't crazy after all," Chuck said.

"Not at all, my friends. Not at all," Eric said, letting the last three words drip out one at a time for better effect. "You see, I figure I'll have this place paid off in about a year and a half if my sales hold up. And I don't have any reason to believe they won't."

"Man, I have to work for a living," John said as he wandered around looking at the various piles of junk. "You've sure made a believer out of me."

"Where did you say this stuff comes from?" Chuck asked, fingering a strange looking metallic object partially buried under some other electronic hardware. Eric stepped over and examined the pile.

"Oh, that stuff. That pile's kind of interesting. I actually got that stuff from the back of a van. The guy selling it said it was government surplus."

Chuck and John exchanged glances and then eyed Eric.

"Oh no, it's nothing like that. I'm sure it's all above board. I've bought stuff from this guy before. He just collects all the things the Government offices are throwing away and then sells them out of his van. I've gotten such good stuff from him before that we've struck up a deal. I pay him $500 for each van-full, basically. Sometimes it's mostly junk, but other times, there's some pretty cool stuff in there. Things that aren't so high tech for the government any more are still great for the average consumer," Eric said emphatically.

Chuck kept eyeing the strange device that he'd pulled from the pile. "What the heck is this thing, Eric? I've never really seen anything like it. It's so light that I'd think it was made of plastic, but it feels more like aluminum or something."

Chuck handed the device to Eric who ran his hands over its surface. It was saucer shaped and looked suspiciously like an old CD Walkman.

"Kinda looks like a CD player, doesn't it?" Eric said while pulling the object closer to his face to get a better view. "I don't see any way to open it, though."

The Walkman had a round glass bubble in its center protruding roughly an inch and a half from the metal surface. The bubble was surrounded by several smooth depressions that looked like touch sensitive buttons, like the kind you'd find on a microwave. The buttons were labeled with strange markings.

Swirls and hieroglyphic-like pictures adorned each one.

"I'm a fan of modern art, but this a little too much," Eric said. "When you can't even figure out how to use the stupid thing. Maybe it's in Chinese or something."

Chuck moved on to another pile of junk and began to root through it, and John had found a long radio antenna sitting on a table and was using it to dig at an itch under one of his casts, but Eric remained mesmerized by the strange find. Running his fingers over the surface, he couldn't find a way to get it open. Flipping it over revealed a perfectly flat, seamless expanse of shiny metal

"Where do you put the batteries?" he mumbled under his breath. Finally, he shook the device, much like a monkey will do when confronted with something he can't understand.

"This thing's solid as a rock," he said to no one in particular. "It doesn't rattle or anything. It must not have any moving parts. What the hell is it?" he said as he turned the object over in his hands, looking confused.

Chuck returned from his junk search and stood beside Eric. "Let me take a look at that," he said, and Eric handed the item back to him.

"It's got to open up somehow," John said without looking up from his scratching. He was now thoroughly engrossed in an itching frenzy.

"Hey Eric, can I keep this antenna?" he asked.

Eric glanced over and saw John thrusting the wire in and out of his cast like a mad man.

"Sure, John, no charge," he said disgustedly.

Chuck feverishly poked at the buttons on the device, which he was wont to do when he couldn't figure something out.

"Oh that's a great idea, Chuck. Let's hope it's not a bomb," Eric said.

Chuck continued pushing buttons at random until suddenly the glass bubble began to glow. Instantly, an image of the earth flashed across its surface.

"Cool!" Chuck exclaimed. "I knew I could figure it out!"

The two stared at the image. It was an incredibly high-resolution picture.

"Damn, that looks good. What is it, some kind of IPS screen or something?" Eric asked.

"I don't know. I can't even see any pixels or anything. It almost seems like you're looking through a telescope or something, doesn't it?" Chuck said, poking his finger at the screen.

John, interest piqued, joined the other two in examining the new toy.

"Look at that," Chuck shouted. Touching the screen with the tip of his index finger caused the image to zoom in by double.

"That's amazing!" Eric exclaimed.

All three of them were captivated now. Chuck touched the screen a second time, and the image zoomed in once again.

"Wait a second, wait a second!" Eric said excitedly as he touched the screen himself. Placing his finger on the glass bubble, he began to drag his finger slowly around its surface. To their amazement, the image on the screen rotated under his finger as if he were touching an actual globe. The picture was now large enough to show the outline of the United States and Canada. A small red circle appeared on the map precisely where it had last been touched, appearing like a small bull's eye. Eric tapped the screen on the image of the United States, roughly where Jackson would be. The image zoomed in again, now showing only the U.S.

"What the hell is this thing?" Chuck said, grinning like an ape. "I don't think you wanna sell this one, man!"

Eric tapped the screen repeatedly. The map enlarged several times in rapid succession. It now showed the view from about the height of your average jetliner. Eric tapped the screen twice more, and twice more, the image scaled up. The screen now clearly pictured the city of Jackson. After delivering a few more well-placed pokes, the image showed Eric's bright yellow farmhouse and blue barn.

"The database for this thing must be almost new," Eric said. "I just painted this place a month ago."

"No way," John said. "If the database was that new, then why would this thing be sitting in some junk pile ready to be sold?"

Chuck and John eyed Eric suspiciously once again.

"What?" Eric said, quickly glancing back and forth between his two friends. "You think I stole it or something?"

"Well, I'm sure someone didn't just throw it away," John said.

"It must just be some kind of mistake. Maybe you should hold on to it for a bit. I'm sure whoever owns it will come looking for it eventually," Chuck added while gazing into the screen. Then something else in the image caught his eye. A little yellow box sat just twenty or so feet from Eric's blue pole barn.

"Let me see that!" Chuck said, snatching the unit from Eric's hands. "You're just tapping on the screen to get it to zoom in, right?"

"That's it," Eric said, offering up his palms as if to show that he had nothing up his sleeves.

Chuck tapped the screen and watched as the image sprang forward, the point of view even closer.

"Hey, that's my hummer," Chuck said, wrinkling his brow.

The screen was showing an area about 200 feet in diameter. That was enough to encompass the house, barn, driveway, and apparently, Chuck's new yellow Hummer.

"Now wait a minute," John said, chuckling. "Enough's enough, Eric. We're on to your little high tech stunt."

Eric looked at the device, then up at Chuck and John. "What are you talking about? I've never even seen this thing before. Chuck's the one who picked it up. How do I know you guys didn't just bring that thing in here with you?"

"It was in one of your piles, man. Now come on, how'd you do it? You got a webcam up on the roof or something?" Chuck asked.

Eric, just a little ticked off, said "Well, you tell me, Chuck, you can see both the house and the barn, so where am I hiding the camera that's overlooking both of them? And how would I have gotten those nifty shots from outer-frickin' space?"

Chuck looked down at the device, blinking his eyes with his

brow furrowed, and began to examine it very closely. He tapped just above the image of his truck on the screen. The image zoomed again and now showed just the edge of the house and barn, his vehicle taking up a good portion of the screen.

"You can almost read the license plate," he said, which he followed with, "This is amazing! What do you think the little red target thing is for?"

"I think that's showing the last place you tapped," John said, standing over Chuck's shoulder. "This thing must be linked to a satellite or something. Chuck, you're the high tech guy. Do they have satellites that would have this kind of resolution? I mean, you can just about see the tread on your tires."

"I don't think they do," Chuck said as the three men gazed at the screen, their wonder growing by the minute.

"Where did you say you got this, Eric?" John asked.

"Well, it came with the last load of government surplus stuff that I bought from the guy in the van."

John and Chuck looked at each other. "No questions asked, eh, Eric?" John said.

"That's usually the deal," Eric returned.

"What's that? Chuck yelled. He'd been watching the screen intently while John questioned Eric. The two of them looked back at the little screen and gasped as they watched a cat meander onto the scene.

"Hey! That's Chicken Little!" Eric called out. Then, seeing the strange looks from John and Chuck, he added, "What? There's nothing wrong with that name! That's a good name for a cat!"

"No way!" Chuck shouted, heading for the breezeway door. Eric and John stood frozen while Chuck gazed out the window. Turning back toward the other two, he added, "No damn way!"

"This thing's showing the images in real time?" Eric asked. "I'm sorry guys, but this is starting to get a little scary. Nobody has anything like this. Do they?"

John grabbed the device. He tapped the screen one time just behind the SUV where the cat was currently standing, licking its front paw. Again, the image increased in magnification, this time showing an area no larger than a ten-foot circle. The cat was clearly visible, even down to its whiskers.

"Hey, the little target's turned green, and one of the buttons just lit up," John said.

"What do you figure it does?" he asked in a rather serious voice. "I'm gonna push it," he added, looking up suddenly, a mischievous look in his eyes. "Ya, I'm pushing it."

"I - I don't know if I'd do that, John," Chuck said. "We don't have any *real* idea of what that thing is. What if it's some kind of weapon or something?"

John looked back at the object again, his eyes surveying its entire surface. There were four buttons, two on either side of the display. The only button that was lit had a little picture on it that looked like the target they had seen on the screen a moment before.

"Maybe we should call some..." was all Eric got out before John pressed his index finger against the flat membranous button.

John heard a sound like a clap of thunder. At first, he thought Eric had been right, that the thing had been some kind of bomb that he'd just set off. The instant he touched the button, he felt a surge like the one you get when someone sneaks up and scares the hell out of you. His entire body experienced the same feeling you get when you hit your funny bone, a burning tingling sensation that coursed through him. He opened his mouth to scream, but before he could vocalize his terror, the sensation was gone. He dropped to his knees and opened his eyes.

A terrible howl reached his ears as if he'd just pushed the needle of a phonograph all the way across a spinning record album. Looking around frantically, John saw Chicken Little's tail pinned under his right knee. The cat struggled momentarily to free itself, then turned and hissed at John before running away.

He still grasped the device firmly in his left hand, but nothing else was the same. For just a second, John looked around, confused about where he was until his eyes came to rest on the tailgate of Chuck's Hummer. Panting, he looked into the screen of the object clutched tightly in his hand. The little green target was flashing, and the button had gone dark once again. John slowly began to realize what had just happened, but could hardly believe it. A thousand thoughts flew through his head in an instant until he heard the sound of Chuck yelling his name. He turned and looked toward the barn just in time to see Eric and Chuck emerge from the breezeway at a dead run.

"What the hell happened?" Eric yelled, grabbing John's arm and hoisting him up to his feet. "You just disappeared! Just like that! Disappeared!" he said again, shaking his head, eyes wide.

"How do you feel? Are you O.K.?" Chuck blurted out as he circled around John, looking him up and down. "You look like you're O.K." Meeting John's gaze, he added, "Say something, man! Are you O.K. or not?"

John held his arms out and said, "I think I'm O.K. Yeah, I'm alright."

Eric bent forward, resting his palms on his thighs and exhaling loudly. Chuck danced around excitedly, wearing an oversized grin.

"You know what this means, guys?" he said, stopping suddenly and pointing the index fingers of both hands at the other two simultaneously "This thing's some kinda teleportation device!" Thrusting his hands toward the sky, he cheered, "Wooohooo! We gotta try it again!"

"Whoa now, speedy," Eric said. "We don't have to do anything just yet. We still know just about nothing about this thing." Then, pointing toward John, he added, "He could have got himself - and us - killed by pulling a stunt like that."

"Oh come on, man! This is a fantastic discovery! We gotta try it again." Chuck said, hopping up and down like an excited six-year-old.

"O.K., O.K. but we gotta figure out what John did and try to do the same thing again. We have to try to be scientific about this. Now John, first off, which button did you push?" Eric said.

"Well, the last time I tapped the screen, it zoomed in, and the button with the target symbol lit up. I'd guess that means it was ready or something," John said, looking up at Eric and Chuck. "I think we should try it again."

"What did it feel like?" Chuck said.

"It's kind of hard to describe. You're just going to have to try it for yourself," John said, grinning.

"Guys, you sure we should be doing this?" Eric asked. "I mean, do you have all your insurance and stuff set up, next of kin and all that?"

Chuck looked at Eric. "I can't believe we're having this conversation! You got lots of people to leave stuff to, Eric? No? Well me neither! Now, are you going to help figure this thing out, or do you wanna run back inside where it's safe and watch some Oprah or something?"

"Fine, that's fine. But if you bastards get yourself all chewed up or something, don't say I didn't warn you," Eric replied, stepping a pace away from his friends.

"O.K., we're done with this conversation," Chuck said. "I'm doing this, and you guys need to help."

Poking his head up, he looked around as if searching for a good spot to land.

"I'm going to try to pop over there," he said, pointing to a big rock sitting in the middle of Eric's acreage. "Any comments?" he asked.

"Nope," John said. "Tap away."

Eric looked over at John. "Well, you're awfully generous with your buddy's life. Remind me not to send you any cookies for Christmas this year."

John just smiled. Eric had always been a bit more cautious than Chuck. But John himself had always been more careful than Eric. John thought suddenly that something inside of him had changed – and he knew exactly what had caused it.

Chuck was tapping away on the Teleporter like a wild man. "It's not doing anything!" he whined.

"O.K., Big Boy!" John said, grabbing hold of the unit. "Let's just slow down a little, alright? Now, what's the screen showing?"

"Nothing right now. In fact, it looks like it's gone off."

John examined the device. "I think one of us pushed this button to turn it on," he said, pushing down and holding the button closest to the target button. It had an insignia that looked like a star. Sure enough, the screen fired up and showed the earth spinning away from some distance out in space.

"O.K., now start zooming in," John said, handing the unit back to Chuck.

Chuck mumbled to himself while tapping. "Americas, North America, Midwest…" he trailed off until after he had made a few more clicks. "O.K., there's the rock."

"Alright," John said. "Now, Eric, let's go stand over there by the rock. Chuck, push the button with the target on it when we get there. And Chuck, if someone drives by while we're doing this, don't push the button, O.K.? We really don't need anyone from the news dropping by or anything, alright?"

"You're from the newspaper, aren't you, John? Eric said smugly. "Maybe you should leave."

"Good, I see you're over your fear and are back to your old smart-ass self," John said. "Let's go."

Eric and John walked across the field, snow crunching under their feet as they went. The rock stood about fifty yards out in the field north of the house. It took just a minute for them to cover the distance. John lagged behind a little, nursing his healing legs. When they reached their target, John looked over his shoulder, first in one direction then the other, and then called out to Chuck, "O.K. Chuck, looks clear. Brace yourself and hit it!"

Chuck bent his legs just a bit, fumbled with the device for a second, and then disappeared in a blink. Instantly, he re-appeared about ten feet in front of them, just off to the side of the boulder. It was as if he had been dropped in from about six inches above the ground. It was a good thing he'd bent his legs, or he'd have probably fallen down. As it were, he landed with a *thump*, like he'd hopped down off the last step of a stairway.

"Wow!" he yelled. "What a trip! Eric, you gotta try this thing out!"

Eric tried to hide his enthusiasm. "Well, if I must," he said, reaching for the Teleporter.

The next hour or so was spent popping in and out of different areas around Eric's farm. The guys figured out that whoever had a hand on the unit would be transported to the new location as well. It also seemed that whatever they were touching, except for the ground they stood on, would be transported along with them. Chuck became extremely excited when he found that he could send himself and his giant vehicle to various locations around the farm. But try as they might, they could not figure out the final two buttons. They had pushed them repeatedly, but there was no response. And in all honesty, they were a little worried about what they might do anyway.

Finally, the three of them decided to give it a rest.

"I'm starving, anybody up for a trip into town for some grub?" Chuck said.

"Yeah, I could eat. Let me lock up the barn," Eric said. "But the burger joint's gonna close in another twenty minutes, and it's a half hour drive even with Chuck at the wheel. Looks like frozen dinners from the A & P for us," he said over his shoulder as he turned toward the barn

"I have an idea," John said, looking over at Chuck. "You know it's about thirty miles into town, right?"

"Yeah, so?" Chuck said.

"Well, just imagine how much faster we could get there, if….." John said, letting the final word linger in the air.

Chuck smiled. "I like your thinking, John-O!"

Eric returned and stepped up into the truck just in time to find Chuck and John tapping in a location on the Teleporter.

"Oh come on, guys. We don't wanna get caught, do we?" he said.

"We already took a look around with the unit. And we're gonna drop in about a mile out of town anyway, so no one's going to see us," John said. And before Eric could protest further, he added, "I ain't eatin' no frozen dinner." Then he pressed the Teleport button.

"Learning to Fly"

Over the next week, the group experimented as much as they could with their new toy, popping in and out of various locations around town, then the state, and even around the country. Eric was starting to stay up at night looking in on his neighbors and keeping a close eye on things around town.

"It's like watching a movie or something. It's very addictive," he said, peering into the teleporter's glowing screen. John and Chuck had been staying at Eric's place since the discovery. The enormous farmhouse offered plenty of rooms to accommodate even the largest of families. John had *popped,* as they liked to call it, back to his home to get Runt and some extra clothes and had set up house in one of the many spare rooms. Chuck bought some clothes from the local thrift store and made a cozy little spot for himself as well.

The three of them quickly grew proficient with using the device. They had even found out what one of the extra buttons did quite by accident. While picking a spot just outside of town to teleport to, they had zoomed in on the top of an old barn. The target turned green, but then something new happened. The button inscribed with a circle made of little dashed lines lit up.

"Hey, guys!" Eric called out. "Take a look at this! I think I found something."

Chuck and John gathered around quickly.

"What is it?" John asked.

"I don't know. I was zoomed all the way in like normal. See, the target turned green just like it always does. Now, if I hit the teleport button, it'd drop me onto the roof, right? But we've never tried to land on anything other than solid ground. So, I was getting ready to move the target a bit when I noticed something different," Eric said while pointing excitedly at the button.

The image on the screen hadn't changed, but the circle button was lit up and blinking.

"Push it," Chuck said.

"Oh, here we go again," John said. "Who's gonna do it?"

"I will," Eric said. "Since I kinda made the discovery, after all."

Chuck and John stepped back a pace and watched as Eric pressed the glowing button. A grin split across his face. "Well, gentlemen, from the look of this we can now get *inside* buildings!"

John and Chuck leaned in, looking closely at the image on the screen. The roof of the barn had disappeared, revealing the contents inside. After another click, the target location indicator turned green, indicating that it was ready to go.

"That's unbelievable," John said. "How, how…," he mumbled, amazed.

"Man, this whole thing just keeps getting better," Eric said. "Now I can be a Peeping Tom!" And with that he zipped his finger across the screen wildly, coming to rest atop a local apartment building. He waited for a second, watching as the target turned green and the circle button began to blink.

"Alrighty! Here we go!" Eric exclaimed with a crazy look in his eye.

John thrust his hand over the screen before Eric could click the button. "O.K., now come on, guys! I'm sure whoever made this thing didn't intend it to be used by perverts!"

Eric looked up at John in amazement. "Come on, man!" he pleaded.

"No way, Eric! What if this thing's connected to something somewhere else? Somebody could be watching everything that passes across that screen. What if this thing is from some alien planet? I'm sure they'd be real proud of how their device was being used. What's next? Are we gonna start using it to rob banks?" John raged.

Chuck and Eric looked at each other and smiled.

"I can't believe this!" John shouted as he began stomping around the room, a scene that looked quite comical, considering the casts on his legs. "We've got a chance to do something fantastic here. And you guys just want to be a couple of pervs! Or even worse, bank robbers!"

Eric and Chuck watched as John played out his tirade. Finally, he stopped and looked at the two of them, eyes wild.

"Geez, John," Eric drawled. "It's not like we were gonna rob YOUR bank."

John stopped dead in his tracks and glared at Eric. Chuck laughed out loud as the grin grew larger on Eric's face.

"You guys suck," John spat. "You really do," was all he could say while shaking his head and trying not to laugh himself.

John's legs grew steadily better. After about two weeks into his stay at Eric's, he decided it was time to get the casts off.

"Have you called a doctor about this, John?" Chuck asked. "I'm mean, are you sure you're ready?"

"Yeah. He said I could come in any time to get them cut off. I'm going to head in there now. You guys wanna come along?" John asked.

"Nah, I'm going to hang around here for a bit and get some stuff ready to sell," Eric said, pulling himself up from the couch. "It's off to the barn for me."

"How 'bout you, Chuck?"

"Sure, I'll go along."

Chuck was always up for doing something. It didn't seem to matter whether it was mundane or not. He considered just about anything a chance for an adventure.

"We'll just be gone for a bit, Eric. I think we're going to stop by and pick up a pizza for dinner. You want anything from town?" John asked while grabbing his coat.

"Pizza sounds good. Just bring it out to the barn when you get back. There's soda in the fridge out there. Maybe you guys will want to help sort through some of my stuff for the auctions?"

John and Chuck looked at each other, then back to Eric, both of their faces wrinkling up like prunes.

"Now come on guys, remember the last time we went junk diving? Who knows what we'll find this time!" Eric said while moving his eyebrows up and down.

"Yeah, whatever," Chuck said and headed for the kitchen.

The teleporter was sitting on the kitchen table. It had become a tool that all three had used daily since its discovery. It was just so damn handy to be able to pop wherever you needed to go instantly. At first, they would go out to the truck and pop themselves and the vehicle to some location just outside of town and then drive in. But they had come to the conclusion that there was no need for the truck. They would just use the teleporter to find an alley or an unoccupied stretch of sidewalk within a few feet of where they were headed and pop to that location. John had even gotten good at popping himself into bathrooms within the establishment that he was visiting to keep from getting his boots dirty or wet from walking in from the snow.

Chuck fired up the device and tapped his way into a storage room within the doctor's office. "You ready, John?"

John stepped over and said, "That's a pretty small office, dude, maybe we should go in from outside. The receptionist may wonder how the two of us got in without being seen."

"Good point," Chuck said while scooting the image around on the screen and centering it on an alley just beside the doctors' office. "O.K. Let's hit it."

John touched the teleporter as Chuck pushed the Go button. The two of them disappeared in an instant, leaving Eric standing alone in the front room.

"I don't know if I'll ever get used to that," he said aloud before heading for the breezeway.

Eric was used to being alone. He'd spent most of his life that way. His parents had died in a car crash early in his life, and he'd lived with his grandparents for most of his youth. He'd dropped out of school in the 11th grade and backpacked across much of the U.S. and Canada. He had learned to depend on himself when things got tough, and he had experienced many occasions where he found himself with his back against the wall. He knew that sometimes you had to do things that seemed less than palatable, but that coming out intact on the other end was usually more important than being right. His lifestyle had kept him from being too close to anyone, other than the few good friends who he knew he could trust. That was the kind of man Eric had turned out to be. Though he acted lighthearted and gentle most of the time, underneath, he was someone you knew you could count on in a fight.

"Looks like everything has come along nicely," Dr. Garbman

said while holding John's right foot in his hand. He twisted and turned the foot then pushed on the heel with the palm of his hand.

"Looks pretty good. I think it's time to get those casts off," he said while retrieving a small circular saw.

John sat on the examining table while the doctor buzzed through one cast and then the other. A nurse was present to wash and clean both legs after the casts had been removed.

The shape of his limbs appalled John. They were wrinkled and white, much like a finger that had a bandage left on too long, though of course much larger in size.

"Don't panic," the doctor said, noticing John's worried expression. "They'll look just fine in the morning."

The whole process only took about twenty minutes, an amount of time during which Chuck had left to go next door to order the pizza. While John waited in the lobby for Chuck to return, he tried out his new legs. They felt very light without the casts, and there was still a little bit of pain, but the Doc had said that could take some time to disappear fully. John paid his co-payment for the procedure and headed outside to look for Chuck. As he stepped out the door, he found him making his way back carrying two pizza boxes.

"Two, Chuck? Did we really need two large pizzas? And I suppose they're both thick crust?" John asked.

"Well, we want something left over for breakfast, don't we?" Chuck asked with all seriousness.

John just groaned and lifted the lid on the top pizza box. He quickly snatched out a steaming slice and began munching on it.

"Hey, can't you wait till we get back?" Chuck whined.

John had done stuff like this before, mostly because he knew it drove Chuck crazy. He especially liked to eat in Chuck's car. That always made him furious.

The two walked until they reached the edge of a building, then ducked into a darkened alley.

"Where's the thingy?" John asked.

"In my coat pocket. I can't reach it. Here, hold these pizzas,"

Chuck said, foisting the pizzas out at John.

"Nah, I ain't falling for that one," John said, thrusting his hand into Chuck's coat and retrieving the teleporter. "O.K. Here we go," he said.

John tapped the screen until he could see Eric's acreage. A couple of taps more brought the house and barn into view. John was just about to zoom inside the blue pole barn when something caught his eye. The door to the breezeway hung open and was tilted off at a funny angle. John used the teleporter to move in a little closer. The door looked to have been pulled from its hinges.

"Something's happening back at Eric's, Chuck!" John said, trying to keep his voice under control. "Take a look. The door's busted!"

"What?" Chuck asked, moving in closer to get a look at the screen. The two watched for a moment as several bright flashes of light appeared from inside the breezeway.

"What the hell was that?" Chuck yelled.

A tall figure appeared in the breezeway. He looked around quickly and then motioned to someone inside the building. A second later two other figures stepped from the portal, dragging a limp figure by the arms.

"Damn, Chuck! I think they've got Eric!" John yelled. "We gotta help him!"

Chuck dropped the pizzas and grabbed John's arm. "Let's go!"

Suddenly, a hand clapped down hard onto Chuck's shoulder.

"What's the problem here?" an authoritative voice called out. "You gentlemen in some kinda trouble?"

Chuck spun around, wild-eyed, and flung the hand off his shoulder before realizing that it was a police officer. Another cop stepped into the alley and flipped on a flashlight, illuminating the entire scene. Chuck and John were both temporarily blinded by the bright light. Shielding his eyes with his hand, John watched as the first officer stepped back and drew his gun.

"Whoa now!" John called out while raising his hands and

tapping Chuck's arm with the teleporter to indicate that he should do the same. "We aren't looking for any kind of trouble officer. We're just on our way home. You just surprised us."

"You want to tell me what you guys are doing hiding out in this alley? I gotta tell ya, it doesn't look too good," the officer with the flashlight said, pointing the beam first at John then at Chuck.

"We don't have time for this, John," Chuck said under his breath.

"What's that? Let's not try anything funny now, boys," the officer with the gun said. In the darkness, John could just make out the other cop moving his right hand down to his gun holster.

Then the first policeman noticed the teleporter in John's upraised hand.

"What do you have there?" he called out loudly. "O.K., you need to drop that, now!"

John's eyes widened as he saw the officer suddenly tense up. The second cop pulled a radio from his belt and began talking. "We're gonna need some back up here. We got a possible 211 in progress."

"John," Chuck said, becoming very agitated. "Come on!"

"I don't know where it's pointing. We don't know where we'd end up," John said in measured tones, never taking his eyes off the barrel of the gun he was staring down.

"Shut up! Both of you need to keep your mouths shut! You're in enough trouble already," the second officer said, shining his flashlight directly into John's face.

"Wait a minute." the first cop said, leaning in a bit to scrutinize John. "Don't you work at the paper or something?"

John clenched his jaw tight.

"Aw shit! Hang on, Chuck," he whispered then pushed the flashing teleport button.

"Splashdown"

An icy chill pierced John's entire body as he and Chuck crashed through the frozen surface of Lake Jackson. The ice was just thick enough to break their fall for a split second. Time enough for them both to clamp their mouths shut before plunging into the dark water. The freezing liquid felt like a thousand needles stabbing into every part of their bodies.

John's heavy winter coat became saturated within seconds as he flailed and kicked in an attempt to return to the surface.

"This is it," he thought. "This is how I'm going to die."

The cold water made his legs ache as if they were being broken all over again.

John broke the surface at nearly the same time as Chuck, both of them gasping for air. John managed to throw an arm on top of a section of unbroken ice that surrounded the gaping hole. His jacketed arm froze to the glassy surface, giving him some leverage and the ability to hang on, but just barely. Luckily the ice was quite thick, several inches at least. Chuck was hanging on to the edge of the hole facing in the opposite direction, sputtering and coughing.

John looked around quickly. He knew he had to get out of the water as fast as possible or risk going unconscious from hypothermia. He had read somewhere that it only took a few minutes in the water this cold to knock you out.

"Chuck!" John choked out, still panting heavily. "You O.K.?"

"Good as can be!" Chuck called back. John noticed a smug sound in his friend's voice. Even in the worst of conditions, Chuck seemed to be able to maintain his sense of humor, regardless of how humorless the predicament might be.

"Shit, Chuck, we're a long way from the shore, Buddy!" John said, his voice breaking up as he began to shake violently.

"Don't I know it!" Chuck said, beginning to shudder from the effects of the freezing water himself.

An awful thought occurred to John. He had no idea of where the teleporter was.

"Chuck, I dropped the teleporter!" He sputtered. "It's probably down on the bottom of the lake by now!"

Chuck glanced over his shoulder and looked at John. "There's nothing you could have done, man! Don't worry about it right now; we gotta figure out how to get out of this water!" And with that, Chuck tried to pull himself up onto the ice. With a great heave, he thrust his body out of the water and dropped down onto a patch of unbroken ice. The brittle surface gave way under him with a cracking sound, and he sank back into the bone-chilling liquid.

"It's not gonna hold us," Chuck said wheezing from his efforts to escape the cold, watery grave.

The two men struggled fruitlessly for several more minutes, quickly expending the last of their energy.

John's mind raced. He knew both he and Chuck were only seconds away from going under. An awful tremor ran through him, and he began to shake uncontrollably.

"Johnny?" Chuck said slowly. There was resignation in his voice now. "It's been a great ride, man." His voice was all but a whisper as it sputtered out through his chattering teeth.

John reached behind him just in time to grab hold of Chuck's jacket as he started to slide under the surface of the frigid water.

"Don't do this, Chuck! Don't give up!" John tried to yell, but his own voice was so thin and shaky that he could barely utter the phrase. But his words did have some effect. Chuck reached out and clung once again to the ice shelf with the tiny bit of strength he had left.

As John hung on to the back of Chuck's jacket, something in the water caught his attention. He squeezed his eyes shut then reopened them again, blinking quickly. The teleporter floated an arm's length away to his left, bobbing just under the surface.

"Hang on, Chuck! Hang on!" John coughed out. He couldn't see any image on the screen, but all of the buttons were lit up and blinking away in the murky water. John knew he wouldn't be able to reach the object and still hang onto Chuck who had stopped shaking and was now completely limp.

"Ahhhh!" John croaked out as he spent the last of his strength. Letting go of the ice shelf, he lunged for the teleporter. Sinking instantly into the dark water while pulling the unconscious body of Chuck under with him, he grabbed the floating object. Squeezing the device with numb fingers, his mind went blank as he succumbed to the cold, his last thought sending a final prayer hurtling skyward.

"The Cliffs"

"Have you ever felt so close to someone that you just can't stop thinking about them?" John asked Eric. "You know what I mean? See, there's this girl at the office that I met about a month ago. I can't stop thinking about her. It's like she's stuck in my head."

Eric thought for a moment then said, "Well, as you know, I'm not the most experienced person you could talk to about the fairer sex."

It was a hot summer day, and John had just celebrated his 30th birthday with his family and a few close friends. Eric had been among them. The two sat on top of Sayers Rock, sweating and breathing hard from their labors. They both loved rock climbing. The area they had grown up in lent itself to a myriad of outdoor activities. A number of foothills were great for hiking, and they were interspersed with sheer rock walls perfect for climbing. They looked down from a fifty-foot outcropping, waiting for Chuck to finish his ascent.

"Come on, you lazy toad!" John called out.

Chuck just looked up and smiled, his mouth hanging open with a silly looking grin.

"And close your mouth. You look like you're missing a chromosome or something!" John added as he lay back on the rock's flat surface, soaking up the bright sun.

"I think I know what you mean, though, John," Eric said, leaning back and pulling his knees up to his chest. "There was this one girl I met at camp one year when I was fourteen. She was so pretty," Eric said, looking off into the distance at an old vacant house perched on top of a lonely looking hill. A little grin parted his lips as he remembered.

"You know, fourteen is one of those pivotal years in your life, lots of things changing in you and about you – growing up and all that kind of stuff," Eric continued. "We were at this dance and, as I'm sure you can remember, I was painfully shy. So I was sitting in a corner all by myself just waiting for the whole thing to be over. Then I spotted this girl watching me from across the room. At first, I wasn't sure, but after a minute or two, it was pretty obvious." Eric paused for a second, looking down. "Yup, she was definitely interested."

"And?" John said, smiling, poking Eric with an outstretched index finger. "And what did you do?"

"And," Eric said exhaling. "I just looked away."

"A New World"

John woke with a start. A burning sensation covered his entire face and forehead. Cracking his eyes open slowly, he was met by the blazing noonday sun. Lying flat on his back with arms stretched out to either side, he had no idea of how long he'd been out. He pulled himself up into a sitting position, head swimming violently. Looking around, he spotted Chuck laying several feet away in a similar state.

"Chuck!" He coughed. His lips felt tight and dry. "Chuck, you alright?" he called again. This time Chuck, who was lying on his stomach, groaned and with great effort, began to lift his head.

"Where the hell are we?" he asked hoarsely, gathering himself up onto his hands and knees while coughing twice. John looked around through squinted eyes. The entire scene looked like something out of a book. A barren desert spread out around them for as far as the eye could see. John covered his eyes and turned around, peering out in every direction.

"Looks like we're in some kind of ruins in the middle of the desert," he said, noticing the large, crumbling, pillar-like columns reaching skyward all around them. Getting to his feet, he staggered over to examine one of the stone structures.

"There are some really old looking walls and stuff here too," John said over his shoulder to Chuck. He gave a backward glance to see how his friend was coming along. That's when he noticed Chuck was sitting in a stone circle roughly ten feet in diameter. And resting directly in the center of the circle was the teleporter. All of its buttons were flashing just as they had been when he'd pressed them in the frozen lake water.

"What do you make of that?" John asked, pointing at the teleporter's blinking lights.

"I don't know. When did it start doing that?" Chuck asked, rubbing his eyes with the backs of his hands and then crawling over to get a better look at the device.

"I think it was when we crashed through the ice and dropped into the lake. The last thing I remember seeing before I popped us out was seeing all of the buttons flashing like that."

"Really?" Chuck asked, concerned. He picked up the teleporter and tapped on the button that should have turned the power on. The unit gave out a series of three beeps that sounded surprisingly negative. Chuck tried again with the same results. "Damned if doesn't look broken to me, John. What'd you say happened again?"

"Well, it was blinking like that when we were in the lake. I just grabbed you and mashed all of the buttons at once."

"Which one did you push?" Chuck said, a look of worry spreading across his brow.

"I don't know, Chuck. We were about to die. I just grabbed it and pushed. I figured anywhere was better than the lake!"

"Good call," Chuck said, looking up from the unit at his friend, the concerned look disappearing from his face. "Better here than dead, right?" He smiled.

"Well, that's how I figured it," John said, stepping back into the circle and reaching for the device. "Let me take a look at that, will ya?"

Chuck handed the teleporter back to John. "Hey, if you're gonna start messing with those buttons, make sure you're touching me first," Chuck said, sensing that John was going to start monkeying around with the device.

"I would hate to end up *here* all by myself," he said, indicating the desert around them with out-swept arms.

John dropped down into the sand next to Chuck. "Probably not a bad idea," he said, draping one of his legs across Chuck's foot to make sure they had contact.

"Now don't get any funny ideas just 'cause you got me out here alone in the desert!" Chuck said.

The two spent the next few minutes trying to get the teleporter to power up. Every button or combination of buttons they touched produced the same three beeps from the unit.

"It's no use, man, the thing's toast," Chuck said, leaning back onto his elbows.

"Sure looks that way, but it's still making noise so it can't be totally ruined."

"Yeah, but I'm betting it's well beyond us to try to fix it. We have no idea how it really works and no tools to take it apart even if we did," Chuck added, standing up and turning as he gazed out into the distance in every direction. "Man, we're a long way out! We must be in Australia or something."

"What would make you say that?" John asked, quizzically.

"Well, take a look around," Chuck said, waving his arms around. "It's daytime! When we dropped into the lake, it was just after dark back home."

"Very astute," John said wryly. Standing up, he began to explore the ruins again.

"What're you looking for?" Chuck said.

John stopped for a second, his hand resting on some strange looking etchings on one of the rock columns. "Last I checked they didn't have hieroglyphics in Australia."

"Egypt, then?" Chuck asked.

"I don't know. Something about this just doesn't seem right, though," John said, still eyeing the markings carved deep into the stone. "Something sure looks familiar about these etchings, though. I'm sure I've seen something like them before."

John studied the rock columns for a moment more and then turned back toward the stone circle.

"You got something," Chuck said, noticing the hound dog like expression on John's face.

John walked back to the circle and picked up the teleporter. He ran his fingers over the symbols on each of the buttons then looked up at Chuck.

"You're kidding," Chuck said, his mouth remaining open after expelling the last syllable. "No way."

John walked back to the column carrying the teleporter in front of him. Chuck met him at the slender rock column, and the two compared the symbols carved in the stone with the buttons on the unit.

They were an exact match.

"Captivity"

Eric awoke with a splitting headache. Holding his head in his hands, he searched for the lump that he assumed must be there to accompany such a terrible aching, but he found nothing. Squeezing his eyes shut, he breathed out slowly, taking in the sounds around him. Water dripped somewhere in the distance, and a low hum resonated all about him. With effort, he opened his eyes and twisted his head from side to side, trying to relieve the pain at the back of his skull.

As far as he could tell, he was in some kind of cell or holding pin. A dim greenish light radiated from a light fixture recessed into the ceiling. The room was roughly ten by ten with a cot situated in one corner. A tall door stood on one side of the room.

Eric stretched, then got to his feet slowly. The pain in his head subsided as he stepped to the portal where a small glass window was positioned, high up, centered in the frame. The glass was cloudy to the point of being opaque. Eric rubbed it with his shirtsleeve, removing as much of the grime as he could. The window became a bit more translucent, at least clear enough to let some outside light into his little room. He could make out shapes moving about outside the door, but little more. Pacing about, he noticed markings on the wall, apparently written in some foreign language. They looked mostly just like scratches and squiggles to his eye, but from their strange shapes, he presumed that he had been taken to some other country. For what purpose, he could only guess.

Eric quickly spent the last of his patience. Not being one to endure too much crap without at least showing his displeasure, he started banging on the door with both fists.

"Hey, you can't keep me here!" He yelled. "I am an American citizen! I demand to talk to someone at the Embassy!" Not knowing how else to threaten his captors, he added, "I've got people who are going to be looking for me!" Eric mumbled under his breath, "At least I hope they're looking for me."

"So, let me get this straight," Chuck said, pacing nervously. "Our little teleporter has the same markings as this ancient column out here in the middle of the desert, right?"

John nodded his head, still mesmerized by the finding.

"And," Chuck continued, pointing a shaking finger at the column, "I'm guessing, from the looks of it, that this stone thingy here is about a jillion or so years old, right?"

John shook his head again. "Plus or minus a few thousand, but I'd just be guessing."

Chuck squinted at John, suddenly remembering his friend was quite capable of being as much of a smartass as he could be when the situation called for it.

The two explored the ruins for another few minutes, but it soon became obvious that they wouldn't find any more answers buried amongst the ancient, crumbling buildings.

"I guess we're just going to have to pick a direction and head out," Chuck said at last. "No use wandering around here any longer, and besides, I'm starting to get thirsty."

"Yeah, but which way?" John said, gazing out across the seemingly endless expanse stretched out around them.

"Good question," Chuck said, staring out over the barren landscape. "That way," he said finally, pointing out into the desert on a bearing that seemed totally random to John.

"And why that way?" John asked, peering in the direction Chuck was pointing. "You see something out there?"

"Nope," Chuck said. "Just got a good feeling about it." And with that, he picked up the teleporter and stuffed it into one of his coat pockets.

"Guess I don't need to be wearing this," he said, tying the still damp coat around his waist. They had tried to wring a bit of water out of the jackets to use for drinking, but with the blazing sun and arid climate, the thick material had dried amazingly quickly.

The two headed out in the direction Chuck had chosen. It was difficult to tell what lay any distance ahead because large sand dunes erupted from the flat desert surface at seemingly random locations all about the expansive plane. So many in fact that it was impossible to look towards the horizon in any direction without having one of them impede your view. The two tried to walk between them as often as possible but would occasionally scale to the top of a dune to try to get a better look around.

"It's strange how these dunes have formed," John said. "You usually see pictures of the desert with dunes flowing one into the next, like the ocean. But here, they're almost like bumps sitting on a flat surface."

"Well, most dunes get their shape from the wind blowing across them. So in a way, it is like waves on the ocean. But you're right, these are different, almost like big sand piles rather than dunes," Chuck said, affirming John's opinion of the strange sand formations.

Nearly two hours into their trek, they were both showing signs of heat exhaustion and fatigue. They figured that they had covered roughly six or seven miles, and as far as they could tell, they had been walking in a nearly straight line. John had a very good sense of which way he was heading and knew how not to end up going in circles. They passed hundreds of dunes during their trek and became ever more convinced that something was strange about them.

John stopped at the base of the closest dune.

"Something's not right about these, Chuck. Take a look. The sand on the dune seems very loosely packed, but the rest of it seems like the stuff you'd see at the beach right along the shore. You know what I mean? The sand by the shore is very densely packed. That's what the sand we're walking on is like – almost as if it's been pressed down over time," John said while picking up a handful of sand. He let it slowly sift through his fingers down onto the hard packed desert surface.

"I've never seen anything like it before. Have you?" he asked Chuck.

"No. It looks like someone has piled the sand into neat little dollops like you would do with a cookie cutter. I mean, take a look at them," Chuck said, pointing at several of the dunes that stood close by. "They all look the same."

The two marched on for another hour or so until John plopped down on the ground at the base of yet another dune.

"I'm exhausted, Chuck. I got to rest for a minute. You have to remember, these legs haven't been rode like this for months. It's a good thing I was in pretty decent shape before the accident or I'd probably be lying dead out here by now."

John took the jacket from around his waist and draped it over his head, blocking out as much sun as he could. Chuck watched him worriedly.

"We need to find some shelter pretty quick, or we're both going to be in trouble," Chuck said. "You take a breather. I'm going to climb up this dune and see if I can spot anything that looks like, well, like civilization."

Chuck began scaling the side of the sand dune. The dunes were about twenty feet in height and maybe sixty feet across at their base. Climbing one wasn't the easiest task because with each step, his foot sunk several inches into the loose sand. After a handful of steps, Chuck gave up on trying to keep the sand from getting into his shoes. He was far more concerned with finding some water and a place where they could get some shade.

Reaching the top of the dune, Chuck turned slowly, peering out in every direction, shielding his eyes with his hand in an attempt to cut down on the glare coming off the hot desert surface.

Man, what I wouldn't give for a pair of sunglasses right now, he thought.

Gazing about the desert, he took note of the sun's position, which seemed a bit low on the horizon for this time of the day. It almost looked as though it was within hours of setting. Chuck did some quick mental math and decided that they must have been unconscious longer than he had initially thought. But the sun had been directly overhead when they woke up, and they hadn't been traveling for more than a few hours. "Must be where we are in relation to the equator or something," he mumbled to himself. He continued to survey the landscape when something in the distance caught his eye. An object glinted in the bright sun.

"Aha! I've got something!" Chuck yelled down to John. "There's something out there dead ahead."

"How far?" John asked, looking up at Chuck.

"I'd guess about two miles, give or take a bit," Chuck said, starting back down the side of the dune. "We should be able to get there within an hour," he added. "And another thing, it looks like we're not going to have the sun too much longer."

"How's that?" John asked. "We just woke up a few hours ago, and it was high noon."

"I don't know, but from the look of it there are only a couple of hours of sunlight left," Chuck said, shaking his head. "At any rate, we need to get moving."

John hoisted himself up from the desert floor and dusted off the sand that clung to his pants. "Let's hit it then."

Another hour brought them within sight of the object Chuck had seen from atop the dune. It was a building of sorts, but nothing like they had imagined. The structure was shaped like a dome roughly thirty feet tall, and the roof was constructed of glass panels. These were no doubt what Chuck had seen glinting in the bright sun. The building was covered with what appeared to be battle scars. In some places, large chunks of concrete were missing, and almost the entire surface was littered with jagged scrapes and scratches.

Long shadows stretched across the building's face. Chuck and John were surprised by how quickly daylight was disappearing.

"It's a good thing we made it here as quickly as we did. It's going to be dark in minutes," John said. "I can't believe the sun's going down already."

"Me neither," Chuck said. "Let's try to get inside."
The two made their way across the last hundred feet to the dome-shaped structure, and hastily found the door.

"O.K. now how do we get in?" Chuck said, searching the hatch for some kind of handle.

"I don't know," John said, beginning to examine the excessively tall door himself.

"Did you hear that?" Chuck asked suddenly, turning back toward the open desert behind them.

"Hear what?" John asked, engrossed in trying to figure out the secret of opening the strange portal.

"I don't know, it sounded like something moving out there in the sand," Chuck answered, tilting his ear in the direction from which he'd detected the sound. "There it is again."

"Sure, now you're just trying to scare me," John said. "Now give me a hand with this damn door. I hope there's some water in there."

"I've got a bad feeling about this, John. Let's get a move on the door, O.K?" Chuck growled.

John realized that his friend wasn't joking and doubled his efforts to open the portal. A moment later, he found a small panel on the inside edge of the door. In the failing light, it was nearly undetectable.

"Looks like there are some symbols on the edge of the door. I can barely see them, though. The light's too bad to tell what they are."

The sunlight was nearly gone, the glowing orb having dropped completely behind the dunes. Chuck was squinting hard into the twilight, searching for the source of the ominous sounds. Finally, he spotted something. A pair of pale eyes stared back at him from out of the encroaching darkness.

"You need to get that door open now!" Chuck said, reaching back and slapping at John. "Something's out there, man, and it's coming this way!"

"Bound"

Eric wandered around his cell, wondering exactly where he might be. His head had cleared up now, and he was running through the last few things he could remember about his abduction. He'd been working in the barn when the door had been forced open, and someone had stepped in. He remembered turning and seeing a bright flash of light and then nothing else.

"They must have hit me with some kind of Taser or something," he said, thinking out loud before quickly searching himself for any sign of the pinholes that would have been left by the Taser's electrodes. He found none. What he did find was a strange looking pattern in the center of his chest. It looked like a bruise but wasn't tender to the touch. The spot was about an inch in diameter and most closely resembled a sunburn.

Eric wrinkled his brow as he ran his fingertips across the marking.

"What could have left a mark like that?" he said aloud, rubbing the spot for a moment before returning to searching around his cell once again. The markings on the walls meant nothing to him. He decided that they had to be some kind of symbolic language and tried to imagine what cultures would still be using such a strange form of writing.

The cot seemed long for the average person and also quite narrow. Eric picked up the thin mattress, trying to find something he could use as a weapon should the need arise. There were several thin metal straps running along its underside. It took some doing, but he managed to pull one of them loose and fold it over several times, leaving a thin blade-like section sticking out. It looked something like a very small sword. The leading edge was not sharp, but it was thin and pointy enough to give someone a good jab. That would be all he would need to get the upper hand and then hopefully overpower his adversary.

Suddenly the light in the cell went out, leaving Eric in total darkness. For a moment, he was disoriented — a fast swooshing sound followed by a sharp "clank" emanated from the direction of the doorway. Eric saw his chance and rushed the opening; arms thrust out in front of him. A strange voice barked something unintelligible, and he heard the swooshing sound once again. Erik misjudged the portal's location in the darkness and slammed full speed into the wall as the door slid shut.

Unfortunately, he hadn't totally missed his mark. His left arm shot through the opening an instant before the portal had shut completely. The closing door smashed against his arm several inches below his elbow. Eric yelled out as a searing pain shot through his arm. The bones cracked with a sickening crunch, the door laboring to carry out its task, its motor straining from the effort. Someone called out in a foreign tongue, and the door slid back open again. Eric dropped to his knees, and the light in his cell flashed back on. He stared down at his mangled forearm then looked up just in time to see a figure in the doorway point something at him.

"Aw, shit," Eric choked out. And then, as with his abduction, there came a bright flash, then nothingness.

"Go, man! Go!" Chuck shouted urgently, his eyes darting around, looking for anything he might use to defend himself. "There's a wolf, or a bear or something big out there!"

John fumbled with the buttons along the edge of the door, pushing one then the next in rapid succession. "I'm trying!" he yelled back, his hands shaking in reaction to the panic he heard surging up in his friend's voice.

"There's more than one, John!" Chuck called out again, the pitch of his voice going up an octave higher than it had been before.

He stared hard into the shadows cast by the dunes, trying to get a look at what type of animals were approaching, and he didn't have to wait long. A tall creature stepped from the gloom into the waning sunlight.

Chuck's eyes widened in terror as he beheld a monster he could only have imagined in his wildest dreams. Even on all fours, the creature was easily eight feet tall. It walked forward slowly, a thumping sound emanating from each talon-shod foot as they landed heavily with each step. Its pale green eyes glowed in the near darkness, looking much like the eyes of a giant snake. A long, sinewy body reminded Chuck of the creatures he'd read about when he was a boy. Thick armor covered the animal's entire body, and a ridge ran down its back in the shape of an ocean wave.

Chuck gulped twice, but could scarcely speak as he and the monster eyed each other. For a moment, the only sound was that of John's fevered tapping on the portals membrane keys mixed with his breaths coming in short, quick gasps.

"Dra-Dragon bug…" Chuck squeaked out, backing suddenly into John and pushing him against the door. Dragon-bug was the best description he could think of at the moment. As he spoke the word, the creature tilted its head to one side much like a cat would do when spoken to, almost as if it understood.

Chuck looked on in horror as several more pairs of eyes appeared behind the first beast. Within seconds, hundreds of green eyes appeared all about the dome-shaped building, but Chuck barely noticed them. The eyes of the original animal had him transfixed.

The creature lowered its head slowly, keeping its eyes locked on Chuck and then, letting out a terrible screeching howl, it sprang.

In the same instant, John yelled, "Got it!" as the door swished open.

Chuck stumbled backward and sent the two tumbling into the structure. Just as quickly as it had opened, the door snapped shut and just in time, as the monster smashed its full weight against the portal. The door flexed slightly against the load but did not give.

John rolled over and got to his feet as several overhead lights flickered to life. A howl arose from outside the building accompanied by the sound of pounding from every direction. Chuck and John huddled within their safe haven, sure that it would be demolished within seconds.

Then something strange happened.

The panels from the glass roof slid downward, then moved flush against the inside walls of the dome. A platform in the center of the chamber rose up through the space left vacant by the glass. The dais stopped just short of the roof and locked into place with a sharp clanking sound. The two watched in amazement as several long tubes jutted out from the central hub of the device now firmly attached to the ceiling. Within seconds, the tubes began to fire out blinding rays of light. Each of the three barrels was mounted independently on a ball-like socket and spun from target to target so quickly that it was difficult to watch them without becoming dizzy.

The noise of the turrets firing ceaselessly at their unseen adversaries was deafening.

A hologram image floated in the center of the dome several feet off the floor. It displayed an image of the scene outside. The viewpoint encompassed an area roughly two to three hundred feet in diameter.

"It's like watching a movie," Chuck said in disbelief as he

watched the scene of terrible carnage taking place just beyond the walls. Monsters were attacking from every direction while the turrets sprayed out red-hot beams to meet their rush. The lasers seared through the creatures' thick armor, separating limbs from bodies like a knife through butter. The action continued unabated for what felt like hours. John actually started to grow weary of watching the life and death struggle being played out before them on the holograph. Finally, he spoke.

"Where the hell are we, Chuck?" he said in a low voice.

His friend shrugged his shoulders, still captivated by the devastation taking place outside.

"Chuck, *where..the..hell..are we*?" John yelled, finally drawing Chuck's attention away from the image floating in the center of the floor.

"I don't know, man," he said, looking John straight in the eye. "But I'll tell you this, it's not Earth."

Eric slid his eyes open slowly and then just to a small slit. It was one of the survival tactics he'd learned. If someone doesn't know you're awake, you may be able to capitalize on the element of surprise.

He swept his eyes back and forth, taking in as much as he could without moving his head. He was in a different room now. The lighting was different, and it had a peculiar sterile smell very much like a hospital, Eric thought. He couldn't detect anyone else in the room, but he was able to make out some kind of apparatus sitting next to his bed.

Eric lay very still, recounting what had happened and wondering where he might be now. Finally, he decided to hazard a movement. He was lying flat on his back with his head turned to the right. Twisting his right arm confirmed his fears. It was strapped down to the bed. Momentarily he determined that all of his limbs were secured fast.

Giving in to the fact that he was totally restrained, he lifted his head to get a good look around. The room was indeed in some kind of a hospital. The bed was overly long and too narrow just as the cot in the cell had been, but it was comfortable nonetheless.

The room contained several large cabinets and a countertop with a washbasin in its center. Items stacked along the top of the cabinets had the same strange symbolic markings that he had seen in his cell. In one corner stood what appeared to be a refuse can with a rather bloody looking piece of cloth partially contained within it. Eric swiftly realized that it was the remains of his shirt.

"Oh yeah," he sighed out. "That's right, my arm."

He tilted his head back and took in a deep breath, then looked down at his left arm, expecting to see a bloody stump where his arm should have been. Before he'd been knocked out in his cell, he'd gotten a pretty good look at the wound. Considering the amount of damage, he knew it would have been necessary to amputate the arm. Cringing, he remembered the sound of the bones crunching and splintering while being crushed by the sliding, metal door.

"Yup, this isn't going to be pretty," he said under his breath then looked down to where his arm lay tethered. To his surprise, he found a complete, intact arm lashed to the bed.

The only problem being, it wasn't his.

The arm was metallic grey in color and appeared to be a smidgen longer and leaner than it should have been, but by far the strangest feature was the three fingers on the hand. It was attached to his own skin rather neatly with no bandages or stitches, just a smooth fit running from his own flesh into the metal socket of the arm.

Eric sucked in a deep breath and clenched his teeth hard to keep from calling out. He dropped his head back onto the pillow and squeezed his eyes shut, trying to get a hold of himself. Then he noticed something else that seemed bizarre. As he lay there with his body tense, he could feel his new hand tightening into a fist. Yes, feel was the right word for it. But how could he feel anything from a prosthetic, he wondered. He looked down at the new arm and saw the fingers squeezed into the shape of a ball, the three appendages interlocking neatly.

A sense of wonder quickly overpowered whatever fear and loathing he might have had for the new arm. Opening his hand just as he would have done with his own arm proved to have the same natural results. The hand opened and lay flat against the bed. No gears could be heard whirring or spinning as the fingers moved. The entire thing moved just as fluidly as his own flesh and blood hand. Of course, this hand had only three fingers. Eric determined that it was more like two fingers and a thumb. The finger closest to the thumb responded much like an index and middle finger would if they had been taped together. The same went for the second metal finger, which acted as a combination of the ring finger and pinky.

Eric watched in awe as he moved the fingers through their range of motion. Even more amazing was the fact that he was feeling each movement. He tapped the fingers against the thumb one after the other and *felt* the small impact through his new metal skin.

Laying his head back against the pillow, Eric pondered the situation. He knew that this new arm was a feat well beyond the capacity of modern man to produce.

"What do you mean, it's not Earth?'" John fired back at Chuck. "The teleporter had to have sent us someplace on Earth. It always has!"

Chuck pointed to the hologram. "Then tell me what those things are out there, John. When's the last time you saw monsters like those that weren't up on the big screen? Those things are real, and they're out there right now trying to get in here!" Chuck said, excitedly yelling over the thrumming sound of the lasers, which were still blasting away.

"And what about this place?" he said, indicating the area all around them. "Last I checked we didn't have laser guns back on Earth! Not to mention holographic screens!"

The two stared at each other from across the room, not sure of how to proceed.

"So, how do you figure we got here?" John asked, at last, settling his voice back down to a more normal level.

Chuck relaxed a bit himself. "Well, the only thing I can figure is that when we fell through the ice something got messed up in the teleporter," he said, retrieving the unit from his coat pocket. "Didn't you say all the buttons were lit up before you pushed one of them?"

"Yeah, I don't even know which one I hit," John admitted.

"Well, I'm just guessing now," Chuck said. "But I'd almost bet that it's somehow set to go home if there's a problem with it. You know what I mean? It probably has some kind of limp home mode or something."

Chuck paused for a second, his wheels turning on this new idea. Suddenly he snapped his fingers and pointed to John. "I'd bet you that's why we landed in that stone circle out there in the desert. That's probably a set point that it knows to return to," Chuck said, finishing up. "That's my best guess."

"Sounds reasonable enough to me. It might also be why it doesn't seem to be working right now. Since it's already here, it won't go anyplace else till it's fixed," John said then followed with, "How about that, a machine that goes home when it's broken."

"It's just a guess," Chuck said, turning the device over in his hands. Then looking up at John, he added, "But either way, you have to admit, we're not in Kansas anymore."

John turned the corners of his mouth down into a sharp frown. "That sounded really stupid, Chuck. But you knew that didn't you?" he asked.

Chuck just smiled, tapping his teeth together like he was biting off small pieces from a carrot.

Well, I guess we may as well take a look around," John said, shaking his head in resignation.

The two began exploring the contents of the dome-shaped building. There were several panels with flashing lights and meters that proved indecipherable because of the cryptic language used to label them. John noted that every surface was covered in a thick layer of dust.

"Seems like nobody's been in here in forever," he quipped. "The dust is like half an inch thick. What do you figure this place was used for?" he asked.

Chuck stopped and placed his hands on his hips. "Looks like an outpost or something, don't you think? I mean, it's out in the middle of the desert with nothing around it but miles and miles of wasteland. I guess I would figure it's a life hutch."

"Life hutch?" John asked.

"Yeah, like a little manmade oasis in the middle of nowhere, a place where people who are lost can get supplies and hang out for a while. They can get replenished and have some shelter. Chances are if we knew how we could use one of those panels over there to call for help," Chuck said.

"Sounds feasible enough, I guess." John agreed.

"Yup, I imagine all those battle scars on the outside of this place are from attacks by those critters out there. The lasers must be some kind of automatic defenses to fend them off," Chuck said.

As if on cue, the laser turrets stopped firing. John and Chuck raced to the center of the dome to get a look at the holograph. Sure enough, there were no more creatures to be seen anywhere, only the bodies of the ones killed by the outpost defenses.

"Where'd they go?" John asked. "They've been attacking non-stop for at least a half hour."

"I don't know, but take a look at that," Chuck said, still watching the floating holographic image.

Chuck and John watched as the scene leisurely turned from a colorless dusky image to a brighter and clearer picture. Within minutes, the world outside was bathed in a bluish light. It wasn't quite as bright as what you'd expect from the breaking morning sun.

"O.K.," John said, pointing at the screen. By this time nothing surprised him. "So I suppose that's the *other* sun, right?" he asked Chuck.

"Well, unless this planet's spinning like crazy, there's no way that light's coming from the same sun we were trudging under on the way here. My guess would be that this planet is in a system with a binary star," Chuck said.

"Oh, would that be it then, Professor Chuck? It is Professor, isn't it? Or would you prefer Doctor?" John said, smugly.

"Professor will do just fine," Chuck said, grinning, then followed with, "The Prof is gonna take a quick look outside. Come hold the door for me."

"Now wait a minute you wild man, let's give it a few minutes before we go racing out there to our deaths. I'd like to take a better look around in here first where it's nice and relatively safe," John said.

"Alright, but only for a minute. I want to get my hands on one of those beasties," Chuck grudgingly agreed.

John began pouring over the control panel while Chuck wandered off toward the back of the dome to the area farthest from the door.

After a few minutes of searching, Chuck found a door leading to a small room, which jutted out several feet from the wall of the dome.

"John, take a look at this," Chuck said. "I think I've found something."

Chuck stood holding a swinging door open, peering inside at the contents of what appeared to be a refrigerator.

"Look, there's a bunch of stuff in here that looks like vacuum sealed food. And I'm betting that's water!" he said, fishing a clear fluid filled vessel out of the cold compartment.

"You really think you should be drinking that?" John asked, curling up his lip.

"Well, here's how I figure it," Chuck said, placing one hand on his hip. "I'm lost somewhere out in space on a strange planet with monsters running around outside in a little building that's barely holding them back. So if I'm gonna die, it's not going to be from dehydration!" He blurted out the last few words to complete the effect.

He twisted the top off the bottle. The cap produced a hissing sound as its seal cracked open. Chuck smiled over at John as he spun the cap free from the vessel, and then drew it to his lips slowly, sniffing it first.

"Sure smells like water," he said. "Here goes nothing, or maybe everything."

Chuck tipped the bottle up, allowing a quantity of the liquid to chug into his open mouth. He stood there for a second, swishing the fluid back and forth between his teeth as though it were mouthwash, then swallowed hard. John leaned forward, watching for any sign of trouble from his friend.

"Well?" he asked.

Chuck raised a finger and swallowed again, this time tilting his head to one side and squeezing his eyes shut.

"Well? You O.K.?" John asked again.

Chuck twitched once or twice and then sank to the floor, grasping at his throat, his eyes bugging out.

"Oh shit, Chuck! I knew this was a bad idea! What's wrong, what are you feeling?" John yelled, crouching down next to his friend. He grabbed Chuck by the arms and began to shake him furiously.

"Are you O.K.? What are you feeling?" he repeated.

Chuck coughed loudly then pulled John closer, his hands

shaking violently.

"I feel…. I feel…." He gasped. Then suddenly he stopped twitching, his eyes opening ever wider. "Johnny?" he called, his eyes searching around as though he couldn't see John even though he was right in front of him, only inches from his face.

"What is it, Chuck? What's happening?" John said, fearing the worst.

"Johnny, I feel… I feel…less thirsty," Chuck said finally, a smile breaking across his face.

John reeled back as Chuck began to howl with laughter.

"You sack of crap!" John bellowed as he swung a well-aimed punch into Chuck's abdomen.

"You - you sack of crap!" he yelled again. He was so enraged he couldn't think of anything worse to say.

The fluid was indeed water as far as they could tell, and they drank their fill. Chuck also hazarded a look into one of the sealed food containers.

"Tastes like chicken," he said, noticing how John was watching him as he took his first bite. "Really though, it's pretty good, you should try some. We need to keep our strength up."

John decided he had little to lose and suddenly felt very hungry.

Shortly after eating, they decided it was time to take a look outside.

The two headed for the hatch and John keyed in the same series of buttons that he'd pushed to get in before.

"How'd you remember which ones to push?" Chuck asked.

"Believe me, Chuck, those little keystrokes are forever imprinted in my brain. I imagine I'll be dreaming about them for years."

John finished pushing all but the last in the sequence of buttons. "Here goes," he said, then pushed the final button. The door slid open speedily, allowing the two to view the scene outside for the first time since the battle had begun. There were hundreds, if not thousands of bodies everywhere. Their size alone was staggering to behold.

Chuck stepped out through the doorway. "O.K., John. Shut the door, and then I'm gonna try to open it again from out here."

"You got the sequence memorized, right?" John asked.

"Yup," Chuck said.

The two waited for a moment for the door to close.

"Maybe I'm standing too close," John said. "Probably has some kind of sensor like at the grocery store."

Sure enough, when he stepped back a pace, the door slid shut.

He then waited a few seconds while Chuck keyed in the code. A second later it whooshed back open.

"That's it then. Looks like we should be able to get back in if we need to," Chuck said. "Now, I wanna get a closer look at one of those buggers."

"Hey, how do you figure those turrets fired up automatically before? You know, when we first got in?" John asked.

"I'm betting we were just real lucky. The place is probably set to seal everything up when it's under attack."

John eyed Chuck momentarily. "Do you have an answer for everything, you geek?"

"Sorry man, it must be tough going through life without any imagination," Chuck said, slapping John on the back a bit harder than he should have. "I owed you that one, buddy!"

The two headed over to the closest creature. This one, in particular, had been sliced nearly in two through its midsection. Bluish blood had soaked into the sand all around the animal. The image was even stranger because of the eerie bluish sunlight that was covering the entire area.

John shielded his eyes while gazing up at the sun.

"Binary sun, eh?" he said. "Awfully blue, don't you think?"

Chuck looked up from examining the corpse. "Well, it all depends on where the star is in its lifespan. I'm betting that's a pretty old star," Chuck said.

John just shook his head.

They continued their examination of the dead creature for some time. The thing was enormous. After giving it a close look, they determined that it was indeed somewhat dragon-like.

The long neck, fangs, and talons looked like images from a page in a medieval history book, but the rest of the beast was quite different. There were no wings, and the body was not covered in scales as Chuck had at first thought, but in a thick exoskeleton. In many ways, it appeared bug-like.

Chuck dug his hands into the wound where the body had been separated into halves.

"Oh, what the hell are you doing?" John asked disgustedly.

"Look," Chuck said. "There are no bones in here. I think this thing really is some kind of insect. But its body doesn't conform to the norms for an insect," Chuck said, stepping back far enough to be able to take in the entire length of the creature.

John watched as the dragon-bug goo dripped from his friend's hands.

"Now how you gonna get that off?" he asked, pointing back to the dome-shaped building. "I don't remember seeing a bathroom in there."

"Oh, I'm sure there's one in there, we just haven't done enough exploring," Chuck said while wagging a dripping finger in John's direction.

Chuck had clearly slipped into explorer mode. John had seen him like this before. His friend was an adventurer at heart, and John figured if he was going to be marooned on a lonely planet with two suns and dragons, Chuck was just the guy to be stuck there with.

"Realization"

John and Chuck continued to explore the life hutch and did indeed find a bathroom.

"Well, looks like the folks who inhabit this planet must not be too awful different from us," Chuck said, staring down at what was certainly a toilet bowl. "You can always tell by the bathroom."

"Oh, and just how many alien toilets have you had the pleasure of using?" John asked.

"Well," Chuck said, a look of deep thought appearing on his face. "I guess this would be my first."

"That's what I thought," John said.

"But really, if you look at how this place is laid out, I'm guessing whoever or whatever lives on this planet isn't terribly far removed from us, physically at least. I mean, the food seems similar, at least in portion size. You have to admit the bathroom looks pretty familiar, and with the size of the doorways and those cots we found there in the back, I'm almost sure they're about the same size as us and probably bipedal," Chuck surmised.

John looked around the bathroom and then back out at the control panels and the refrigerator. "I guess I could see that."

"And," Chuck continued, "it's now obvious to me that the teleporter came from here. Everything points to it. So these folks have definitely been to Earth at some point in time. Who knows, maybe they look enough like us to get by without even being noticed."

John paused for a second, thinking hard. Chuck had gotten his wheels turning now.

"So, you figure those guys we saw toting Eric out of the barn may have been," John said, looking up at Chuck. "aliens?"

Chuck drew in a deep breath then let it out slowly. "Eric. Damn. I hope he's O.K.," he said, rubbing his forehead. "You know what? I bet he's right here on this planet somewhere. And with any luck, he's alive."

"So why would you figure they'd have come after him?" John

asked.

"Well," Chuck said, reaching into his coat pocket and drawing out the teleporter. "That part's obvious," he said, holding the flashing device out toward John.

"Greetings"

A gentle touch on his new metallic arm stirred Eric from his sleep. His body tensed instinctively against the restraints, his fists balling up, ready for action.

"Lie still." A soft female voice spoke to him. "You're in no danger."

Eric squinted into the bright examination light that was hanging just behind the speaker, allowing him to see only a dark silhouette of her head and upper torso. His pulse quickened as she touched his new arm, running her fingers over the seam between his own flesh and the shiny surface of the prosthetic. He looked down and watched as her long thin fingers glided over his skin.

"It's working along nicely, don't you think?" she asked.

Eric was speechless. For what may have been the first time in his life, he was unable to gather his thoughts enough to muster an answer. It was a strange place for him to be since he'd always tried to stay one step ahead of life, ready for anything. And now, all he could do was blink randomly up at the individual standing over him.

"You're going to be fine," she said, sensing his disorientation and fear. "You'll get used to your new arm very rapidly, I'm sure. Can you feel it?" she asked, trying gently to calm him down.

Eric took a deep breath and regained his composure.

"Yes, I can feel it," he said, letting his breath out slowly. "I can feel it," he said again, this time feeling a bit more relaxed. "Where am I?"

"You're safe. And we're very sorry about the accident with the portal. We never intended for you to be hurt," she said.

"Who's 'we'?" Eric asked, feeling a bit more at ease.

"All will be made clear soon enough," she said. "But you need to rest now. Someone will be in shortly to speak with you." And with that, she turned to leave.

"Wait!" Eric called after her. "Can't you at least untie me?"

The nurse turned around for a moment, and Eric was able to

get a better look at her. She was tall, and though Eric was six feet in height, she was at least as tall as he was and had a slender build. Not slender so much as slight, perhaps, though in a more wispy, graceful fashion. Her eyes were enormous while her nose and mouth seemed a tad smaller. Overall, she appeared humanlike but was clearly different. Eric imagined that someone standing next to her would look squat and thick.

"I'm sorry," she said, in a soothing, gentle voice. "I cannot."

She then turned again and stepped through the portal into a hallway, the door sliding shut behind her as she went.

Eric's mind strained to comprehend what had just transpired. He was now positive that he was no longer in the presence of humans. The question remained, though, whether he was still on Earth or not. He wondered if he might be in some kind of underground compound or if he'd been transported to another world altogether.

Looking around the room for a second time, he took in some of the technology surrounding him. First of all, the new arm was simply amazing. He flexed it time and again and watched as it instantly responded to his mental commands as if it were tied directly to his brain just as his own arm had been. The craftsmanship on the prosthetic was also incredible. No seams or machining marks could be detected on its surface. Other objects around the room showed the same levels of complexity and perfection, as well.

Eric had always been fascinated by technology. From the time he was a boy and had gotten his first erector set, he had loved everything about moving parts and electricity. When he was old enough to go to school, he found the science classes to be the most interesting. Everything else seemed boring to him. How things worked and how they were put together had been the one thing in his life that had truly held his interest.

That's how he originally got into selling items in online auctions. He'd simply collected so many bits and pieces of what others would call junk that he needed to make room for more. Many of the items he happened to get a hold of would-be broken or missing parts, and he would spend weeknights and weekends trying to fix them. Then he'd sell them just to buy more. He was a high-tech handyman capable of fixing just about anything, from computers to washing machines.

Lying in his hospital bed, Eric couldn't help but wonder about what technology went into the items littering the shelves and cabinets around him. It also gave him something else to think about besides his predicament.

John fished around in yet another closet that he and Chuck had found tucked away inside the rim of the dome. They'd gone back to exploring, looking for gear that might help them survive outside of their safe haven should they need to leave. And of course, they both knew they couldn't stay in the life hutch forever. As the teleporter was currently nonfunctional, they would have to trek out on foot again eventually. But the idea of heading out to the dragon-bug infested desert seemed less than palatable.

Chuck was messing around with one of the control panels that were interspersed throughout the dome. They all looked similar with a flat panel littered with touch-sensitive buttons that were not surprisingly very much like the buttons on the teleporter.

Chuck dusted off the top of one unit and sat down on a metal stool that was anchored into the floor. His eyes wandered over the panel, trying to make some sense of the pictograms and symbols that dotted the flat surface. Finally, he began pressing buttons randomly, one at a time. He would press one then watch to see what effect it had. Most of them seemed to do nothing, and Chuck guessed that they needed to be keyed in using some sequence to mean anything. He imagined someone sitting in front of a computer keyboard, randomly pushing keys while expecting something spectacular to happen.

"This is going nowhere fast," he said to himself. "John, you having any luck?" he asked over his shoulder.

"Well, depends on what we were hoping to find," John called back from across the dome.

John had been poking away at some buttons on the front of a sealed cabinet about halfway around the inside of the dome. The cabinet was roughly seven feet tall and eight feet wide, with large double doors covering its face and a key panel situated almost dead center just off the edge of one of the doors. John had managed to get the door open and was holding what appeared to be a rifle. He was smiling like a kid at

Christmas who'd just received his first BB gun.

"Dude!" Chuck yelled, springing up from the stool and running across the room. "What the hell!" he called out again.

He was almost dancing in place with excitement, barely able to keep himself from grabbing the weapon out of John's hands.

"Relax," John said, stretching the word out. Then he reached into the cabinet again, retrieving a second rifle and handing it to Chuck.

"See, there's one for you too," he said in a voice you would use with a spoiled child. "Just don't point it at anybody."

Chuck grabbed the gun and began immediately sighting down its barrel, making gunshot sounds.

"How do you figure it works?" he said, examining the weapon closely.

The rifle was roughly four feet long and looked to be made from some kind of composite material. It was very light for its size. It was pale metallic green in color and was shaped as though the entire thing had been formed from a single piece. The stock flowed neatly into the main body of the weapon, and a sighting scope ran along the length of the barrel.

"Well, first off, I don't think it uses any kind of bullets. I can't see where you'd put anything in. And secondly, there's a little button on the side next to the thumb rest that looks suspiciously like the power button on the teleporter, same symbol and all."

"You figure we should fire one up?" Chuck asked, pointing toward the door.

"Heck yeah, I do. These could be our tickets outta here," John said.

Chuck headed for the door almost at a run, carrying his new toy in one hand, followed closely by John, who was sporting his own weapon.

Chuck opened the door and stepped out onto the hard-packed desert sand. To his amazement, he found himself nearly face to face with another creature of the desert. This one was feeding on the carcasses of the dead beasts from the battle. It was different from the others and had to be at least three times as large, towering nearly thirty feet at its shoulder. A giant, tooth-lined mouth tore enormous chunks of meat from the dead bodies littering the desert.

When it saw the two men emerge from the building, it stepped back momentarily as if startled, then reared up onto its hind legs. The sight was truly terrifying.

The beast howled a guttural sound that made John and Chucks' vision shake. Then it came crashing down onto its front legs with an earth-shattering impact. The resounding thump was so great that it shook the legs out from under both of the men.

John lay on his back, temporarily stunned, but Chuck was quicker to react. He pointed the weapon toward the animal and pushed the power button. Pulling its stock under his arm, he made ready to take a shot from the hip.

"No!" John yelled as he rolled over and pushed the gun barrel away from the creature who by this time, was just staring blankly at them. Apparently, it had performed the only defensive move it knew how to do.

The weapon discharged a red pulse of light into the sky, making the sound of a bass guitar string being plucked hard. The shot went just right off the beast, narrowly missing its thick midsection. In response, the creature stomped backward several steps, then turned and ran.

"What are you doing?" Chuck yelled at John.

"That thing's just a carrion feeder. It's not trying to hurt us. And besides, look at the size of it. You probably would have just made it mad," John responded while getting to his feet.

"We need to figure out just what these things can do before we go blasting away at everything in sight!" he said, brandishing his gun in front of him.

"O.K. O.K., you're probably right," Chuck said, trying to calm himself down. "I just got a little, overexcited there for a second."

"Right," John said. "Now, why don't you take a shot at one of those dead critters out there. Then maybe we'll have a better feel for how these things work."

Chuck stood up and shouldered his rifle, pointing it toward one of the large bodies that lay strewn about the desert before them.

"O.K., here goes," he said, gently squeezing the trigger. A pulse of red light shot from the bulbous end of the gun. Traveling at the speed of light, it struck the dead animal's body in essentially the same instant Chuck pulled the trigger.

Chuck had aimed for the midsection of the creature, and he struck his target squarely. The beam left a hole about the size of a silver dollar in the animal's body and passed completely through it. Within a second, the wound closed under the weight of the surrounding tissue.

"Whoa!" John said, amazed by the destructive energy of the laser. "We sure don't have anything like that back on Earth."

Chuck stared dumbfounded at the smoking wound left by the beam.

The two walked out to the body to get a better look at the damage. Sure enough, the laser had punched clean through the entire body and had, in fact, gone on to impact the desert floor some distance away, leaving a scorch mark on the sand.

After several more minutes of target practice, the two decided that they were pretty comfortable with operating the guns. Upon further examination, they determined that the power source for the weapon was somehow self-replenishing. A small green bar marked the side of the gun just above the trigger. Each time they fired the weapon, it would momentarily drop by about half, and in nearly the same instant, it would spring back again, showing full strength.

Chuck tried several times to deplete the bar by rapid firing a dozen or more shots, but the laser recharged so quickly that he could never exhaust its readiness.

Several other buttons lined the side of the weapon, but as with much of the alien technology, their purpose was indecipherable to the two men.

"Hey, I'm gonna head back in and see what else may be in that cabinet," John said as Chuck tested his aim on yet another dragon-bug body.

"O.K.," Chuck said without looking up. "I'll hold down the fort out here."

"Oh," John said, turning to head back for the dome-shaped building. "Try not to blast anything that doesn't really need to be blasted. Remember whatever you shoot may have lots of friends out here."

Chuck waived a dismissive hand over his shoulder. "Yeah, yeah," he said, continuing with his target practice.

Back inside the life hutch, John headed to the cabinet where he'd found the laser weapons. Passing by one of the control consoles, he saw something that caught his eye. One of the buttons that had been dark was now lit up and blinking. Perhaps all of their button mashing had not gone unnoticed after all.

John stepped to the console and looked at the symbol imprinted on top of the flashing switch. It was a little circle surrounded by other concentric circles, each one drawn with a dashed line. To John, it looked a lot like the symbol for a radio antenna or some type of broadcast. He stared at it for a second then reached down and pressed his finger against the flat surface.

The flashing button turned from red to a continuous green. Nothing seemed to happen for a few seconds, but then a small screen under the panel flickered to life. John wiped the dust from the screen to get a better look. An empty chair could be seen in the image. He wrinkled his brow, trying to figure out what he was looking at.

A moment later a tall figure appeared on the screen. John looked on in wonder. The being on the other side of the screen was obviously not human, though not terribly far removed in shape or size. Large eyes, a small mouth and nose, and a very slender build clued John in that he was looking at one of the alien masters of this planet. The look on the alien's face showed that it was just as surprised to see him as he was to see it.

"Chuck! Get in here! You need to see this!" John called out to his friend without taking his eyes off the screen. Chuck appeared in the doorway a moment later.

"What's up?" he asked, setting his laser rifle down on one of the many countertops.

John tipped his head quickly without speaking, indicating toward the view screen.

Chuck stepped over and stared down at the screen and was rendered speechless by what he saw.

"Hello?" John said, finally breaking the silence. The figure waved hurriedly at someone else off-screen and spoke a string of syllables that were unintelligible to John and Chuck, its eyes darting back and forth between them and the unseen recipient of its message.

Another figure appeared alongside the first, and the two stared wide-eyed, as if unable to believe what they were seeing. They made a few back and forth exchanges before one of them leaned forward as if reaching for something. The view screen's image went blank, leaving the two Earthlings staring at the dusty surface, the green light now having gone back to black.

"Well, apparently our conversation is over," John said, looking over at his friend.

"Revelation"

The door to Eric's room slid open once again. By his account, it had been roughly two hours since the alien nurse had left. A tall thin being stepped through the portal and stopped momentarily to gaze at him from across the room. It then walked to his bed and sat down on a rolling stool, much like any other doctor might do.

"How are you feeling?" he asked, holding before him what appeared to Eric to be a tablet computer.

"I'm doing alright," Eric returned. "How are you?"

The doctor smiled at this, apparently not expecting such a warm response.

"I'm quite well," he said, tilting his head forward just a touch as if he were saying "Thank you for asking."

"Do you know why you're here?" the doctor said.

"I can imagine." Eric said, "But you have me at a disadvantage. Can you tell me where I am?"

The alien doctor leaned back on the stool and looked around the room for a moment.

"I don't see why not," he said, smiling. "After all, you're turning out to be much different than we had at first assumed."

"How's that?" Eric asked.

"Well, first things first," he said, and leaned forward, reaching for the restraints that kept Eric strapped fast to the bed. Lifting his gaze up from the first clasp, he asked, "I assume it's safe for me to remove these?"

Eric made his choice quickly. In any other place, he might have lied his way out of the situation in order to get free, but somehow, he knew he could trust this individual. And besides, he had become fascinated by the whole idea of what was happening to him.

"Of course," he said, with all honesty. "I just want to know what's going on."

The doctor smiled again then began to remove the restraints, starting with his feet and undoing the ones holding his arms last. Eric reached over and rubbed the area where his new arm connected to his own flesh.

"Quite amazing, isn't it?" the alien spoke. "Would that we could produce more of them."

Eric squinted at the doctor questioningly. Noticing Eric's inquisitive look, the doctor sat back onto the stool once again.

"Let's start at the beginning," he said, smiling wide. "Literally. You see," the doctor said, "There's much to say about your history." He leaned forward again, his eyes meeting Eric's with intensity. "Are you sure you wish to know about your origins?" he asked. "Many would find the truth – disturbing."

"Yes, I want to know," Eric said.

"Very well," the alien said. Then he turned toward the door. "Altare?" he called.

The door slid open, and the nurse who had previously spoken with Eric re-entered the room. The doctor said something to her in a tongue so foreign that Eric could not have possibly translated even a word of it.

"Oh," he said, noticing Eric's wrinkled brow. "I'm so sorry, I forget myself." Then looking back to the nurse, he spoke again.

"Could you please bring us something to eat?"

"Yes, doctor," she said, then turned to leave.

"Alright, shall we begin then?" he asked Eric.

"Whenever you're ready," Eric said, sitting up in the bed and arranging the pillows behind him.

"You see," the doctor started out, "you must take some things for granted in what I'm about to tell you. You may find them to be a leap of faith; other items are factual data from what we've been able to ascertain from our own records." The doctor then took in a deep breath.

"It would seem that everything in the universe has the same creator. Though we are scattered all over the cosmos, we are, in form and function, essentially the same."

"But you look different from me?" Eric asked.

"Yes, of course we do. You see, there are thousands of variables that play into the evolution of a species. But at the heart of it, we all started out from the same seed. The differences have come from where and when we were planted, so to speak. Also, our own actions as a race play a significant role in what we have become today. Planetary climatic changes along with encounters with our world's other indigenous life have also shaped our existence. Your own planet, for example, has had many ice ages that have left their mark on your evolution. You see differences in skin color and body structure depending on where an individual has come from, geographically speaking.

Our own race appears to have been one of the first to be created. As far as our recorded history tells, we have been traveling through the cosmos visiting other worlds for tens of thousands of years, perhaps even hundreds of thousands," the alien said, then took another deep breath. "Of course, that is all different now."

"Different?" Eric said.

The alien doctor shifted on the stool. "Later," he said, shaking one of his long fingers at Eric. "We'll get to that later."

"Now then, we've been visiting your planet for some time. We even had an outpost there to study your progress. Unfortunately, it was lost to us thousands of years ago in a cataclysmic event."

"Oh my God!" Eric said grinning. "Do you know where it was located?" Eric asked.

"I don't know for sure, but it was on a small island that sank due to an underwater volcanic eruption of some sort. Many lives were lost."

Eric's leaned in closer. "Atlantis?"

"Yes. Yes, I do believe I have heard it called that somewhere before. You've heard of it then?" The doctor asked, nodding his head in acknowledgment.

Eric leaned back against his pillow in disbelief. "Well, I've heard tales of it – everyone has. It was supposed to be a city populated by a highly advanced race. It sank into the ocean because of an earthquake."

"Yes, that was one of our outposts. And you can imagine the technology that was lost when that city went down," the doctor said, staring intently at Eric.

"Yes, I can," Eric said, noticing how the doctor was watching him. "What?" he asked.

"Have you ever seen anything that you might find unusually advanced for your own race? Perhaps something like this?" the alien said, slowly drawing an object out from under his robes.

"The teleporter!" Eric yelled, then quickly gathered himself, realizing that he'd just given away more information than perhaps he should have.

"Hush now," the doctor said, trying to calm Eric down. "This is not the same unit you have seen. It is indeed akin to it, though." He then looked Eric in the eye watching, for his reaction to the next question.

"Do you know where the other device is?" the doctor asked slowly, giving Eric a chance to think about how he should respond.

Eric stared at the teleporter and wondered how he should answer the question. He knew full well that his friends had the device, or at least they did before his abduction.

"I'm not sure," he lied.

The doctor watched Eric for a moment, giving him a moment to collect his thoughts.

"These devices appear to be quite rare," he said at last. "Let me tell you a little about what we know of them," the doctor added, settling back on the stool once again. "But first, I'll need to fill you in on a bit of our own history. You see, our race is quite ancient. We can tell this from some of the technology you see around you right now. That arm, in fact," the doctor said, reaching over and touching Eric's new metal arm, "is tens of thousands of your Earth years old."

"What?!" Eric exclaimed. "But it looks brand new."

"That is a testament to the prowess of our ancestors. The creation of such a thing today is quite beyond us," the doctor said. Seeing the lost look on Eric's face, he added, "Perhaps I should go back even further."

The door to the chamber slid open, and Altare stepped through, carrying a tray filled with strange looking vegetables and two vessels filled with fluid. The doctor handed one to Eric; then he took a long swallow from the other. "Thank you," he said, dismissing Altare.

"You see, our history, and perhaps the history of all intelligent life in the universe is heavily rooted in conflict. We, like your own race, have struggled with our differences for ages. The small amount we know about our own past leaves us with little to pass on to future generations."

"I don't understand," Eric said. "You seem to be so advanced."

The doctor chuckled at this. "Yes, it would seem so to one from the outside."

He set his drink back on the tray. "Would you like to take a walk with me, Eric?" he asked.

Eric noted that it was the first time he had called him by name. "I would," he responded.

"Watch your legs now. Much of your strength was lost when your arm was damaged," the doctor said.

Eric slid out of bed and gently put some weight on his legs. "I'm O.K.," he said, noticing the doctor's inquisitive glance. "I'll be fine."

The two made their way out through the portal into a dimly lit hallway. They passed through a series of doorways on either side and finally to one large portal at the end. The doctor pushed several buttons, and the door slid open, revealing a large courtyard hundreds of yards long. Eric stared wide-eyed at a huge garden spread out before him. The scene reminded him of what the hanging gardens of Babylon must have looked like. There were hundreds of varieties of plants growing up from well-manicured beds on the ground and dozens more suspended from the transparent ceiling of the building, which was a full fifty feet in height. The place looked like a giant greenhouse.

"This is where we grow much of the food for the city," the doctor said, letting Eric soak in the sight.

"These are part of my responsibilities," he added, sweeping his arm in front of him, indicating the whole room. "The entire planet is a desert, which is why we must produce everything we need within the city walls."

Eric stepped to the side of the building and rubbed his hand against the glass plate, removing a swath of condensation.

"Has it always been this dry?" he asked as he began to walk down one of the rows of plants while the doctor followed alongside him.

"No," the doctor said, walking for a moment with his head down as if deciding the best way to convey his next thought.

"We have very little knowledge of our past. As I said before, the little we know speaks of savagery and destruction. Our people waged terrible wars against each other and in doing so, desecrated the land to such an extent that it may never return to its former state. This much we know: the planet used to be green and lush much like your own. But the weapons used thousands of years ago burned nearly all life from the face of the planet. And what remained was altered beyond recognition. Only a few outposts of our once great civilization remain. And even these are in grave danger of disappearing forever."

"How is it that you know so little of your past? There must be records, books, or something," Eric asked.

"No, those artifacts are nearly all gone. Only a handful remains. These walls were built only just before the ultimate weapon was used against our kind. One of the warring factions unleashed a bio-toxin killing over ninety percent of our population. Unfortunately for the inventors of the plague, their disease covered the entire globe and decimated their own ranks in the same fashion.

"How did anyone survive?" Eric asked.

"As far as it is known, only a few of the very young lived through the cataclysm. These children were not yet old enough even to read. Apparently, there was some natural immunity in them, or perhaps their systems were able to somehow adapt to the disease. Either way, they grew up without knowing anything about their own culture, without any transfer of knowledge from parent to child."

"But what about all this technology? How do they know how it works?"

"For the most part, we do not understand our own sciences. Many of the devices around you, even ones as complex as your arm, are so advanced that they require no understanding of how they work. It is only necessary to understand their purpose, and then in most cases, the question of how to use them becomes obvious."

The two walked through the remainder of the garden. Eric tried to understand how such a great civilization could have destroyed itself. But then thinking of his own world, he realized that with the push of a button, thousands of years of learning and culture could be erased. He suddenly felt very sad.

"Come, I'd like to show you something else," the doctor said.

They walked down another long hallway, this one only sparsely lit by small fixtures overhead.

"We're going to an older, less used part of the city now. You'll find that it's not in a good state of repair. We must salvage what we can from one section of the city in order to shore up the areas where we live the most."

The corridor ended at a junction where a vehicle waited. It sat atop a track that was much like a monorail.

"Please, step in," the doctor said, gesturing toward one of the two available seats. Eric climbed in and sat down.

"We rarely use these transits to the outer reaches. Most of the city's inhabitants find traveling there disheartening."

With the press of a few buttons, the vehicle came to life.

"So, if this thing breaks down somewhere, how do you fix it?" Eric asked.

"With great difficulty," the doctor said. "We've found most of the city's systems to be self-perpetuating and very rarely require maintenance of any sort."

Eric's mind reeled at the idea of machines that were intelligent enough to fix themselves, or that something could be engineered so well that it would last virtually forever without any type of repair.

"So how old would you guess this vehicle is?" he asked, noticing a thin layer of dust coating many of the monorails controls.

"I would assume it to be roughly two and a half thousand years old," the doctor said.

Pressing a final button, the monorail began to move. It accelerated so smoothly that Eric barely felt the motion at all. There were no vibrations or sounds of spinning gears as he would have expected. It was as though the unit ran exactly the same as it did on the day it had been produced.

Sliding along at breakneck speeds, the monorail swiftly escaped the bounds of the building in which it had been housed. Soon Eric and the doctor were cruising along through a glass tunnel just a few feet off the ground. Eric could see the parched desert land passing rapidly by outside. In the distance, he could make out a wall much like one you would expect to see fortifying a castle. An occasional flash of light could be seen coming from the top of the wall, even in the bright noonday sun.

"What's happening over there?" Eric asked.

The alien doctor looked out through the glass toward the wall. "That, my Terran friend, is what is trying to destroy the last of us."

The slowing of the monorail drew Eric's attention away from the city wall. They were approaching a tall, slender building with a large, mushroom-shaped section at its peak. Dozens of skywalks sprung from the bulbous room and ran some distance to the outer wall. The monorail slid gently into a hatch at the base of the building and came to a halt.

"Come," the doctor said, stepping out of the vehicle. Eric followed close behind the doctor, noticing that his pace had quickened somewhat.

The two entered a lift in the center of the building and with the push of a button, jetted skyward. Within seconds they stopped inside the chamber Eric had seen from the monorail. The room was about sixty feet in diameter and was constructed almost entirely of what appeared to be glass. Fifteen or twenty aliens were positioned around the room at various consoles. Some were coming in from or going out to the tubular walkways.

"Dr. Arcos," an alien standing close to the lift greeted them, his eyes widening when he saw Eric.

"It's fine, Lokar," the doctor said, seeing his surprise at the visitor. "He is with me."

Though he couldn't understand the exchange, Eric assumed that they were greeting one another. He took note that the beings in this room were clad in body armor. Each one also carried a sidearm and a rifle slung over his or her back.

"This way," the doctor said to Eric, pointing toward one of the hatches leading out to a walkway.

As they started toward the door, two of the aliens in the room dropped into line behind them.

"Oh, that won't be necessary. We won't be out long," the doctor spoke once again, this time speaking the sentence first in his native tongue, then again in English for Eric's benefit.

The Alien soldier offered a laser pistol to the doctor. "Very well," the doctor said, taking the gun and tucking it under his robes.

The door slid open, and the two stepped out onto the walkway.

"You see, my friend," the alien began their conversation again, "we know little about our heritage. We do know this much, however. Our lack of foresight has brought us to where we are today. It seems our planet is growing weary of our lack of consideration for it and for ourselves."

The doctor walked quickly, obviously a bit nervous about heading out onto the city's outer walls. Eric could see a portal at the end of the walkway, and as they closed the distance, the bright flashes of light he had seen from the monorail became more intense. With them came a thunderous sound like someone striking a large drum and then quickly silencing it. The explosive sound repeated again and again as they approached the portal. Eric became nervous, a bit afraid of what he might see on the other side of the door.

Reaching the end of the walkway, the doctor stopped and turned to Eric.

"Are you ready?" he asked, retrieving the gun from his robes.

Eric nodded his head up and down quickly, not speaking for fear that his voice would shake.

Arcos reached up and touched a button on the key panel, and the hatch slid open. The sound of the laser turrets boomed into the walkway so loudly that Eric had to cover his ears. The two stepped onto the city's outer wall and looked out over the desert. Eric watched in amazement and horror as hundreds of creatures poured toward the city from all directions.

Turrets spaced at fifty-foot intervals along the wall poured bright red laser beams continuously down at the advancing creatures.

"What is this?" Eric asked, fighting the urge to run back through the hatch into the walkway. "What are those things?"

"Those are the products of twenty thousand years of evolution and mutation on the once modest life forms of this planet. What you're seeing is the reason we live within these walls and dare not venture from them.

"They just keep coming!" Eric shouted over the roar of the laser cannons.

Thousands of the creatures' bodies lay scattered about the desert in every direction.

"Yes, they do. They will attack like this several times a day and then again at night. There are many different creatures out there, each seemingly with its own grudge against us," Arcos said, staring off toward the horizon. "Shall we?" he asked, pointing back at the door.

Eric was only too happy to pass back into the relative safety and quiet of the walkway. Once inside, he leaned against the rounded glass wall to catch his breath.

"So you're saying that your ancestors built all of this to keep those creatures out?"

"We cannot know for sure, but I would surmise not. I believe the city's defenses were most likely constructed to keep our own kind out," Arcos said. "It was only luck that they have also worked so well against the mutations that roam our world now."

"What powers them? I mean, how can they have been running for thousands of years with no repairs?" Eric asked.

"They do not seem to require repair unless one is damaged. And then we have no way of mending it. Much of the ability to use the technology is within our grasp, but the understanding required to repair it is not. We can't even get inside one of those turrets to attempt to see how it works," Arcos said while pointing through the glass tunnel at the cannons still hammering away at unseen enemies.

"You see, much like the rest of our technology, these weapons have a simple keypad embedded in them. From this pad, you can stop or start their operation and, we presume, perform maintenance. We have also seen, quite by accident, that the right combination of keystrokes will open access panels on each machine. But since we do not understand much of our own written language, we cannot decipher many of the codes required to open and therefore maintain this equipment. So much is coded into the programs trapped within the metal hull, and we are unable to access them."

Eric noticed that one of the turrets several hundred feet down along the wall was not firing and that it looked rather oddly shaped when compared with the rest of the cannons.

"What about that one?" he asked. "Why isn't it firing like the rest?"

"That one has been damaged. Occasionally one of the desert creatures will make it to the wall and will attack one of the turrets. This happens very rarely, but with our inability to fix the systems and the increasing number of attacks, a breach seems imminent," Arcos said.

"If we only had some way of understanding more of the symbols on these devices, we could open and perhaps repair them," he added.

"A Rosetta stone, of sorts," Eric said. "You need a Rosetta stone."

The doctor looked at Eric. "Rosetta stone?"

"Yes, in our own history, a piece of stone was found that had the same inscription carved in several different languages. It allowed humanity to understand an ancient, lost form of communication."

"Interesting," Arcos said. "A 'language' stone."

"Your ancestors' knowledge of technology must have been incredibly advanced," Eric said. "So advanced that some of it could be figured out even without being able to read the instructions. It's like at home – most people don't have any idea of what's happening in the appliances and machines they use every day. I can imagine that with technology as advanced as this is, it would be nearly impossible to figure out what makes it tick without a thorough understanding of that same subject. It's a Catch 22."

"A Catch 22?" Arcos asked.

"Oh, I mean you're in a spot where you can't fix something because you don't know how to go about doing it, and you don't know how to go about it because you've never been exposed to the science behind it," Eric said. He then added, "What you need is a good schematic to start with."

"Yes, if my understanding of your word *schematic* is correct. If we had documentation on these systems, we could better understand them," Arcos said.

The two headed back to the central hub in silence. Eric was trying to sort through everything that had been thrown at him in the last day. He stopped suddenly in the middle of the walkway and turned toward Arcos.

"So, why bring me here?" he asked directly.

Arcos stopped and looked at Eric "The *teleporter*, as you call it, is a very powerful device. As you now know, it can transport the user not only around the face of a planet but to other worlds as well. Again, much of what the device can do has been discovered through trial and error. Unfortunately, we've lost many individuals and units while trying to uncover its secrets. When you discovered one on your planet and began to use it, we became very interested."

"But how did you know we had it?" Eric asked.

"The units act as a beacon when they're powered on, much like what you would call a homing device. We can detect their presence with special equipment here in the city," Arcos said. "We were then able to travel to your position to retrieve the device."

"I'm guessing you wanted it back because it's so powerful," Eric said.

"Of course. I'm sure you can imagine what an individual could do with such a thing if they were given to performing evil deeds."

"But how did it come to be left on our planet?" Eric asked, transfixed by the story of the teleporter.

"The outpost we spoke of earlier. When it met its fate, many artifacts were lost along with the city. Though it was many thousands of years ago, there was no way of knowing where the unit was. That was also during a very turbulent time in our own history. From the little we know, many of our colonies were lost to us during those war-torn centuries."

"So, do you know where the device is now?" Eric said, trying not to give anything away.

"Well, we've found that the units return home when they are damaged. So the device is in fact, here. Somewhere out there in the wasteland," he paused before continuing as if measuring how his next words would be taken. "Along with your friends."

Eric was speechless.

"Well, how about that," Chuck said, looking over at John. "So much for making a surprise entrance, huh?"

"Let's just hope they're not going to kill us and eat us," John said.

The two stood staring at the blank screen for a minute more, fiddling with the keyboard in a feeble attempt to reconnect with the aliens. Finally, John said, "We ought to grab what we can carry and get the hell out of here. Don't ya think?"

"Sounds like a good idea to me," Chuck said. "I'm wondering how long it will be before more of those monsters decide to come back for another round."

"Yeah, let's roll," John said. "But I want to make sure we're not missing anything important while we're here. Let's take one more good look around."

"I'm on it," Chuck said, heading for one of the cabinets they'd been unable to get open.

John began tapping feverishly on the keypad for the second door of the weapon cabinet. Trying the same sequence of keys he'd used to open the first door didn't work. The panel would make a low beeping sound after he'd punched in three symbols.

"Must be something good in here," he mumbled to himself, keying in yet another series of symbols. Finally, the door popped open. Examining the contents of the large cabinet, he was startled by what he saw. A pair of metallic red eyes stared out at him from the deep recesses of the enclosure.

"Chuck, take a look at this!" John yelled over his shoulder.

In the instant it took Chuck to appear at his side, the eyes began to glow.

"Oh man, I think its firing up!" Chuck said, backing off several feet.

John and Chuck watched as a robotic biped stepped from the cabinet and stood before them. It was roughly seven feet tall and built like a tank. Two thick arms hung down to its knees. A small head with the two red eyes was positioned between the heavily armored shoulders atop a tiny but thick neck. The legs and torso appeared to be made for heavy work.

The robot turned its tiny head toward John and spoke several words in what sounded like the same language he'd heard the aliens using on the monitor. John looked at Chuck, eyebrows raised. Chuck shrugged his shoulders.

"Do you speak English?" John asked very slowly, enunciating each word.

"Yeah, I'm sure it's been programmed with the Queen's English! You moron! Maybe you should ask it if it knows French!" Chuck blurted out, laughing. But his chortle was cut short as the robot responded with a metallic sounding "Yes."

The two were taken aback, unsure of how to proceed until John asked another question, "How many languages do you speak?"

"Five thousand, two hundred, and fifteen." The robot responded.

"What do you do?" John asked.

"Invalid input, restate query," the robot said back to him.

"Can you help us?" John asked again.

"Invalid input, restate query," was the only response.

"Any ideas?" John asked Chuck.

"Well, maybe it's more of a doer, than a thinker," Chuck said, stepping up to the machine.

"Pick up that rifle," he said, pointing to one of the weapons in the cabinet.

The robot turned back to the enclosure, retrieved one of the laser guns, and then returned to Chuck and John.

"Looks like some kind of worker robot or something," Chuck said. "Probably good for lifting heavy stuff and moving things around."

"Hey!" John said suddenly, "I wonder if it can guide us out of here. Maybe it can take us to those aliens."

"Maybe," Chuck said, "But how are you going to ask it? It doesn't seem to understand a lot of what you're saying. I'm betting its vocabulary is pretty limited."

"Well, there's got to be someplace on this planet more

populated that here – a city or town or something," John said, turning back to the robot.

"Go city," he said, trying to keep his words as simple as possible. The robot paused for a moment then responded by voicing a series of strange sounding locations, followed by a single word spoken in English: "Choose."

"Those must be the places it knows about," Chuck said. "How do we know which one to pick?"

John was thinking hard now. Rubbing his chin with his thumb and forefinger, he looked up at the robot and said, "Closest."

The robot turned and started lumbering toward the door.

"Yes, that's it! Now we're getting somewhere!" John shouted.

"Yeah, but who knows how welcome we're going to be if and when we get there," Chuck said a bit worriedly. "And, you may want to stop him before he gets too far. We need to load up on some supplies. Who knows how long we may be walking."

"Good idea," John said. "Stop!" he called to the robot who obediently halted in his tracks just feet from the front door.

Rummaging through the remainder of the cabinets, the two found several more items they thought might be useful on the trip. They loaded everything they could into some shoulder packs they'd found and ordered the robot to carry the bulk of the load. Chuck found a wheelbarrow-like contraption that they attached to the robot as well. It was large enough for them to sit in and had a reflective cover that could be pulled up to block out the sun, much like a giant baby stroller.

"This should keep us from getting burnt to a crisp," Chuck said, lifting the sunshade up and down. "You about ready?"

"Yes, I suppose so," John said, looking around the domed building a final time. "I just hate to leave the security of this place for whatever's waiting out there in that desert."

"I know, but we can't stay here forever. We'd be out of food in no time," Chuck said, grinning wide. "And then I'd have to eat you."

"Coming Clean"

"What do you mean, along with my friends?" Eric asked quickly, his voice sounding more urgent than he wanted to let on.

"It appears that your two friends activated the unit when it was damaged. And as I've said, we've found that the teleporters (as you call them) are programmed to return to their place of origin when in need of repair."

"So where would that be?" Eric asked.

"Well, that's difficult to say with any certainty," Arcos said. "You see, most of the cities where the devices were produced no longer exist. At least not as they once did. Nearly all of them are rubble now, reduced to foundations of stone jutting from the desert sand."

By this point, Eric had lost all hope of hiding his relationship with the other two men.

"So, you're saying they're out there in the desert with all those creatures around?"

"That would seem to be the case," the doctor said. "But, do not worry, it appears that they've made it to one of the ancient safety houses."

"And what's that?" Eric asked, still quite worried.

"A waypoint of sorts. A place for travelers lost in the desert to find safety and summon help."

"Well then, we need to go get them!" Eric said.

Arcos put his hand on Eric's shoulder. "I'm afraid it's not that easy. They are a half a day's travel away, and the wasteland is very dangerous, as you have seen." The doctor indicated back toward the creatures still streaming toward the wall. "All we can do for now is hope."

"Surely you have some way to get to them," Eric shouted. "What about using a teleporter?"

"The teleporters no longer operate on this planet. They can only be used to travel from here to another world or back again. It is another byproduct of our warring history. A field surrounds the entire planet. This field will not allow accurate transit via teleportation devices. Our elders believed they were too powerful and nullified their capabilities here on our world."

"We can't just sit here! We've got to do something! With all the technology you have, are you telling me there are no airships, no armored vehicles, nothing?" Eric wailed.

Arcos lowered his head and closed his eyes, exhaling deeply. A moment later, he returned Eric's gaze. "I am sorry that we are not as you at first believed us to be. The terms of our existence are worse than you may even now imagine. It is hard to understand, but we have very little left to give." Turning slowly toward the hatch, he looked out over the city's walls. "Do you know why we brought you here?" he said without looking back. "We brought you here so that we might use the teleporter ourselves, to escape from this world when the time comes."

Even though he wasn't human, Eric could hear the humanity in the doctor's somber voice. The thrum of the laser turrets pounded away while they both stood in silence, worlds apart.

"Into the Void"

"Alright, let's hit it!" Chuck called to John, who was still digging around in one of the cabinets. "Time's a wasting!"

"I'm coming! Man, keep your pants on! I just don't want to leave anything behind that we may need," John shouted back, somewhat irritated.

"We've got food, we've got guns. What else is there?" Chuck said in his best Southern accent.

John stepped toward the door, a laser rifle slung over his back, and a pistol strapped to his hip. "So I guess we're riding, huh?" he asked Chuck.

"Yup. As far as our metal friend will take us," Chuck quipped while patting the robot on the back.

John watched his friend hopping around excitedly, tossing the last few items into the cart behind the robot.

"You're really enjoying this, aren't you?" John asked.

Chuck stopped for a second. "In a way," He said. Then he nodded his head. "Yeah, in a way, I am. You can't buy this kind of adventure back on Earth. I mean, look around you, John." He said with a wild look in his eye. "My God man, we're on an alien planet with a robot and laser guns and monsters! We may be the first humans to have ever met aliens! So yes! I am very excited!"

"O.K.. are you done with your speech, Pocahontas?" John asked. And before Chuck could answer, he said, "Good, then let's get moving while we've still got some light. Who knows how long that's going to last."

John gave one last look around before stepping through the portal. He turned and pushed the 'close' button, stepped back, and watched as the door slide shut behind him. He and Chuck then climbed on the back of the cart.

"Go closest city," John said to the robot, who promptly lurched to a start, nearly causing Chuck to tumble out onto the hard packed sand.

"Quite the traveler, aren't you?" John laughed as Chuck tried to regain his composure.

The robot stuck to a rapid pace once it got going. Within seconds they were all moving along at what Chuck guessed to be around five miles per hour, a very good pace indeed.

"I wonder how far it is to the nearest city?" Chuck asked John. "You figure our friend here knows?"

"Can't hurt to ask," John said.

Chuck cleared his throat and leaned forward in the cart. "Closest city distance?" he asked.

"Fourteen miles." The robot reported.

"Should take about three hours at this pace," Chuck said. "And I'm guessing we'll have plenty of light."

"I sure hope so," John said, clutching his laser rifle. "I hate surprises."

"Last Hope"

Eric stared down at his new arm, trying to think of something else to say. He was overcome by everything that had happened since having woken up a short time ago. The idea of an ancient race of advanced aliens teetering on the edge of extinction seemed inconceivable.

He'd imagined that someday the discovery of life beyond Earth would bring with it the promise of peace through the understanding of higher technologies. As it turned out, for this race, that very technology had been their undoing. As he watched the laser guns pounding away at unseen enemies just beyond the wall, Eric wondered if his own world would meet a similar fate.

"There must be some way to help them," Eric said at last.

Arcos lifted his head and met Eric's stare. "My friend, you have seen what awaits us in the desert. You are asking for something we cannot give. Your people seem much more resilient than we've expected. Perhaps they will find a way to make it to us or to one of the other cities."

"Are we the closest to them?" Eric asked.

"Yes, the closest populated city, but there is no way of knowing which way they will travel. Without an understanding of our maps or the systems in the safe house, I don't see how they could determine the proper path."

"But you said that your people had seen them and knew where they were. Why couldn't we contact them and give them directions?" Eric asked, urgently.

"The ones who were contacted by your friends were frightened by the sight of them and ended their communication immediately. I have tried to reestablish the link, but apparently, they are no longer in the safe house."

"How could you know that?" Eric asked again.

"It is only a guess. But as I've said, your friends seem to be quite capable of taking care of themselves," Arcos said.

Their conversation was cut short by an alarm sounding throughout the hall. Seconds later, the walkway was filled with armored troops heading toward Eric and the doctor.

"What's happening?" Eric shouted

"Come!" Arcos yelled, grabbing Eric by his prosthetic arm and pulling him back toward the hatch leading to the outer wall.

The portal sprang open, and the two ran onto the battlements. Peering over the plane, the doctor exclaimed, "Oh no. It is as I feared!"

Eric swept his gaze back and forth across the horizon until at last, he saw the object of the doctor's dismay. A huge robot lumbered toward the city, still some miles away.

The doctor was using a spotting scope attached along the edge of the wall, gauging the robot's progress. Eric quickly found another and squinted through it to get a better look at the approaching menace.

To Eric, the huge animated creation looked like something from a science fiction magazine, towering fifty feet in height with cannon barrels protruding from pods on each of its massive shoulders. A large weapon was clutched tightly in its right appendage while the left arm was formed into the shape of a giant spike.

Eric took his eye away from the scope and looked around the now deserted plane. The lasers had stopped firing and stood pointed directly at the oncoming behemoth. They hummed with readiness, apparently waiting for the thing to breach some invisible line, at which point they would open fire.

"Where did all the other creatures go?" Eric asked, eyes still searching the desert for some of the arachnid life forms.

"They have run away in fear," Arcos said without looking up. "Would that we could do the same."

Eric pressed his eye against the scope again as soldiers poured from the open portal behind him. They began to line the walls for hundreds of feet on either side. Most of them carried laser rifles, which they quickly shouldered and sighted out toward the robot — a few carried heavier ordinance such as large tubes reminiscent of bazookas.

Eric's breath caught in his chest as he watched them prepare for battle, each one wearing a grim look upon his alien visage.

"What is that thing, Arcos?" Eric asked, his voice sounding thin and strained.

"Yet another one of our follies," Arcos said, his voice nearly a whisper. Then remembering himself, he added, "You see, our ancestors have left us more than one legacy. We've seen these devices before. They were created to batter down the walls of an enemy city and dispatch the inhabitants within. They were created after the time it had become unsafe to venture beyond the city walls because of the mutated indigenous life forms.

Arcos smiled a wan painful looking grin. "When it was no longer safe enough in the wasteland to attack our neighbors in person, we built these monsters to do it for us."

"How many of them are there?" Eric asked, watching as the robot drew nearer. It was now close enough that he could hear the groaning of its joints as it moved, along with the heavy thuds of its footfalls.

"No one knows for sure," Arcos said. "They seem to travel randomly until they come across something to destroy. Their programming is unknown to us. In the past, they've been discovered in the desert at rest, sometimes sitting still for years or even hundreds of years without moving. Their locations would be marked only to find that they had moved again at some later date. Occasionally only by feet, but other times they would seem to disappear altogether only to turn up thousands of miles away. We've lost three of the last remaining cities to them in my lifetime," the doctor said, retrieving a rifle from one of the soldiers standing close by. "They are much more deadly than the creatures you witnessed before," he said, then turned to face the oncoming threat, now easily within view. "You must go back to the roundhouse. Wait for me there. I will come for you if I can," Arcos said.

The doctors' voice was deadly serious now, not the gentle caring timbre Eric had come to expect in the last few hours.

"Go!" he said then turned back toward the city wall. Eric paused for a second, then started to back away toward the portal. Within a few steps, something inside him forced him to halt his retreat. Gritting his teeth, he returned to the wall. Arcos glanced over questioningly.

Eric glared back. "Give me a weapon, Arcos. And I will fight beside you," he said, holding his metallic arm out to the doctor.

Arcos weighed Eric for a moment then nodded sharply. He called out something in his native tongue without taking his eyes off Eric. A soldier stepped up quickly and offered another rifle to the doctor.

"No, this one is not for me," Arcos said, still eyeing Eric. "Give it to the human."

"The Battle"

The silence was broken only by the humming sound of the laser cannons and the thumping that accompanied the robotic behemoth's approach. Eric shouldered his weapon in anticipation as Arcos flipped the power switch to the on position. They stood side by side, waiting for the word to open fire. They knew that when the laser turrets opened up, they would be within range themselves.

Eric was breathing quickly through his nose. He hid his terror as best as he could. Glancing down the line of soldiers, he saw similar looks of fear on all their faces. This was indeed going to be a fight.

The robot was now close enough for them to see battle scars painting its armored body. Black scorch marks covered most of its surface. Several spots had a melted look, but Eric could find nothing that looked like a weak spot. There was no way of knowing how long this contraption had wandered the deserts of the planet or how many cities it had destroyed. A thousand thoughts ran through Eric's mind, but he was loath to voice any of them out loud.

What was the best place to try to hit the machine? How close would it have to be for the lasers to do any damage? Did we really have any chance of taking it down? Eric figured that these unasked questions would be answered all too soon.

The metal beast stopped suddenly, and for several moments, it stood motionless, facing the city wall. A light breeze wafted through the ranks of soldiers who stood waiting for the sign to commence firing. Eric clenched his teeth and for a second prayed that the robot would not resume its deadly march.

Momentarily, it began to bend at the knees and squat down into what looked like a Tai Chi stance. The shoulder-mounted cannons both moved ever so slightly as if picking out separate targets. A bright green ball of light formed at the tip of each barrel accompanied by a low humming sound similar to the laser turrets arrayed along the wall. The iridescent green shape grew in brightness, then with an ear-splitting crack, streaked out from both cannon barrels and sped across the desert expanse toward the city.

An instant later, the defensive turrets sprang to life, pouring out bright red pulses of light energy that instantaneously covered the half-mile distance to their target.

One of the soldiers barked out something that must have meant 'open fire,' as the entire wall lit up with laser light.

The charged particles shot from the robot's cannons struck the wall in two different spots. One smashed into a turret sitting hundreds of feet down the wall to the left of Eric's position. The other made impact on the face of the wall itself.

The shockwave from the second shot dropped nearly everyone along the battlements to their knees.

Eric staggered to his feet and watched as a plume of smoke rose from the demolished turret. It had been completely turned to slag, along with a dozen or so soldiers who'd been unlucky enough to be alongside it. A new sound drew his attention back to the battle. The robot raised the weapon clutched in its metal paw and fired a burst of laser beams in the direction of the city's defenders. It swept the gun across from right to left with deadly accuracy, sending pulses of green light burning through several soldiers and pummeling another turret into rubble.

Eric repeatedly fired at the metal contraption with no apparent effect then watched in horror as two more balls of green light began to form in the Howitzer-like barrels mounted atop the marauding machine. They were only partially visible due to the number of red laser beams striking on and around every inch of the robot's body. Eric fired several more volleys, trying to place each shot where he thought it might do the most damage, though there appeared to be little if any effect from any of the defenders' weapons.

Two more shots rang out from the shoulder-mounted pods, each slamming into a different spot of the wall. Another defensive turret was vaporized, this time only a few dozen feet to the right of Eric's position. The second shot pummeled the wall again, sending tremors heavy enough to cause Eric's vision to blur.

"Arcos!" Eric yelled over the sounds of battle. "We're not hurting it at all!"

Arcos' finger moved like lighting over the trigger of the rifle. For just a second, he glanced toward Eric without stopping his dizzying rate of fire as if to say "I know" then re-sighted the weapon and continued firing.

Eric shot glances up and down both sides of the battlements, watching the soldiers firing lasers and small shoulder-mounted rocket-like projectiles toward the robot, all to no effect. Another blast of green lasers sent a half dozen soldiers to their deaths.

"There must be some weak spot on this thing!" Eric called out. "Everything's got a weak spot!" he yelled again, this time catching Arcos' attention.

"Weak spot?" Arcos called back over the din. "What do you mean?"

"A weak spot!" Eric said, grabbing Arcos by the shoulder and pulling himself up next to his ear. "Like the tanks we have back on our world!"

Arcos stopped firing and squinted his large eyes at Eric quizzically. Eric lowered his rifle and pointed his thumb back to the portal, indicating that they needed to go inside.

"I cannot!" Arcos yelled. "I must defend the city!" he said, pointing back to the giant behemoth on the plane. As he did, the robot resumed an upright stance and began slowly pounding toward the city once more, launching a shower of green lasers as it approached.

"I must defend the city!" There was desperation in Arcos' voice.

"How did you defeat the other ones?" Eric asked. "How did you kill the other robots that have attacked?"

"This city has never been attacked by one of them before. We've only heard the stories from survivors of other cities that dealt with them." Arcos said.

Eric shook his head back and forth questioningly. "Well, how did they defeat them?" he asked.

Arcos ducked down behind the battlements as a green ball of light streaked by, crashing full force into the wall fifty or so feet down from their position. A large section of the wall crumbled under the blow, leaving a ragged stair-stepped gap winding all the way down to the desert floor.

Eric grabbed Arcos' shoulder, gripping it firmly with his own flesh and blood hand. "How did they beat them?" he said again, holding Arcos' gaze by sheer force of will.

Arcos' eyes went suddenly wide as if he'd just accepted a fate that he knew would someday come. "They did not," he whispered.

Even though the tumultuous battle raged around them, Eric could hear the resignation in his voice. He watched as Arcos bowed his head, clenching his teeth in bitter anger.

Eric squeezed his eyes shut, trying to imagine how a race so advanced could one day be destroyed by their own creations. A moment passed before either of them made a move.

"A weak spot," Eric said, his face only inches from the top of Arcos' bowed head. "There must be a weak spot," he said again, trying to revive his newfound friends' spirit.

Arcos lifted his head and stared back into Eric's gaze. "I know of no weak spot, my friend." The resignation still weighed heavily on his once noble voice.

Eric turned and snuck a peek through the crenulations at the mechanical nightmare. It had cut the distance to the wall nearly in half and was marching resolutely with no sign of stopping. A chill shot down Eric's back as the urge to turn and run cut through him. He thought of how the people of this planet had been disconnected from their own history for a thousand years. They probably knew very little about how to fight or defend themselves from an attack like this. Even though their ancestors had created the monstrosity lumbering toward them, they knew nothing of how it was created or how to combat it. They only knew that it existed. They used the only weapons and tactics they could understand to defend themselves.

The idea that such an advanced race had lost its ability to fight seemed strangely idyllic. Perhaps there was something they could learn from him after all.

In an instant, he knew what he had to do. He reached out and squeezed Arcos shoulder once again. The doctor looked up expectantly.

"A weak spot, Arcos. I'm betting that the armor is much thinner on the robot's back," Eric said, letting a sly grin cut across his face. "If we can just get that monster to turn its back on these turrets," he said, pointing at the laser cannons firing away as they conversed. "If we can do that, we may just have a chance."

Arcos blinked rapidly at Eric. "Why would the armor be thinner on its back?" he asked. But Eric had already jumped to his feet.

"I'm gonna need five tough guys," he said, looking around at the soldiers arrayed on either side of him.

Another green particle canon ball coursed passed them, but Eric was unfazed. He was in the zone now and knew exactly what he had to do.

"You, you, and the three of you!" he shouted while indicating a handful of the alien soldiers standing close by. "Come with me!"

The soldiers looked from Eric to the doctor and back again. Eric turned to the doctor and yelled, "Tell them to follow me and not to shoot until I give the signal!"

Arcos stood with his mouth hanging open, and his palms turned up in confusion. The soldiers nearby gazed on, waiting for something to happen.

"Do it!" Eric yelled again. This time he yelled with such authority that it made the soldiers stand up straighter, even though they had no idea what was being said.

Arcos stared hard at Eric for a second longer, measuring what he was about to do. The two locked eyes for an instant then Arcos snapped his head forward with a quick nod.

"Go with him! Do not fire until he fires!" he barked to the soldiers. "Go now!"

Eric didn't waste another second. Bending down, he scooped

up one of the rocket launchers that had been dropped by a slain soldier, flung it across his back, and headed toward the gap in the wall at a dead run. The soldiers fell in behind him, their thinly armored legs easily keeping pace. Their passing was noticed by nearly everyone atop the battlements.

Reaching the large crack, Eric stopped and turned back to Arcos. He knew this might be the end of him, but without this last chance, he knew it would certainly be the end of this city. He caught the doctor's eye and raised his gun over his head. Tilting his head back, he let out the best war whoop he could muster. The soldiers around him stepped back a pace in bewilderment. Arcos, standing fifty feet away, climbed onto one of the crenulations and raised his own gun. Keeping his eyes locked on Eric, he pumped the gun up and down and yelled out in kind. The call spread out amongst the soldiers as each one raised their weapon and roared out their anger to the sky.

Eric smiled a warrior's grin and leapt down into the gap. He hopped like a rabbit from one broken piece of stone to the next, each time dropping down a few more feet. His five alien soldiers clamored down behind him, vaulting like lemurs from one section of broken stone to the next.

The fighters atop the wall opened fire again with redoubled efforts. A blazing stream of red lasers and rockets pounded the metal monster. For a moment, the hail was enough to slow its approach to a crawl.

Eric and his crew reached the desert floor and took advantage of the sudden flurry to make their move. They sprinted full tilt at a 45-degree angle to the left of the robot which was now within a hundred yards of the wall. Eric's lungs pumped frantically for air as he gave it his all. Ignoring the burning in his legs, he pushed on, knowing that this was a do or die attempt. Within seconds they had pulled clear of the monster and were nearly a hundred feet behind it. The thing appeared not to notice their movement as it was fully engaged with the cities defenders. It had pulled even closer and was now firing well-aimed shots at the turrets, taking them out one by one.

Eric and his team swung wide, running until they were directly behind the beast.

Eric checked his stride and raised his hand, trying to catch his breath. The soldiers skidded to a halt alongside him, hardly winded, but their eyes were wild with anticipation. Surveying the robot's rear armor, Eric made a decision. He slapped himself on the back just between the shoulder blades then poked his gun toward the robot repeatedly, indicating where to fire. The soldiers nodded their heads vigorously in acknowledgment.

Eric shouldered the rocket launcher and nodded sharply at his alien comrades to do the same. He then yelled out something unintelligible, but his intent was obvious. All six of them opened fire simultaneously. Five lasers and a rocket struck the robot just under the base of its neck. Several chunks of armor exploded away from the behemoth's body and rained down to the parched desert floor.

Eric called out again as he and his group sent another volley toward the robots back. The thing reacted amazingly fast. Even if the city's defenders didn't know where its weak spot was, the metal monster surely did. Spinning at the waist, it swung its incredible bulk around within a second to face a threat to its lightly armored hindquarters. Eric waved his arms out to either side, indicating that this would be a good time to scatter. The message was received, and the alien soldiers were all too happy to run for their lives. The robot sent several blasts of green light in their direction but found it hard to target such highly motivated, fast moving objects. It blasted away haphazardly, turning large parcels of sand into glass with each shot.

Eric looked up at the wall in time to see his efforts had paid off. The moment the robots back was turned, the City's defenders began to concentrate all their firepower against the middle of the monster's back. Dozens of rockets streaked simultaneously from the wall as hundreds of laser rifles lit up, pouring out fiery red beams of light. Even the large turrets seemed to know the best place to target, as they refocused their beams toward the monster's vulnerable back.

Eric watched aghast as a bright red spot appeared in the center of the robot's chest, the metal turning white hot. The monster seemed to hesitate for a moment before turning back toward the wall as if somehow realizing its mistake. But it was already too late.

"Run!' Eric yelled, turning to scramble away from the scene.

The five soldiers fell in behind him as the robot's chest exploded like a bomb. Eric had only covered a few paces before the shock wave caught him, mashing him to the ground like a linebacker and knocking the wind out of his lungs.

Huge pieces of metal plate armor crashed down about him with sickening thuds. Eric rolled onto his back just in time to see the robot, now totally engulfed in flames, drop down to its knees. Its entire midsection and head were missing, along with one of its arms.

The thing teetered for a moment before falling forward onto what remained of its torso, several smaller explosions rocking its heavy frame as it was consumed by fire.

The turrets atop the wall stopped firing and returned to their ready positions. The alien soldiers lowered their weapons as well, each one wide-eyed with disbelief.

Eric blinked hard and took in a deep breath, letting it fill his lungs while trying to calm the shaking of his hands. One of the alien soldiers in his group stepped up beside him. Eric peered up at him and saw the worried look upon the alien's face. The soldier paused for a second, then bent over and offered him a hand. The air seemed to crackle with electricity as Eric reached up and clasped the forearm of the alien. The soldier returned the grip to Eric's arm and leaned back, pulling him up of from the sand covered desert floor.

A cheer rose up from the battle-weary soldiers along the wall as they fired wild, random shots of red laser light into the air in celebration of their unexpected victory.

"Sleep"

"Wake up, sweetie. Come on, hon. We need to go get some breakfast."

John's eyes opened slowly, allowing in just a smidge of the bright morning sunlight. Sarah pattered around the bedroom, clad in her housecoat and slippers, a towel wrapped around the top of her head.

John smiled in abject contentedness as he contemplated what the day ahead would hold for them. Sarah loved getting up early on Saturdays and being one of the first people to arrive at the Old Mill restaurant. She felt that there was something magical about the old building with its water wheel and stone foundation. She liked to imagine what life had been like there a hundred years ago when the mill was still in use, when men in overalls would throw sacks of cracked grain and flour onto delivery wagons. When you could listen to the sound of water pouring over the spinning water wheel, then down onto the rocks and back into the river from which it had come.

Sarah liked the idea of simpler times. Things seemed to make so much more sense then, or at least that's how she imagined it.

John yawned and stretched out his legs like a cat will do when it first awakes.

"Come on!" Sarah said, this time pulling the blankets off John, who immediately curled up into the fetal position and groaned, "I'm getting up, just give me a bloomin' second!"

Another several minutes had passed when John noticed that things had gotten very quiet. He cracked an eye open and gazed about the room. Sarah was standing at the foot of the bed; her hands planted firmly on her hips. Her eyes squeezed half shut and a look of overall disgust curling up the edges of her mouth.

John lay there a second more, contemplating the ramifications of what might happen if he didn't spring into action that very instant. A moment later he made his decision and rolled lazily up into a sitting position, rubbing his eyes and yawning again.

He turned his head slowly to the left and looked sheepishly at

Sarah, a playful smile just starting to part his lips. In response, Sarah squeezed her eyes down to mere slits, trying to look mean, but quickly enough, lost her composure.

"You!" She yelled as she leapt toward John, arms raised for an attack.

"No!!" John yelled, rolling onto his back as she crashed down on top of him, digging her fingers into his sides until he laughed and convulsed uncontrollably. Finally, Sarah sat up, straddling John's midsection, peering down at her prey. John looked up expectantly, wiping tears of laughter from his eyes and trying to catch his breath. Sarah tipped her head to one side, eyeing John the way Runt would do on occasion and said, "I love you."

A thump roused John back to consciousness. The blinding light reflected off the desert sand seared into his eyes, causing him to blink rapidly.   For a moment, he couldn't figure out where he was. Only a second ago he'd been home with Sarah, wrestling on their feather bed.

Another thump shook him fully awake as the wheels of the cart rumbled over another stone. The dream faded fast as John squeezed his hands into tight fists, trying to hang on to the feeling of peace and happiness that had accompanied his fitful slumber. His friend sat on a box of supplies roughly a foot higher in the cart than John. He was watching intently over the vast plane, keeping an eye out for anything that might come their way. The laser rifle lay across his lap, and he kept a hand on it at all times, ready for anything.

The rhythmic footfalls of the robot continued as John clenched his teeth, trying not to let the emptiness left behind by the dream consume him. Tears ran down over his lips and dripped from his chin as he wept silently, hoping that his tough friend wouldn't notice and call attention to his pain. It had been two months since the accident, but to John, it sometimes felt like only hours.

John sniffed once, trying to keep his nose from running onto his shirt, then shifted his eyes to Chuck to make sure he hadn't noticed. To his dismay, he found his friend was watching him out of the corner of his eye. John quickly looked away out over the side of the cart, suddenly ashamed. To his surprise, he felt Chuck clamp a solid hand down on his shoulder. John turned back, meeting his friend's gaze. Chuck squeezed his shoulder once and dipped his head slightly, as if in acknowledgment of his friend's suffering. John exhaled sharply then gave a quick nod back.

The two traveled on for another hour in relative silence. Chuck finally broke the dull thudding sound of the robot's steps with a question.

"How much farther to the city?" he asked, leaning toward the robots back.

The metal man responded quickly. "One point seven miles," he answered.

John poked his head over the edge of the cart, looking around the side of the robot's thick torso. "Shouldn't we be able to see something from this distance?" he asked.

Chuck stood up in the cart, trying to get a look over the robot's head, sheltering his eyes with his hand as he scanned the horizon.

"I would certainly think so," he said. "Even if the buildings were only as tall as the one we came from, we oughta be able to see something by now."

"Maybe there's some kinda cloaking device or something." John offered.

Chuck looked worried. "Yeah, maybe," he half mumbled. "Maybe this robot's full of crap."

They traveled on for another ten minutes, both men still visually scouring the scene in front of them, desperately looking for some sign of life.

"Hey!" Chuck yelled. "I think I see something!" Reaching forward, he tapped the robot with the butt of his gun. "How far now?" he asked.

"Three hundred and twenty feet." The robot said.

John rubbed at his chin, his eyes darting around the nearly empty desert plane before them. "That can't be right!" he called to Chuck, "All that's out there is another bunch of ruins, just like the ones we started out in!"

Chuck shook his head side to side in confusion. "No, no something's wrong here! Robot, you say this is the closest city?"

"Correct," the robot replied.

Chuck waved his hands in front of him, indicating the nearly empty desert expanse that was broken up only by a few small crumbled stone foundations and stubby columns.

"Where's the city then?" He yelled.

"One hundred and sixteen feet," the robot responded.

John's eyes widened as he realized what was happening.

"Oh shit, Chuck. Oh shit…" he said slowly.

"What?" Chuck said irately, overcome by disappointment. "This damn thing's lied to us or something!"

"No, Chuck. I don't think it has," John said calmly. "Robot, stop," he said, as the mechanical biped halted immediately. John hopped out of the cart and stepped several paces in front of the robot, laughing out loud.

"What the hell are you laughing at, you moron?" Chuck yelled, getting down from the cart himself.

John turned back to the robot and asked. "Robot, what's the name of this city?"

"Tira-Lindore" the robot replied.

"And what's the population of this city?" John asked, clasping his hands behind his back while pacing back and forth in the sand like a detective questioning a witness.

"Population of Tira-Lindore is one hundred and sixty-seven thousand, at last count," the metal box dutifully replied.

"What's this about, John?" Chuck called out, more irritated than ever.

John pursed his lips and raised a finger to silence him. Chuck gritted his teeth in reply.

"Now." John continued. "How long ago was the last population count?" John said, leaning in closer to the robot for effect. "In earth years," he added quickly.

"One thousand two hundred and eighty-one earth years," the robot said without emotion.

The metal contraption obviously had no idea how much weight this information carried for the two men.

Chuck stood with his mouth hanging open as he was known to do when totally dumbfounded.

"And what is the population now?" John asked a final question.

"Two." The robot said.

"Well, there you have it," John said. "And I'm guessing that number two means you and me big boy!" he added, pointing first at himself then at Chuck.

"Aw shit, John!" Chuck spouted. "This damn place has been dead for a thousand years!"

"Well, we don't know that now, do we, Chuck?" John said with all seriousness at first then changed his tone. "It may only have been dead for *five hundred*," he continued, letting a smartass tone soak each word before he spat it out. "But I'm guessing you may be right," he said as he bent over and picked up a chipped piece of stone. Turning it over in his hands, he said smugly, "From the looks of it, it probably is more like a thousand."

Chuck stood still for a moment, sucking on his teeth, then said, "Ya know, John, I oughta just kill you right now!" And with that, he started pulling the laser rifle off his shoulder as if he were going to take a shot at John.

"Oh, Chuck," John said, savoring the moment. "Now if you did that, you'd be out here all alone. And," John added, "and our robot friend here would have to do a recount."

The look on Chuck's face sent John into hysterics. He'd been in need of a really good laugh, and the ridiculousness of their situation had just afforded him one. Chuck watched while John laughed like a maniac, ultimately falling to his knees, sobbing with laughter.

"O.K., John Boy!" Chuck sneered. "I'll give you *this* one since you seem to be enjoying it so much," he said before turning to explore the ruins.

"Robot, is there anything here we can use?" he asked while he waited for his friend to collect himself.

"Please restate question," the robot responded.

"Is there anything here – food, water, weapons?" Chuck said.

"The answer, upon initial survey, is negative," the robot said slowly as if mulling over its options.

This sent John into another laughing fit, which this time was so strong that he was actually reduced to lying prostrate on the ground, quivering like a mass of Jello.

"It's not that funny; you pinhead!" Chuck yelled at his friend, but couldn't help giggling a little at the robot's response himself.

A minute later, John had gathered himself up into a sitting position and was only chuckling in small bursts. Chuck climbed back into the cart and, shielding his eyes from the sun, turned slowly around in a circle trying to determine what direction to go in next.

"Robot," he asked finally, "do you know where the closest city with inhabitants is?"

"My data is incomplete or inaccurate," the robot said.

"Oh, now you tell us!" Chuck shouted. "Well, then, I guess we just keep wandering around the desert until we find something that's alive, right?" he said, looking over at John.

"Well, we certainly know there are lots of living things out there," John said, rubbing tears of laughter from his eyes with his sleeve. "The problem is it looks like most of them wanna eat us."

As if on cue, the robot spun at the waist back toward the direction they'd traveled from and spoke, "Objects approaching, one point two miles and closing at a rate of twenty feet per second."

John sprang to his feet, and both he and Chuck leapt into the cart.

"What are they? And how many?" John asked, all the humor gone from his voice now.

"Native life forms, unable to ascertain quantity – many," the robot said.

"Native life forms, like the ones that attacked the building before?" Chuck asked.

"Affirmative," the robot replied.

"Oh boy, there's no place to hide either!" Chuck yelled, "Maybe we should head for the ruins. There's part of a building over there that still has some walls."

"That's as good a place as any, I guess!" John said, jumping from the cart and heading for the ruins at a dead run. Chuck grabbed one of the supply sacks they'd brought with them and followed quickly after his friend.

The remains of the building appeared to offer reasonable cover from an enemy who might be firing at you. Of course, this enemy would be trying to rip off your limbs instead of sitting back taking potshots. It was, however, the best the men could come up with considering they had only moments to take cover. The walls were roughly seven to eight feet high and formed a nearly complete rectangle except on one side where there was a break of about four feet across. Luckily, it was on the side facing away from the attackers.

With any luck, the two would be able to hold them off. Chuck took his station at the left front corner. He was able to keep his head and shoulders above the wall by standing on piles of stone and rubble littering the inside of the eroded structure. John did the same in the opposite corner. Both were breathing heavily at the thought of the fight to come. They had seen the ferocity of the insect-like creatures when they had attacked the well-equipped, well-defended life hutch.

"You figure we're gonna be able to beat these guys?" John asked between quick short breaths. Chuck glanced over at him and flicked the power switch on.

"I guess we're gonna find out, buddy," he said, forcing a smile.

They could see a dust cloud on the horizon now. John thought that it looked like the ones you'd see in an Old West movie when the Calvary was riding to someone's rescue. Unfortunately, he knew that no one would be coming to pull their butts out of this fire.

Flicking the power switch of his weapon on, John shouldered the rifle and gave one final look around the ruins for someplace that might be more defendable or maybe a spot where they could have a better chance of hiding.

Chuck, remembering their robotic cart-hauler still standing a hundred feet or so in front of the ruins called out, "Hey! Robot! Protect us!"

The robot turned momentarily toward Chuck, who was pointing feverishly at the approaching threat stirring up its oncoming cloud of dust and sand. The metallic worker calmly un-tethered the wagon from its midsection and started plodding slowly out into the desert in the direction they had first come from.

"How 'bout that?" Chuck said, smiling over at John. "We may just get out of this yet!"

"I don't know, Chuck, I don't have a great feeling about this," John said.

"Aw, come on!" Chuck said, looking around the scene. "You can't buy adventure like this!"

Seeing John's disgusted look, he added, "I mean, how many people do you know who've gotten chewed up by monsters on an alien planet? Huh? How many?"

"O.K., I get your point." John said rather solemnly, and then added, "Chuck, if we don't make it through this, I'll see you on the other side."

Chuck winked quickly at John and re-shouldered his weapon. "We got this, buddy."

The robot had traversed maybe a few hundred feet into the desert by the time the first bugs came into view, and there were lots of them. From their viewpoint behind the wall, the creatures appeared to be the same type that had attacked the life hutch.

"Guess they've come back for a little more," Chuck boasted as he watched the robot come to a halt some distance away. Seconds later, the thick torso of the robot split open and rotated down. Two stubby tubes slid upwards along its back and locked into place on top of each shoulder.

"Can you believe what we're seeing here?" Chuck asked in amazement. "And I thought this guy was just some kind of workhorse!

"Yeah," John said, a worried look still pasted across his face. "But look how many are coming."

Chuck scanned the horizon once again. He could now see hundreds, if not thousands, of the creatures pouring toward their position.

"Yeah," he said, a hint of resignation now registering in his voice.

A moment later the robot opened fire, its lasers cutting down dozens of the creatures within seconds. But for each one that fell, another two monsters took its place.

John and Chuck started firing into the rush almost at random. They squeezed off shots as quickly as they could pull their triggers. Red beams seared through thick hides as horrible animal screams rent the air. The attackers slowed their pace somewhat under the withering fire the two men and the robot heaped upon them.

"Damn!" Chuck yelled. "What'd we ever do to these guys to make them so mad?"

John didn't respond. He was almost in a trance, aiming, firing then aiming again. It all somehow reminded him of the video games he used to play as a child.

Thirty seconds passed before the horde was on top of the robot. Even with the bright beams firing out in every direction, the metal protector was consumed. The two looked on in awe as the beasts swarmed over the robot's body like a plague of giant locusts.

The metal warrior disappeared momentarily under the rush of bugs then exploded. A giant fireball mushroomed into the sky, followed by a shock wave that sent hundreds of the monsters to the ground, seared beyond recognition. The force from the blast knocked both men from the wall, landing them flat on their backs. The rifle was knocked from John's grip just as the wind was pummeled out of Chuck's lungs. The wall itself took a beating. A large section just in front of John began to tip inward, a crack forming raggedly along its sandblasted face.

"Crap!" John yelled while back peddling like a crab on a

sandy beach, trying to outrun the falling chunks of stone. An entire section roughly eight feet wide hung precariously for a moment before it crashed inward. John blinked his eyes, trying to clear away the dust from the collapse, but before he could get to his feet, the ground beneath him began to shift.

"Chuuuuuck!" John yelled as he slid in toward the spot where the wall had fallen. A sinkhole had opened up under the ruins just where the rocky structure had come down. Sand poured into large cracks in the desert floor, and so did John. Chuck got to his feet just in time to see his friend disappear completely under the edge of a large chunk of broken stone.

"John!" Chuck yelled, scrambling over the rubble toward the shattered earth. He had no more than reached the crack when his attention was drawn back to the remains of the wall. Silvery black, talon shod arms appeared at the edge, followed immediately by the heads of several creatures. Chuck recoiled in fear, realizing that he was about to be devoured or torn apart, or whatever these beasts would do to him. He knew this much at least – it wasn't going to be a nice death.

"Not yet!' he yelled, flailing his arms in an attempt to bat away one of the talons reaching for him. "Not yet!" he yelled again, then dove headlong into the dark crevice that had only moments before swallowed his friend.

"The Longest Day"

Chuck landed with a thud. Luckily, the hole had filled up with sand from the surface, making a dirt ramp for him to slide down. It was nearly pitch black, and the air was filled with choking dust.

He groped around in the dark, trying to find his friend while the creatures thumped around above him, ten feet away up on the surface. They shrieked and wailed in dismay at the loss of their prey.

Chuck's eyes quickly adjusted to the darkness, allowing him to see a small area that made up his immediate surroundings. The crack in the desert floor above allowed a trickle of the bright desert sun to enter in. The monsters still pawed at the edges of the fallen wall trying to move it in an effort to retrieve the two men.

Chuck called out, "John! Where the hell are you?" as he felt around in the darkness, searching for his friend. He found John quickly enough. Or maybe not, as it seemed that the Beasts were starting to make progress with moving the stone. They had already managed to slide it about a foot, opening the hole just enough to poke their long necks inside. The gap allowed a little more light into the underground compartment. Chuck found John face down, and he rolled his friend over onto his back. John coughed hard but didn't open his eyes.

 "Get up, you pantywaist!" Chuck hollered at his friend, but he got no response. "Well, this is just great, you're gonna make me carry your ass, aren't ya?" he yelled again, shaking his head. He scooped John up and tossed him over his shoulder like a sack of grain.

"Damn, you're heavy!" He groaned under the weight of his friend. "But you ain't leaving me here alone!"

Chuck stumbled away from the ever-widening hole above him as rapidly as he could, considering the extra burden of John's body. He'd only taken a few steps before realizing that it was quite dark outside the small ring of light that streamed in through the gap overhead.

Shuffling along in near darkness, Chuck wheezed for air, trying to get as much distance between them and the hissing creatures still prying away at the earth only yards behind them.

He poked his feet out in front of him, trying not to stumble over stone fragments, the whole time wondering if he was about to step off an unseen overhang only to fall to his death inside the dark subterranean canyon.

John sputtered again, this time repeatedly hacking, his body tensing with each cough.

"Put me down," he choked while squirming around on Chuck's shoulder.

"Gladly," Chuck said, dropping to his knees and plopping John onto the hard floor as gently as he could in his nearly exhausted state.

They were a good thirty or forty feet from the opening now. Chuck turned to see if the bugs had made any more progress at enlarging the hole. Through the dust-filled room, he could make out their shadows darting back and forth, repeatedly breaking up the solitary beam of light.

"Come on, John, we have to keep moving," Chuck whispered hoarsely, the thick dust sticking in his throat.

"O.K. Give me a second," John groaned, rubbing the back of his head. "Just give me another second. Everything looks dark. I can barely see."

"That's because everything is dark, you goof! We're in some kind of underground cavern or something. Now let's move! We have to put some distance between us and those critters before they break through," Chuck spat out between gasps.

John panted for a second more then pushed himself up to his feet. "O.K. I'm ready," he said, then looked around in the near darkness. "Any idea which way to go?"

The question was answered for him by the sound of one of the creatures punching through the stone behind them, opening the crack to nearly double the size it had been before.

"Any direction away from that!" Chuck yelled.

The two scrambled as quickly as they could through the dark passage. The farther they traveled, the darker it became. Soon they were in complete darkness, bumping against unseen objects all around them. It seemed as though they'd been moving for some time though only a handful of seconds had actually passed. Finally, John dropped to his knees, his head spinning, partly from the disorientation of scrambling along in the dark and partly from the blow he'd taken to the head during his fall.

"Wait!" he yelled. "Chuck, I gotta stop for a second."

Chuck, who had been groping his way in front of him, stopped and turned back to his friend. He strained his eyes through the black passage but could no longer see any light. They'd made a handful of turns during their flight, leaving Chuck with no idea of where they were in relation to their starting point. He listened intently but couldn't detect any sign of pursuit.

"You figure they're still after us?" John asked as if reading his friend's mind.

"No, I can't hear anything, and I'm sure they'd be making a hell of a ruckus if they were," Chuck said.

Indeed, the only sound to be heard was the labored breathing of the two men. Chuck let John rest for another moment, then said, "O.K. We should probably get moving again. But I think we can slow our pace a little."

John rolled onto all fours and began to push himself off the floor when he felt something under his left hand. His fingers curled instinctively around the tubular shaped object.

"Wait a sec. I think I've found something," he said.

"What is it?" Chuck asked.

"I don't know," John said as he ran his fingers over the find. "But it doesn't feel like something you'd find in a cave."

He stood up, still holding the object. It was roughly ten inches long and seemed to be made of metal. It was much too smooth to be naturally occurring.

"Let me take a look-see?" Chuck asked, reaching in the direction of John's voice.

John proffered the object to his friend who turned it over in his hands, trying to figure out what it might be.

"Listen," John said, noticing a sound he hadn't picked up on before. The two stood silent for a moment. "Sounds like something's humming, like machinery or electricity or something, ya think?"

"Yes, it does," Chuck said, sounding rather baffled. Kneeling down, he ran his hands over the ground. "John, feel the floor and tell me what you make of it."

John dropped to the floor and slid his fingertips around the dusty area. Finally, he tapped a knuckle against the ground several times and listened as it returned a faint metallic ring.

"Metal?" he questioned Chuck.

"Sure sounds and feels like it, doesn't it?" Chuck said. "I'm thinking we're inside an underground building, not a cave."

"Of course!" John exclaimed, "Who's to say the entire structure of the city was above ground!"

"Yeah, so the question is, how much farther in do we go? It's awfully dark, and it's just a matter of time before we step off the edge of something or run into something that's living down here that doesn't want company," Chuck said.

"Well, I don't particularly care for our other option either. I don't know about you, but I don't think I could take on one of those creatures back there in a fist fight," John responded, his voice ringing out hollowly in the darkness.

"Yeah, you're right about that," Chuck said, then paused for a second to consider their options. "This room must be pretty big. You can hear an echo."

"If we only had some light, we might be able to negotiate our way through," John said. "I mean, it must come out someplace. Maybe we could give the beasties the slip."

"Oh, I'm an idiot!" Chuck said, suddenly. Then John heard a jingling sound as Chuck fished around in one of his blue jean pockets.

"What are you doing?" John asked.

His answer came in the form of a bright light that suddenly illuminated the area immediately around them.

"Got me one of these cool little waterproof LED key chain flashlights a couple of weeks ago," Chuck laughed. "I just knew it would come in handy!"

Chuck flashed the light back and forth around the room. The beam of its tiny bulb, though powerful, couldn't reach three of the four walls.

"Man, this place is pretty big, must be better than fifty feet across," Chuck said while panning the light back and forth, momentarily splitting the darkness of the room.

John stared into the darkness, half expecting to see something standing out there just at the edge of the light, momentarily illuminated as the diffused beam swept past. A chill ran down his spine at the thought of it.

"Come on. Let's get moving. This place is starting to give me the creeps," John said. "Who knows how long this place has been standing empty."

"Well, if it's like everything else around here, it's probably been over a thousand years," Chuck said, giving one final sweep around the room with the flashlight then allowing it to come to rest on the wall directly in front of them.

"Which way?" he asked, pointing first to the right then to the left with the beam of the flashlight. An unbroken wall ran along in both directions for as far as the light would carry.

"Can't hurt going to the right, I suppose," John said. "Lead on, great bringer of light."

"Right," Chuck said, then turned to the right and began trekking along, keeping about five feet between him and the wall to his left.

It wasn't long before they came to a doorway. It was more of a hatch really, much like you would see on a ship or a submarine. Chuck scanned the outline of the door with the flashlight. Its entire surface was covered with deep gouges.

"Looks like someone's been here before us," John said, running his fingers along the slashes in the thick metal door.

"Here, hold this," Chuck said, handing the small flashlight to John.

John stepped back as Chuck gave the door a push with the barrel of the rifle. The door swung in slowly, the hinges groaning under the weight of the portal. John leaned to the side and pointed the flashlight into the room. Once again, the light illuminated a short distance into the chamber before the darkness beyond swallowed it whole.

"It's like shining a light into the ocean or something. It really gives me a creepy feeling not knowing what's beyond the beam," John said, slowly panning the flashlight back and forth.

"I know what you mean," Chuck said. "But what choice have we got?"

A clanking sound brought their attention back to the darkness of the room just behind them. Chuck shot John a worried look. John spun around and cast the flashlight's beam behind them, whipping it back and forth, searching for the source of the sound. A single eye caught the light and cast a yellowish color back at the two men.

Chuck raised the rifle to his shoulder just in time as the creature lunged forward, its legs making a clanking sound on the metal floor as it rushed straight for them. The ferocity of the blast from the laser rifle took John by surprise. In the enclosed space and darkness of the underground chamber, the weapon's fury took on epic proportions. Chucks first shot was followed quickly by several more in rapid succession, as if he had just remembered that he could squeeze off rounds as fast as he could pull the trigger. Two of the red beams hit their target, sending a shower of sparks into the air, briefly illuminating the entire room.

The metallic thing covered the distance between them in an instant.

"Look out!" John yelled as the monster reared onto its spindly back legs and lashed out in their direction. The air hissed as it swung a whip-like appendage toward them. Chuck ducked just in time as the arm raked the wall behind him, but John wasn't quite quick enough and suffered a glancing blow by the jagged flail. Only the tip grazed his left arm as he dodged off to his right. Luckily the blow had not been aimed at him, or he'd surely have lost his arm. As it were, his limb had been sliced open just above his elbow.

John yelled out in pain as the flashlight slipped from his hand

and skittered across the floor. The room plunged into darkness instantly. Chuck opened up with the laser again, firing wildly, the bright flashes blinding John and him with their stroboscopic effect. Several shots found home, sending a shower of sparks in every direction.

John reeled as he watched the mechanical creature shudder to a halt, two glowing holes passing through its center. Several more hot blast marks covered its limbs and torso. The sizzling metal gave off just enough light for John to find the flashlight, which had been kicked a few feet away during the scuffle.

Chuck exhaled audibly, still pressing the weapon hard against his shoulder.

"Give a little look around with that light will ya, John? I'd hate to think another one of those things might be waiting out there for us."

John gave a quick sweep of the room with the light and was left dissatisfied by the results. The light couldn't quite reach the edges of the chamber, leaving both men with a terrible sense of unease.

"Nothing out there within the flashlight's reach anyway," John said, walking slowly toward the heap of smoking metal. A couple more paces and the two were staring down at what appeared to be a very large metal spider. It had eight legs and a thick center section. The four back legs were heavier, while two of the front arms were obviously made for slashing. The other two arms carried heavy pinchers at the end.

"You figure it's a guard of some kind?" Chuck asked.

"I don't know, but that may be why those bugs from the surface didn't try too hard to follow us in here," John said.

"Did he get you?" Chuck asked.

"I think he may have," John responded, turning the flashlight on himself to examine his arm. "Aw damn!"

Blood ran freely from the wound on his arm, dripping from just below the elbow down to the metal flooring.

"That's gonna leave a scar," Chuck said, holding John's arm up closer to get a better look at the incision. "Yup, we're gonna have to stop that bleeding, and we have to do it quick. I ain't carrying your heavy butt again," he said, looking up at John with a sneer. "Now hold still," Chuck said while tearing a large strip of cloth off the bottom of his T-shirt.

"You're not planning on bandaging me up with your dirty, sweaty shirt, are you? I know how bad you are about doing laundry, Chuck. I hate to even imagine how many germs there are crawling around on that one sliver of shirt alone!"

Chuck grabbed hold of John's arm and began to rap the cloth tightly around the wounded area. "Man, you've been married too long. I remember when we were young..." Chuck started, then seeing the look in John's eye, quickly cut off the rest of his thought. "Oh, I'm sorry man."

"Yeah," John said, nodding his head ever so slightly. "Me too." He then gave Chuck a swat on the arm with his good right hand and said, "You gonna tighten that thing up or let me stand here and bleed to death?"

Chuck cinched up the cloth tourniquet. "There, that oughta hold you until we can find something better."

"Or maybe we'll find a nice hospital down here somewhere," John laughed. "O.K. Let's get moving before another one of those spider things finds us. Oh, and don't forget the rifle. It's definitely coming in handy these days."

"Hell of an idea!" Chuck said, retrieving the weapon from where he'd dropped it on the floor. "Here, take the flashlight."

The two continued their trek into the underground portion of the ancient city for what seemed like hours. In the darkness, time passed slowly, and the farther they progressed, the more frazzled their nerves got. One turn after another brought them to dusty ruined rooms, some with partially collapsed ceilings or gaping holes in their floors. The complex was enormous. John imagined the area above ground must have been truly extensive if this underground portion had only been its basement.

They seemed to be traveling deeper as they went, encountering many stairwells along the way, each one leading down further into the darkness. After a while, they walked in silence, ears and eyes ever alert to a possible attack. The time they had spent in the darkness was starting to take on a toll on both of them. Finally, John spoke up.

"Hey Chuck, I need to take a little break. My arm's going numb, and my legs are getting wobbly."

Chuck, who had been walking a pace or two ahead, turned around to face John. John could see that his friend was growing weary as well.

"O.K.," Chuck said. "Probably not a bad idea. Here, let me take a look at that cut."

John held his injured left arm out toward his friend and shone the flashlight on the wounded area. Chuck slowly peeled the blood-soaked, makeshift bandage away from the wound.

"You sure you oughta be doing that?" John called out, his body tensing up as a fresh trickle of blood started to seep from under the bandage.

"Yeah, maybe you're right. We need to find something else to use as a bandage soon. We can't keep that tourniquet on there forever, or your arm's going to turn green and fall off!" Chuck barked back. He then felt up and down John's forearm. "You see, it's starting to get kind of cold already."

"Well, I'm not sure how soon we're going to find a box of medical supplies down here, and if we do, they're probably well past their expiration date," John joked, trying to make light of the situation.

"Alright, let's sit down here for a few minutes, but then we gotta keep going," Chuck said. "What other choice have we got? There has to be another way out of this place."

John plopped down onto his bottom. He was nearly exhausted from the trek and from blood loss from the slash on his arm. Chuck stayed standing, peering out into the darkness in an attempt to keep watch for anything that might be lurking out there waiting to pounce.

"You think we ought to shut off the flashlight for a bit?" John said. "It's starting to look a little dim. I'm guessing we're not going have too much battery life left here in a bit."

"Probably not a bad idea," Chuck said.

John flipped the little switch, and the two were cast into total darkness. John clenched his teeth together to quell the panicked feeling that rose up in his throat. He fingered the switch on the flashlight, fighting a desperate urge to turn it back on, but was just as afraid of what he might see if he did. Chuck must have been thinking the same thing.

"Pretty scary down here in the dark isn't it, dude?" Chuck asked, his voice sounding hollow in the darkness. "I mean, I guess kid fears never really go away, they just hang out there in the back of your mind, waiting for a time like this to come knocking."

"Sure enough," John responded. "Sure enough."

"You remember that time when we were kids?" Chuck started. John loved it when Chuck reminisced about their youth. No matter how bad the actual events he would recount had been, he would always put a funny spin on them.

"That time we played Ghost in the Graveyard and Eric got super scared. If I remember it right, he was the ghost, and you and I and a bunch of kids from the neighborhood were playing. Remember?" Chuck asked, giving John a little poke on the shoulder.

"Yeah, I remember," John said, feeling suddenly very tired.

"We were playing out there in that open field behind your parent's place, the one with that old barn and abandoned house. Eric had gone out there and hid somewhere by that house and was waiting for us to come find him," Chuck said. He paused for a second, letting the memories flow over him. "Man I loved that game. Things were so simple and easy then. Anyhow, Eric was out there waiting for us, and we were just about to start the game when he came running back up to the whole group yelling about something being out there by the old barn. We all went out there with flashlights, but of course, we never found anything," Chuck finished the story then added one last thought.

"Being here now kinda reminds me of how he must have felt. Feeling just sure something is waiting for you out there in the darkness." Chuck exhaled shakily.

John, sensing his friends' fear, did what any good friend

would do. "You want I should turn the flashlight back on? Or maybe I could just hold your hand," he said with all the seriousness he could muster.

Even in the darkness, John could almost see the smile breaking across Chuck's face.

"You're a dick, John," he said. "And I hate you."

"I know you do, buddy. I know," John said, leaning his head back against the cold metal wall. Closing his eyes, he drifted quickly off to sleep without a thought as to what might happen if he did so.

"Parents"

"So when are you kids going to give us some grandbabies?" Sarah's mother exclaimed.

That was the first thing she would say each time they visited.

"I don't know, Mom," Sarah said, brushing past her mother and into the front room while pulling off her thick winter coat. "Why don't you call Jimmy and see why he hasn't produced any grandbabies for you?" Sarah said, placing lots of emphasis on the word *grandbabies*.

"You know Jimmy's not ready for kids. I don't even know why he married that girl. She's never been right for him," Janet continued in her usual tirade. "I tried to tell him long before they decided to get married, but as always, you kids never listen to me," she added, this time glancing over accusingly at John.

John knew better than to acknowledge the look. It was just what Sarah's mother wanted, a confrontation. "Good morning, Mrs. Wilson," he said instead, trying to head her off at the pass before things got too heated.

He had begun to dislike their visits as of late. Sarah's mother was becoming increasingly persistent about her desires for grandchildren. And since she and Mike had had only two children, Sarah and Jimmy, they had to hang their hopes for grandchildren on at least one of them.

Jimmy had been married for years but had yet to father any children. And Janet was still holding out hopes that Jimmy and his wife would split up so he could pursue a more "proper" lady. It was true, of course, that Jimmy did indeed have poor taste in women. He'd had countless bad relationships and been married twice by the ripe old age of thirty-one, so it was easy to see why his mother was so concerned about him having children with one of his lady friends. The last one was easily the worst of the bunch. She was only nineteen to start with and seemed more concerned with drinking and smoking pot than having children. Of course, at that age, most people aren't looking for children, even though many somehow manage to find them accidentally. And to add to their problems, Jimmy's new wife hated Janet, so the two rarely visited, giving even more fuel to Mrs. Wilson's fire.

John knew how much family meant to Sarah, so he bit his lip during most of their visits. But it was getting harder to sit idly by while Janet pummeled them with questions about everything from how much money they made to why Sarah would wear such an unattractive coat. But tonight Mrs. Wilson had set her sights set on grandchildren.

"It's going to be a great holiday season," John thought to himself. Looking out the window while Janet droned on, he watched as a gentle first snow began to fall.

"Hero"

Eric struggled to his feet with the help of the warrior alien. The cheer from the wall was deafening. A broad smile covered Eric's face. It'd been a long time since he'd been seen as a hero or even been acknowledged for anything at all. Actually, he'd never been seen as a hero as far as he knew. More of an outcast was how he'd always imagined himself, certainly not someone who would save a city from certain destruction. But here he was, holding a rocket launcher in the air over his head, as a crowd of aliens whooped and hollered, "Eric! Eric!" Even though none of them could speak his language, they now knew his name.

A sharp pain pulled his attention away from the revelry for a moment. Looking down at the back of his left leg, he saw a large piece of metal sticking out from the meaty part of his calf muscle.

"Damn," he said aloud.

The alien next to him saw the wound at the same time and called to the city wall for help. The warrior then placed a hand under Eric's armpit to help buoy him up. Another soldier stepped in from the other side and did the same, taking most of the weight off Eric's injured leg.

The soldiers quickly shuttled Eric from the field, heading back toward the crack in the wall at a rapid pace. The other three warriors fell in behind them, each one watching over his shoulder looking for new threats. Eric realized that even though the giant robot was gone, the fear of an impending attack by the arachnid-like creatures was always at hand.

The group crossed the desert floor back to the city in short order. At the wall, Arcos had lowered down a rope with a harness attached to meet them. Sensing the urgency of the situation, Eric tossed his rocket pod to the ground and buckled himself into the harness. Giving a thumbs-up to Arcos, the crew on top of the wall hauled him up, and not a moment too soon. He was only ten feet off the ground when the bugs returned. At first, only a few poked their insect heads above the sand, but then dozens began to appear on the horizon. The remaining soldiers clambered up through the crack in the wall as the large laser turrets spun to life and began firing short bursts toward the new threat.

The group of five warriors scrambled safely back to the top of the wall as Eric was hoisted up. During the lift, Eric was a little nervous that one of the creatures might make it through the withering laser fire and snatch him out of the harness before he could make it to safety, but his fears were unfounded. In fact, the attack proved short-lived. Only a matter of seconds after it had begun, the attackers went back underground and disappeared.

Atop the wall, Altare waited for Eric with a small medical kit in hand. Arcos and several soldiers pulled Eric over the crenulations and set him gently onto the stone walkway of the battlements. A small crowd of smiling alien faces gathered around him, all of them excitedly chattering amongst themselves while observing their new hero's treatment.

Altare knelt beside Eric and began to examine the wound. It was not as bad as it had at first appeared. Only a sliver of metal had actually penetrated his leg, knife blade-like in its thickness. Altare met Eric's eyes and giving a small nod, said, "I must remove this." Eric nodded back, still smiling in jubilation at his great success. Nothing, not even a piece of hot shrapnel stuck in his leg, could take this moment away from him. In fact, it somehow made it all the more poignant.

Altare wrapped a small bandage around the still smoking piece of hot metal and quickly pulled it free from Eric's leg. It slid out easily, leaving a clean cut that began to bleed profusely. Altare handed the fragment to one of the soldiers and retrieved a device from the med kit. It looked like a high tech staple gun to Eric, but he had no idea what its actual purpose might be. Altare ran it across the bleeding wound on his leg. The bleeding stopped instantly where the device passed, sealing the wound almost completely. Altare left a small gap at the base of the wound where blood continued to flow but at a much slower rate. Seeing the questioning look on

Eric's face, she said, "The gap will allow your body to heal more naturally. Without it, the wound would continue to bleed on the inside, allowing a chance for a clot." She paused before the last word as if measuring it for correctness. Eric found her mastery of the English language amazing.

He watched closely as she wrapped the now much smaller wound with gauze and then placed a large adhesive patch over the entire area. Eric thought to himself that it wasn't terribly different from how the wound would have been treated back on Earth. Perhaps flesh was flesh, and there was only so much that could be done in the repair of it.

Arcos called out to the gathered soldiers and said something that Eric took to mean, "Return to your posts." The bulk of them headed off in different directions, many back to the round room while others arrayed themselves at distant intervals along the wall.

"That was an amazing thing you did, my friend," Arcos said after the soldiers had dispersed. "I feel that the Kro-an would certainly have breached the wall had you not performed that act of bravery."

"Kro-an? Is that what that thing is called?" Eric asked, standing up using his good leg while hanging onto the wall for support. "Bravery? I don't know about that, maybe a little crazy though," he said, smiling at Altare. She lowered her head suddenly as if embarrassed, a little smile parting her lips.

"Call it what you will, Eric," Arcos said. "But this I know, you have saved many lives this day. I feel that there is much we could learn from you." Then Arcos lowered his head.

"What is it, Arcos?" Eric said, sensing that something was wrong.

Arcos lifted his head and met Eric's gaze. "I am truly sorry for the manner in which you were brought here. It was something less than noble. And now you've risked your own life in our defense."

Eric paused for a second. "All's well that ends well," he said, clapping his hand on Arcos's shoulder. It was a cheesy saying, but Eric figured that no one here had heard it before, and it seemed to fit the circumstances pretty well.

"You should rest now, Eric," Altare said finally. She then turned to Arcos added, "Doctor, shall I take him back to his room?"

"Certainly, of course," Arcos said. "Take the northern corridor. It's much more scenic."

"Yes, doctor," Altare said, turning back to Eric. "Follow me, please."

Eric found that he had little trouble walking after the fragment had been removed from his leg. The amazing medical device that Altare had used had mostly sealed the wound. He was able to move along with only a slight limp.

Altare led him back through the round room and into the lift. Neither of them had much to say on the elevator ride down to the ground level. Altare glanced up once or twice during the ride and made small talk, asking about his leg or how he was adjusting to the new prosthetic arm. Eric answered in short bursts, just like he would do when on an elevator with an unfamiliar female back home. Conversing with the opposite sex had never been his strong suit, but somehow chatting with this alien female didn't seem quite as difficult. Perhaps it was because there weren't any preconceived notions on either side.

"So, how is it that you know my language so well?" Eric asked as the lift stopped at the ground floor.

"I am somewhat of a historian as well as a nurse," Altare said. "I oversee a rather large collection of books and scrolls that were retrieved from your world when we still had a colony there. I've spent much of my spare time studying the languages of your planet, English being one of them – my father has as well."

"Your father?" Eric asked, pointing back up the shaft toward the round room.

"Yes, Arcos is my father, a very astute observation, Eric."

"Well, it only makes sense, seeing how he also appears to have a good command of my language," Eric said.

"Yes, and who knew we would someday be able to use our language skills with an actual human," Altare said excitedly.

"When we were informed that a teleporter, as you call it, was found on Earth and that the human using it was to be retrieved, we were both very excited."

"Do your people still travel to other worlds?" Eric asked.

"Very rarely. And then only to try to retrieve technologies that were lost or are dear to us. As in your case, there are very few functional teleporters in existence. They are used only in emergencies, and even then we have difficulty knowing exactly where we'll end up. We lost the first group who was sent to find you. So as you can see, it is very dangerous for us. Many of the units no longer function, and we have no way of repairing them."

"How did you lose the first group? Where did they end up?" Eric asked.

"We have no way of knowing," Altare said, sadness weighing down her voice.

"How did you know that we had one of the units?" Eric asked, his mind racing as he tried to put all the questions he had into some kind of logical order.

"When a teleporter is used, it gives off a signal that can be detected by equipment here, much like a homing device. That way if one is lost and then found again, we can find it and hopefully retrieve it. That is what we were attempting to do in your case, but instead of getting the unit, we got you."

"Arcos says my friends are here somewhere. Is there any way to find them?" Eric asked, probing to see how much Altare knew about the situation.

"As I'm sure the doctor has told you, we have no safe way to travel beyond the city walls, and the teleporters no longer work for movement about the planet. So if they are out there, there is little we can to do help them. We can only hope they are as resilient as you and that they can somehow find a safe haven."

"That's not what I was hoping to hear," Eric said, a worried look appearing on his face. "I'm not accustomed to sitting still and letting circumstances have their way with me."

John awoke slowly. Opening his eyes brought him to a world filled with complete darkness; he was momentarily frightened by the lack of light. Blinking into the darkness around him did nothing to quell the sudden upsurge of fear. It took a second for him to remember where he was. The whole thing was disorienting, opening, closing then reopening his eyes, every movement of his eyelid resulting in the same outcome – pitch black.

He felt something clenched in his right hand and remembered the flashlight. Quickly flipping the small switch on sent a bright beam out at ground level. The light passed over his outstretched legs and cast a strange, frightening pattern across much of the bare metal floor.

Something stirred off to his left. John couldn't bring himself to look over to see what it was. The sound came again, and this time, it was obviously very close by. John sat petrified, his fist tightening up on the flashlight.

"What are you doing, man? Turn that damn light off!" Chuck croaked out over a yawn.

John exhaled loudly, easing his death grip on the flashlight. "You pinhead! I thought you were a monster or something!"

"Well, you're half right. I *am* something," Chuck said, stretching out the word "am."

"How long have we been asleep?" John asked.

"I'm not sure, but probably two or three hours," Chuck responded while getting to his feet. "How's the arm doing?"

John hadn't noticed before, but now that his attention was called to it, he found his arm to be quite numb and cold. "Not too good, I'm afraid."

Chuck leaned down and touched the skin on his friend's forearm. "Hold that flashlight up here for a sec, will ya?" he asked. John directed the light onto the wounded area while Chuck slowly untied the tourniquet and began to unwrap the wound.

"It's gonna start bleeding again if you do that," John said, wincing at the thought.

"I know, but your arm's turned blue. We should have taken this off an hour ago," Chuck said in a worried voice. "Now hold still, we need to get at least a little blood back into that arm for a bit. We can always re-apply another tourniquet later."

"So my choice is either to have my arm fall off from the tourniquet or bleed to death?" John mumbled. "I have to tell you, I'm not very happy with either of those options."

Chuck continued to work on John's arm without responding to his friend's grumpy commentary. The wound was still seeping as he removed the temporary bandage, trying not to reopen the laceration. A large crusty scab had formed across most of the cut, but fresh blood ran from under its edge each time Chuck pulled on the makeshift tourniquet.

"Quit moving around. We need to get this thing off, and the more you move, the more chance it has of breaking open again!" Chuck admonished John.

"Well, I'm sorry, MOM!" John spat back. "But it hurts like hell! O.K.?"

Chuck ripped another long piece of cloth off his shirt. "Alright, let's give it a minute to see if you can get some circulation going in your arm again. Why don't you flex your hand a bit? That should help."

John repeatedly squeezed his left hand into a ball. Fresh blood ran from the wound each time he made a fist.

"Geez, that hurts!" he said through his teeth. It feels like someone's stabbing me all over my arm with little tiny knives!"

"That's good. That means you're getting some feeling back," Chuck said.

John was losing a considerable amount of blood. He turned the flashlight up toward Chuck's face. "Dude, you think you might wanna tie it off now? I'm starting to feel a little woozy."

"Ah, don't be such a sissy," Chuck said, quickly re-dressing the wound. This time he used the cloth strip more like a bandage than a tourniquet, covering the wound repeatedly, then snugging the whole thing down with a little knot. "O.K. You shouldn't have as much trouble with it going to sleep now. Let me know if it does."

"Right," John groaned. "So you can torture me some more."

This time John's voice carried less bite than before. He was relieved that the ordeal was over, at least for now.

"I think we should get moving," John said after resting for another minute. "I really need to find something better to cover my arm with."

"Yeah, let's move," Chuck said, giving his friend a hand up off the floor. "Onward and downward, I suppose?" he asked.

"No other way to go," John said, weariness tugging at his voice.

Chuck knew his friend wouldn't be able to go on forever in his condition, but he also knew they had no choice. It was an uncomfortable feeling for him. He was used to relying on himself and having everyone else carry their own weight.

Trying not to think about what would happen if John began to bleed severely again, or even worse, if he suddenly collapsed, Chuck trudged on ahead, keeping the pace as easy as possible, hoping for a change in their luck before things got real ugly.

The two had passed through several more cavernous rooms when the flashlight dimmed suddenly, its volume of light reducing drastically.

"Shit!" John said, slapping the side of the flashlight with his good hand. "I think we're about to lose our light!"

John continued to slap the flashlight harder and harder until Chuck barked at him, "Dude, you're gonna bust that thing if you keep whacking it like that!"

As if on cue, the light went out completely just as Chuck had uttered the last word of his sentence.

Even though he couldn't see him, John knew Chuck was glaring at him from across the room.

"Oops," John muttered lowly into the darkness then slapped the flashlight twice more in a futile attempt to revive it.

"O.K., then," Chuck said after a moment of silence. "Let's think for a minute. Do we have anything else we can use for light?" Chuck's voice was surprisingly calm, given the gravity of their situation. "Anyone? Anyone?" He called out after not receiving an answer to his question. John couldn't help but laugh out loud at his friend's ability to find humor in their predicament, no matter how twisted it might seem.

"You think we can light something on fire?" John asked. "Maybe we can use the laser rifle to start a piece of cloth going."

"Well, that'd be a great idea if I still had any T-shirt left! I already feel like a Go-Go dancer!" Chuck said smugly. "Maybe we can feel our way around this room for a minute just to see if there's another way out, seems like the stairs have been located in the back left-hand corners of the last many rooms. Follow me over there as best as you can," he continued. "Here, you can see the little green lights on the laser rifle. Walk toward me, and we can head back there together. It won't do to get separated in the dark," Chuck mused then added as an afterthought, "I'd hate to shoot you by accident."

"Hey! That didn't sound very convincing!" John whined as he made his way across the room toward his friend.

The two men shuffled to the back corner, but upon arriving there, they found no stairwell.

"Shoot," Chuck said. "I guess the only thing we can do now is start feeling our way around the room. Maybe there's a doorway or another hatch or something."

The next several minutes were spent in complete silence except when one of the men would stumble over a chair or run into a panel or desk jutting out from one of the walls. Feeling their way along looking for an exit was proving fruitless.

They'd nearly completed their tour of the room when Chuck suddenly stopped moving, John bumping in his back. "What's up?"

"Shhh," Chuck hissed under his breath. "I think I heard something."

The two stood motionless as storefront mannequins, listening intently for any sound besides their own breathing. They didn't have to wait long. A light clinking emanated from across the room in the direction of the open stairwell from which they'd first entered the room.

"Move to your left," Chuck hissed again, this time with urgency.

"What?" John responded

"Move!" Chuck shouted, giving John a quick shove on the shoulder in the direction he'd indicated.

John stumbled sideways from the unexpected push as Chuck opened up with the rifle. The bright flashes from the weapon illuminated the entire room as he blasted away toward their as yet unseen pursuer. The first several shots fired in rapid succession lit up the room like a roman candle. John looked on in horror as he watched several of the bug-like metallic creatures pour across the room toward them, their stealthy cover now blown. Several more squeezed their way through the stairway, pulling up just behind the first.

Chuck fired as quickly as he could pull the trigger, sending bright red beams into the monster's armored hides. The first two sunk to the ground shrieking like lobsters going into a boiling pot of water only to have three more take their place.

John stood petrified, his eyes aching from the constant change from bright red light to dark, then back again. He knew moments into the battle that Chuck wouldn't be able to hold them off much longer. Their numbers and the ferocity of their attack were too great.

Using the near constant flashes from the laser rifle to see, John scoured the room for something he could use as a weapon. He had no intention of going down without at least swinging a punch.

The room was cluttered with the obligatory chairs and detritus much like the last many chambers had been, but nothing fell to hand that looked suitable for defense.

"Damn, what I wouldn't give for a sharp stick right now!" John mumbled to himself, still desperately searching the room. Then he saw it. On the wall to his left, roughly twenty feet away, an air duct was positioned above one of the desktop control panels. He hadn't noticed them in the other rooms, but after seeing one now, John figured that they must have been there. He and Chuck had been so focused on finding doors or stairs that they hadn't considered looking up for air conditioning vents or air returns.

John scrambled across the room toward the vent and hopped onto the console protruding from the wall. It held his weight fair enough as he wrestled with the metal grating covering the ventilation ductwork. After a couple of quick hits from the palm of his hand, John managed to pull the cover loose. It clanged to the floor, momentarily drawing Chuck's attention away from his life and death battle with the bugs.

"You go, John!" he yelled out over the tumult, seeing that his friend may have found a way out for both of them. Launching another volley of shots into the body of the lead creature, he inched his way backward toward John and the new exit route.

The bugs, sensing the imminent escape of their prey, redoubled their efforts, piling on top of one another in an attempt to get past the searing laser beams to devour their quarry.

John peered into the open shaft of the ventilation duct, trying to guess where it might head. All he could see in the thin light from the laser blasts was that it went straight back for some distance. That was good enough for him. Placing his arms firmly against the inside of the metal duct, he hoisted himself up into the mouth of the vent. Traveling head first, John noted that his body blocked out most of the light from Chuck's weapon. Squirming forward in near darkness with the twang of the rifle reverberating off the metal ductwork all around him, he hoped he was moving fast enough to give his friend room to enter as well. The noise was like being inside a giant soda can rolling down a rocky slope. A second later, after a particularly violent flurry of laser blasts, the firing stopped. John swallowed hard, still worming his way into the duct.

"Chuck! You O.K.?" He yelled into the darkness, hoping his voice might still be heard. A series of grunts reassured him that Chuck had at least made it into the shaft. John felt helpless that he was unable to give Chuck a hand getting into the duct, but the fit was so tight that he had no way of turning around. The best thing he could do now was to keep moving forward to make as much room as possible for his friend.

"I'm in! Keep moving!" Chuck called out in a wild voice.

John felt something damp on his arm and knew he'd torn the wound open again. He had no idea how much blood he was losing, but right now, that didn't matter. His only goal was getting as much distance as possible between the bugs and himself.

The two squirmed along through the ductwork, covering another dozen feet while the creatures behind them shrieked and tore at the ventilation hole. Luckily, the walls surrounding the vent seemed quite solid. It would take a long time for them to get through, if ever.

"Something's wet in here," Chuck said, at last, the panic in his voice now somewhat subdued.

"I know, that's from me," John said without thinking.

After a moments pause, Chuck said, "That's O.K., man, it can happen to the best of us."

"I mean it's my blood, you idiot! What'd ya think, I wet my pants or something?" John shouted back at Chuck, his voice ringing loudly through the vent. But before Chuck could answer, John found himself tipping forward onto an unseen ramp in the ductwork.

"Aww shiiiittt!" he yelled, sliding headfirst into the abyss, the skin on his arms making an awful squealing sound like a child's bare legs on a hot metal playground slide. He was crammed pretty tightly into the round ductwork and kept bouncing off the sides of the tube, each rebound sending a shock wave through his body.

John plummeted down the steeply angled ramp; arms thrust out in front of him. The trip took only a few seconds, but it was time enough to gather considerable speed. Moments later, he crashed through a vent grate and shot out onto the floor of another dark room, landing with a crash. Luckily, the angle he'd been ejected at sent him into a fast roll went he hit the ground. He tumbled wildly, spinning over and over again like a log, before coming to rest flat on his back.

Lying prostrate on the floor and trying to catch his breath, John tried to determine if he was still alive or not.

"Damn it," he groaned out weakly.

And even through closed eyelids, he could tell that a light source had just been turned on. Chuck yelled down the chute after him in a panicked voice, "John! John! You alright?"

John popped his eyes open, figuring that anything that happened next would be better than crawling through that ductwork while bleeding to death. His first sight was a bright white ceiling. Not like the dingy, dirty rooms he and Chuck had been in before, but a very clean area indeed. Rolling his head to one side, he saw numerous panels flickering to life on the wall next to him. The ground was also quite clean. No dust or dirt marred the pristine metallic white flooring of this room.

Chuck's voice rang out again, louder this time. "John! You O.K. or what?"

A moment later, Chuck's head appeared in the hole where the vent cover had been.

"Hey!" he exclaimed. "What the hell is this?" he said, sliding the rest of the way out of the duct while John sat up rubbing his head.

"You look like hell," Chuck said, seeing John's battered form sitting on the shiny white floor. "I didn't realize how dirty you'd gotten."

"Well, you don't look so great either," John shot back.

Chuck looked himself over quickly. "Yeah, you're right, especially with your blood all over me!" he griped.

"Sorry 'bout that, couldn't be helped," John said, sending little daggers at his friend with his eyes while gently tapping around the re-opened wound on his arm, a steady stream of fresh blood dripping from under its bandage.

Chuck stepped over and tore another long strip of fabric off his shirt. It now looked more like a loose-fitting halter top than a T-shirt, ending just under his chest. John couldn't help but chuckle, watching as his friend slowly dismantled his wardrobe.

"What?" Chuck asked, pulling the last few threads loose from his tattered shirt. "What's so funny?" he asked again.

"Nothing," John responded. "I just love watching you work," he said.

"Alright. Let's have the arm," Chuck said, walking over and reaching an expectant hand down to John.

John offered up his bleeding arm and surveyed the room while his friend tied off the wound.

"Damn!" John winced. "Not so tight!"

"It's gotta be tight," Chuck said with all seriousness. "You're losing a lot of blood."

Chuck finished his task then looked around the room, his eyes stopping to rest on a hatch located in one corner. Letting go of John's arm, he stepped over to the hatch and began to examine it.

"Looks like we've stumbled on to something here, doesn't it?" he said to no one in particular. "This area of the city is obviously still functional, but it seems to be just as deserted as the rest of the place."

Chuck continued to examine the doorway when one of the panels on the wall caught John's eye. Stepping closer, he noticed a bank of what appeared to be surveillance cameras.

"Dude, take a look at this!" he said excitedly, his eyes darting back and forth amongst the small flickering screens, each one showing a different area.

"Looks like there are at least a dozen more rooms intact down here, and that's assuming there's a functional camera in each one," John said.

Many of the screens showed only static, leaving the men to wonder if the room had been destroyed or if the camera simply was no longer functioning. John watched the monitors closely, trying to determine what might be contained in the rooms. Several of them housed control panels and metallic chests with unknown contents. One room, in particular, was lined with dozens of tubes. Each one appeared hazed over, a few of them with small green lights at their bases.

"What do you figure those are for?" John asked Chuck, only to find his friend had already returned to examining the sealed portal.

"What do ya think? What's our next move?" he asked again.

"Well, obviously there are no stairs out of this room. I figure we have to try to get through this door because I'd sure hate to have to crawl all the way back up to the surface," Chuck said, eyeing the portal. "Looks like it's airtight, doesn't it?" he asked John.

John ran his finger over the edges of the door. "Sure does. How do you figure we're gonna get it open? I mean, I can't begin to decipher the alien-speak on any of the controls."

Chuck looked perplexed for a moment, then took a few steps back. Pulling the laser rifle from his shoulder, he said, "You may want to clear out of there," as he poked the gun repeatedly away from the door.

"O.K.," John said, stepping back several paces. "So much for subtlety," he drawled.

Chuck gave him a questioning glance. "What? You figure we're gonna wake somebody up or something?"

John hesitated a moment as if thinking about it, then said, "Nah, if anyone's been in there for a thousand years, they're probably dead by now anyway."

"Yeah," Chuck said, raising his nose into the air and looking at John over the tip of it. "That's what I figured too. But thanks for your input. Now, why don't you take another step back, just in case. 'Sides, you're starting to make a nasty little blood puddle there."

John did so, stepping over the small pool that had formed on the floor directly below his dripping wound.

Chuck wasted no time. He leveled the weapon and pointed it at the door handle. "Here goes!" he said, squeezing the trigger. A bolt of red light pulsed out from the muzzle of the weapon and slammed into the latching mechanism. The entire assembly disappeared in a puff of smoke, leaving a nice round hole. In the same instant, a rush of air escaped from the chamber beyond the door.

"Airtight indeed," Chuck said, looking over at John.

The flow of air pushed the unlatched door open an inch or two, its hinges groaning. Chuck, for all his bravado, kept the laser rifle firmly planted against his hip and aimed toward the slightly ajar door. The two waited for a few seconds to see if they had indeed awoken anything by their act of breaking and entering, but no sound came from the other room. John moved forward and knelt down, looking through the still smoking hole left by the laser rifle's bolt.

"Can't make out too much," he said, poking his head around, trying to get a better look. Standing up, he grabbed the edge of the hatch. "Shall we?" he asked, opening the door without waiting for an answer. Chuck crowded up next to him just in case there was something waiting on the other side of the portal.

The door was thick and heavy. It definitely had been created to act as a seal.

"Pretty good fit to have lasted for a thousand years, don't you think?" John asked.

"Sure is," Chuck said. "And they can't even make a top to keep the water out of my convertible back home."

John flashed a wicked look up at his friend. "You have a convertible?" he spat disgustedly.

"I knew that one would get you," Chuck said, giggling. "And you know what else? It's red!"

"I'm done talking to you," John said, pointing a finger in the direction of the door. "Let's go," he added, stepping through the portal.

Instantly, lights all throughout the chamber sprang to life. Chuck pushed his way into the chamber behind John, thrusting the laser rifle before him.

"Hang on there, Tonto!" John yelled, grabbing at the barrel of the gun to keep Chuck from accidentally blasting him. "They must be on an automatic switch, just like the other room."

"Damn, John. My nerves can't take too many more of these surprises!" Chuck mused.

A moment later, several panels on the wall just inside the door lit up. Small electroluminescent needles began to spin while various buttons glowed green and red.

"Looks like the whole place is trying to wake up," John said, stepping over to one of the panels. "I wish I could read alien. Maybe we could make some sense of these things."

Chuck wandered around the room while John examined the control panels.

"You notice how clean it is in here?" he asked. "I mean, there's no dust at all."

John ran his fingers over the edge of the panel he'd been watching in an area where he expected he might find residue from a thousand years of disuse.

"You're right. The place is clean as a pin. It must have an air filtration system of some sort. 'Course I can't imagine any air cleaner that would keep someplace clean for a millennium."

"The air in here does seem pretty stale. It's like a clean room where they'd make computer chips. You don't figure the place has actually been sealed up for better than a thousand years, do you?" Chuck asked. "Look around; this stuff looks almost new."

John scanned the room, taking in the high tech control panels. "It must be that old. The life hutch we were in was that old. And what about the ruins above us? It seems like it would take at least a thousand years for those buildings up there to have decayed to the point they are now."

The two men continued their search, but the large room turned out to be mostly empty. Only a few odd chairs sat around the room right where they'd been left ages ago. They did find another sealed door in the corner opposite the one they'd entered through. This one had a more intricate locking mechanism with a string of five glowing red buttons above the latch.

"That sure looks like a combination lock to me," Chuck said. "Probably some code we need to enter to pass into the next chamber."

"So you gonna blast this one too?" John asked, his voice soundly strangely thin.

Chuck looked over at his friend just in time to see him begin to sway.

"John? You alright?" he asked, reaching over and grabbing John by the shoulder. He was teetering like a Christmas tree in a cheap plastic stand, his eyes straining to focus.

John blinked twice. "I don't think so…" he said, then collapsed.

"Goodbye"

Eric watched while his grandfather pulled on his heavy black jacket, filling the air with the musty, unused smell of old clothing that's been hanging in the closet for some time.

"Where are we going, Grandpa?" Eric's four-year-old voice squeaked as he reached for his own coat.

His grandfather looked down at him, one sleeve of the jacket hanging loose while he wrestled with the cuff links on the other arm. He sucked at his teeth for a second, pondering the best way to tell his four-year-old grandson that his parents had been in a car accident and that he and his grandmother were going to the hospital to identify the bodies.

He knelt down in front of Eric and placed a shaky hand on the boy's shoulder. "Eric," he began. "Something's happened to your mom and dad. Grandma and I need to go to," he paused, "visit them for a while. Your Aunt Lucy is coming over to stay with you while we're gone."

Eric turned his head toward the living room where his Grandmother was seated on the couch, already wearing her winter jacket. She was sobbing uncontrollably into her handkerchief and rocking back and forth on the edge of the cushion. Eric's grandfather stood up, his hand still resting on his shoulder.

"You be good for your aunt now," he said, wagging a finger at Eric. "We'll be home in time for dinner."

"O.K., Grandpa," Eric said. Even at his young age, he sensed that something was wrong. Little did he know that he would never be going home with his parents again.

The next few days passed quickly as he was handed off first to his aunt, then back to his grandparents, then off to some other little known relative. Then came the funeral, which he could just barely understand. When he would ask, everyone kept explaining to him that his mom and dad were "sleeping," but when day after day, they never woke up, he began to get worried. His little mind kept trying to grasp the idea of death in terms he could make sense of. Finally, his Uncle Joe responded to his queries in a way he could understand.

Uncle Joe had always been one of those no-nonsense kind of people who didn't believe in ghosts or monsters or things that went bump in the night. He'd always been gentle with Eric when he'd had a question, not treating him like a baby. Eric knew he'd get a straight answer from him, as he always had. Uncle Joe could explain things to him that no one else could. At the wake for his parents, Eric managed to find his uncle amidst the crowd of visitors.

"Uncle Joe," Eric asked tugging on his uncle's shirtsleeve. "Can I ask you something?"

Joe set his plate full of finger foods down gently on a nearby table, then turned back to Eric. "What can I do for you, my little man?" he asked.

Eric stood very still, his hands poked tightly into the pants pockets of the little black suit his grandma had dressed him in. His eyes wandered over his uncle's dark outfit. Everyone in the room was dressed in dark colors.

"Uncle Joe," he began, "When will mom and dad wake up?" he asked, then quickly added, "Everyone says they're sleeping."

Joe looked around the room, seeing the faces of so many relatives that he'd not talked to for months, maybe even years. He then looked back down at Eric.

"Come on, let's take a walk," he said, offering his open palm to Eric.

Eric placed his small hand into his uncle's soft grip, and the two headed toward the front door. Eric's grandpa watched them go, knowing that his son would be able to convey to the boy all the things he couldn't say himself.

The day outside was glorious. The sun shone through a perfectly blue sky dotted here and there by a smattering of small white clouds. Winter was nearly over, and spring was already starting to cast its wonderful palette of colors onto the brown and grey colored earth, the first signs beginning to show in the yard full of light green grass only recently coming back to life.

"Nice day, isn't it, Eric?" Joe asked as they strolled slowly down the front steps and out into the yard.

"It's nice," Eric responded, squeezing his uncle's hand tightly as they headed across the lawn. It'd been days since anyone had held his hand.

The grass was damp with light morning dew. Eric watched as his shoes turned from light brown to black as the water soaked into them, especially on the tips.

"Eric, how much has grandpa told you about what happened to your mom and dad?" Joe asked the boy as they walked along.

"He said they had an accident in the car and that they got hurt," Eric said. "And now they're asleep."

The pair walked on for another minute or two in silence, Joe trying his best to think of a good way to explain things to his nephew.

"You see, Eric," Joe said at last. "Do you remember the time you found that bird out by the barn at Grandpa's?"

"Yes," Eric said. "It wasn't moving. Grandpa said it was dead."

"That's right," Joe said, then added, "Do you know what that means? That word 'dead?'"

Eric thought for just a second. "I guess it means when something stops moving."

"Well, that's part of it," Joe said, stopping suddenly and kneeling down in front of Eric. "You see, Eric, everything that is alive right now will die someday," he began. "That tree over there will eventually grow old and die, and the cat up there on the porch," he said, first pointing out the tree and then the cat. "They will all be gone someday."

Eric looked down at the ground, trying to comprehend the idea. "So me and Grandpa and Grandma will all die someday?"

"Yes, we will all stop moving someday. Sometimes that happens because we get real old, but sometimes it happens because we get hurt real bad," Joe said, placing his hand under Eric's chin and lifting his head up so he could meet his eyes. "Do you understand what I'm saying?" he asked.

Eric's eyes wandered from Joe's gaze to a nearby tree, then back again. "Are you gonna die, Uncle Joe?" he said at last.

Joe leaned back on his heels and took in a deep breath. "Yes, Eric. I'm going to die someday too," he said with eyebrows furrowed, a deep wrinkle creasing his forehead. "But Eric, what you have to remember about life is this," he said suddenly leaning forward and grabbing Eric by the shoulders, pulling him close. "You have to remember that it's not how or when we die that counts," Joe said as he leaned back to look Eric in the eye once again. "What matters, my little man, is how we choose to live."

Eric saw what he thought was a tear in the corner of his uncle's eye and knew what he was saying must be very important. And though it took many years for him to really understand what his Uncle Joe was trying to say, those few words he'd spoken to him on that early spring day had more impact on his life than anything he had ever learned since.

Eric stretched hard and let out a long, satisfying yawn. A pain shot through his leg, reminding him that he'd taken some damage the day before. It was amazing how much healing had taken place already. He vaguely remembered Altare coming and going several times during the night to remove a blood-soaked bandage and then redressing the wound with a fresh one.

Lying flat on his back as the morning sun streamed in through a large glass window, Eric pondered what he needed to do next. It took only a moment for him to determine that he had to find his friends. Dead or alive, it was up to him to find them. The aliens were apparently content to live out their lives within the city walls, cowed by the threats that lurked outside, but Eric was not. Especially when the few people that he really cared about were out there somewhere, probably in great danger.

The whoosh of the sliding door drew Eric's attention away from his thoughts. Altare stepped silently into the room, and she was carrying a tray of food. Eric watched as she glided across the floor toward his bed, astonished by how graceful her movements were. She set the tray down and smiled at him.

"How did you sleep?" she asked, her voice full of concern.

"Well. I slept quite well," Eric said, returning her smile. "How long was I asleep?" he asked.

Altare thought for a moment, then said, "Well, by your own time, you've slept about twelve hours. By our time, that would be nearly two days."

"Do most of your people sleep when it's dark outside?" Eric asked as Altare began to examine the wound on his leg.

"No, we require no sleep at all. We do have quiet times that we use to reflect, but not what you would call sleep."

Eric looked puzzled. "So where did this bed come from then?" he asked quizzically.

"You are sleeping in one of our hospitals. What you're sleeping on isn't what you would really call a bed, it is more of a recovery table," Altare said. "But since we knew your race requires sleep, we improvised."

Eric pushed himself up into a sitting position. "Go figure," he said, shaking his head.

"Go figure?" Altare asked.

Eric chuckled, "No, no, it's just a way of talking. A colloquialism."

"Colloquialism?" Altare queried, a little dimple appearing between her two large brown eyes.

"Never mind," Eric said, waving his hand back and forth as if to dismiss the thought. Altare just smiled.

Finishing the work with the bandage, Altare asked, "Are you hungry?" as she pushed the tray a little closer to the bed.

"Yes, I am. But maybe we could go outside to eat?" Eric asked.

"Certainly," Altare said, pushing the tray away from the bed to give Eric room to move.

Eric slid his wounded leg out first, then the other, and finally, put weight on both. Altare placed a hand on his shoulder in case he should suddenly lose his balance. Her touch was very gentle. Eric was not used to being touched by anyone, let alone a female, alien or not.

Altare stood very close while he tested his footing, close enough that he could feel her breath on the bare skin of his shoulder.

"Do you feel alright?" she whispered, still standing close enough to make Eric feel a bit uncomfortable. "Can you stand on your own?"

Eric closed his eyes for a moment before answering. It had been so long since anyone had been this close to him. He breathed in a wonderful scent that made his head swim. It was a fragrance he'd not noticed from her before.

"Are you wearing some kind of perfume?" he asked Altare without looking up.

Altare lowered her head slightly and looked away to the side. Eric could see the pale skin on her face turn to a beautiful shade of pink.

"Do you like it?" she asked.

"Yes, it's very nice," Eric said, suddenly aware of his own heartbeat as Altare's hand rested on his shoulder. A chill ran through him from that touch, almost causing his breath to shudder.

The door to the room sprang open with a hiss. Altare inhaled sharply through her nose, obviously startled by the sound herself. An armored guard stepped into the room carrying what appeared to be a notepad and some other electronic gadget. He lowered his head, bending into a slight bow, and said something that sounded apologetic.

Altare quickly removed her hand from Eric's shoulder and leaned back a few inches away from him, striking a more "professional" looking pose. She said something to the guard who then stepped forward, head still bowed and handed her the items. The two exchanged what sounded to Eric to be polite goodbyes, then the guard turned and exited back through the portal.

Altare stepped back a pace and examined the items quickly; her eyes traveling from the notepad, to Eric, then back again. Reading the message inscribed on the top sheet, she finally looked up and met Eric's questioning gaze.

"Dr. Arcos and Geopre have requested my presence on top of the wall. There are many wounded that need assistance," Altare said worriedly.

"Geopre?" Eric asked.

"He is the leader of the city's defenses. He was with you when you battled the Kro-an. In fact, he was the one who helped you from the ground after the robot was destroyed," Altare said. Then noticing the puzzled look still crossing Eric visage, she added, "Apparently he was quite impressed with you." She lowered her head once again and said softly, "As were many."

Eric raised his eyebrows, a smile appearing on his lips. "Well, I don't know what I'd have to offer, but I'd like to go with you to see if I can be of any help."

Altare handed him the electronic device that the guard had

brought with him, her hand gently brushing against his in the process. "I had hoped you would come. You'll need this. It is a translator. It will speak to you in our language and will convert your language to our own. It will be much more efficient than having Dr. Arcos or me try to translate for you."

Eric inspected the device, turning it over in his hands. "Thank you, Altare," Eric said. "For everything."

A moment passed where nothing was said until Eric turned and pointed to the door. "Shall we go?" he asked. "Maybe we can eat something on the way."

"Certainly," Altare said, Eric's voice compelling her into motion.

The two each grabbed an item off the tray and headed for the door. Altare retrieved her medical bag before stepping through the portal.

"You don't know this, but we've been under almost constant attack since the wall was breached. The creatures seem to sense the weakness in our defenses and are trying to exploit it."

Eric crunched into a piece of what he took to be some kind of fruit. It tasted like an apple, though it was blue in color. "Must be something to do with that goofy sun out there," he mumbled to himself.

"What's that?" Altare asked. "What does 'goofy' mean?"

"Oh, it's nothing," Eric said, smiling. "I was just making an observation about your produce."

"I see," Altare said, wearing a sweet little smile.

The two headed toward the railcar through one of the glass tunnels. Eric could see several dead insect-like bodies lying out next to the breach in the wall. Apparently, some of them had managed to get through before being cut down. Dozens of soldiers formed ranks around the gap, weapons at the ready. Many of them had taken strategic positions in the shattered stones themselves. These few were repeatedly firing at unseen enemies.

"I had no idea the breach was this close," Eric said.

"Yes, and our greatest fear is that once the Kalwaers are loose within the walls, it will be very difficult to contain them. The turrets will not be of any assistance, and we will have to fight them with only hand weapons," Altare said, quickening her pace a little, the graveness of the situation showing on her face.

Eric quickened his step to keep up, and they reached the railcar in good time. The two hopped in, and Altare pressed a series of buttons. The railcar leapt forward with the same precise, smooth motion that Eric had noticed before when riding with Arcos.

A short ride brought them to the base of the round room. The lift then carried them up to the same level as the top of the wall where they exited and headed into the tunnel running out to the battlements. Eric could see at least a half dozen downed aliens scattered among the others. Here and there someone tended to one before shifting to another.

Altare was almost at a run now, the sight of the wounded soldiers spurring her on. Eric was barely able to keep up with her as her long legs covered an extra foot with each stride.

The two burst out onto the scene and jumped into action. Altare dropped down next the closest injured soldier and quickly examined his wounds. Eric spotted a laser rifle lying next to the warrior and scooped it up then stepped up to the wall, filling in the empty spot left by the soldier that Altare was now mending.

Peering out over the battlements, he saw a scene of total carnage. The bug-like monsters were racing toward the wall from every direction; all headed straight for the damaged section. Beams fired out from atop the wall and at ground level as the defenders tried in earnest to blunt the rush.

A huge pile of carcasses lay roughly a hundred yards out in a half moon shape. Very few of the creatures made it closer than that distance, and those that did were cut down rapidly. But as Eric had seen, at least a few had managed to get all the way to the wall and had even traversed to the inside.

Eric wondered in what way these ground-dwelling monsters had hurt the wounded. His question was answered quickly enough. The creatures were using a tactic he'd not seen from them before. Long spines covered their tales, and they were whipping them at the defenders like a porcupine would toss its quills. The spines traveled with amazing velocity toward the wall, raining down like arrows against the battlements. All of the wounded had been struck by one or more of these flying darts.

Ducking under cover of the crenellations then popping up again, Eric aimed and fired each shot with precision, just as he had been taught to do in his short stint in the military. The aliens around him seemed to fire almost at random, wildly blasting away, most of their shots missing their intended targets. The turrets were actually doing most of the damage to the attackers, and then only because they had so much firepower that any body part they hit would explode. Without them, the city would almost certainly be overrun.

Watching the soldiers reminded Eric of the extent to which the warriors were untrained and unskilled. Even though they'd had a thousand years to learn how to use the weapons at hand, they'd never had anyone to train them. It was as though they were trapped in some kind of medieval Dark Age, without the benefit of their predecessors' knowledge.

It was amazing that they'd been able to figure out all the complex systems that they had. Still, there is art to warfare, and it was obvious that a constant struggle to maintain borders along their city's walls was not enough to teach them any tactics other than those that they were exhibiting now. And those battle skills were sadly lacking.

Eric realized that he was no longer firing and was instead staring down the line of unguided and misdirected "soldiers" on either side of him. He paused for a second to reflect, then began firing again. He placed each shot with great accuracy, learning more about his adversary with each blast of the laser rifle. Within a handful of shots, he found that the insect bodies did a good job of shedding the lasers, a hard carapace covering their sensitive internal organs. The legs were more fragile, as was the neck, but these were almost impossible to hit.

Snapping off several shots at the head of one of the closest creatures brought it down instantly, its skull nearly exploding from the blast. But the creatures' heads, which bobbed along on their long, skinny necks, proved to be very difficult targets. It was like trying to shoot a plate of spaghetti out of a waiter's hand as he hurried across a crowded restaurant.

Drawing on his military experience, Eric formed a plan. He watched as one of the nearby soldiers fired a shot from a rocket launcher into the horde. The resulting explosion killed several of the creatures, but more importantly, slowed down or even stopped the advance of many more around the impact site.

In the precious few moments, while the creatures paused to regroup, Eric fired several carefully aimed shots, taking the heads off two or three of the Kalwaers within seconds.

This delay made it much easier to target the rifle, especially since there was no need to make any type of correction to the shot. The laser bolt raced to its target essentially in the same instant it was fired. The shooter didn't have to lead his target or worry about elevation.

With his new tactic, Eric was popping the head off an attacker with almost every shot. Around him, the alien soldiers began to take note. One, in particular, stepped in beside him, a puzzled look on his face. Eric continued to fire as the soldier looked back and forth between his weapon and the mounting number of bodies that were fast accumulating on the desert floor.

Noticing the looks from the soldiers around him, Eric stopped firing and turned to the alien who was standing closest. He looked vaguely familiar somehow, even though most of the aliens looked the same to him. Except for Altare, of course. The warrior spoke then, a strange string of syllables and consonants conveying no meaning.

Remembering the device that Altare had given him, Eric dug into his pocket to retrieve the translator and popped the small headphone over one ear. He positioned the microphone before his mouth. Holding up his index finger, he pushed the on button. Altare had already set the unit as a translator between English and the alien's home language.

Finally, he gave it a test.

"Can you hear me?" he spoke in a normal voice.

A second after he finished the short sentence, the translator croaked out something that sounded like alien-speak.

The alien soldier smiled and said something in return. Again, the device picked up the sentence and translated it, delivering the message through the headphones.

"Yes, I can hear you. I am Geopre," the soldier said in his ear much to Eric's delight. It was like having an entirely new world opened up to him. The device seemed to know who was talking and would not translate the other voices it picked up just outside of the conversation. Another piece of technology that Eric was sure couldn't be deciphered even by the most intelligent of the aliens. What a shame, he thought, to be essentially standing still for a thousand years instead of marching ahead to newer and even more fantastic technologies.

The alien's voice brought Eric back into the moment.

"You are killing so many of the Kalwaers," Geopre noted, a wrinkle creasing his brow.

Eric looked at the small group of aliens gathered around him. Many more lined the walls still blasting away at the attackers.

"You are using a new tactic?" Geopre asked.

"Well," Eric started, feeling a little uncomfortable with all the attention he was receiving. "I wait until one of your men fire a round from one of those rocket pods. The explosion causes the surrounding Kalwaers to stop their advance for just a second. That's how I'm able to target their heads so easily."

Geopre squinted at him, then turned back to the wall hoisting his gun and pointing it out at the creatures. He motioned to one of the nearby warriors to come to attention. The soldier stepped up to the wall and readied his weapon, waiting for a signal from his commander. Geopre sighted down the barrel of his laser rifle, and without looking over, gave a sharp nod to the warrior standing next to him. The soldier launched a rocket toward a tightly packed group of Kalwaers.

Eric watched as it snaked its way across the desert to the target, landing almost exactly where it had been pointed. Dozens of the creatures were either blown to pieces or knocked to the ground. The sound of the explosion took a moment to reach the city's defenders. In the instant before the Kalwaers regained their footing, Geopre pushed his advantage.

Firing off one shot, he narrowly missed one of the Kalwaers heads. He quickly re-aimed and fired again, and this time his shot slammed dead center into the monsters thick skull, blowing a hole clean through it. Another round sent a second creature to the ground just as the Kalwaers started moving again, making their heads too difficult a target to hazard.

Geopre turned to Eric as a murmur ran through the soldiers who had witnessed the spectacle. A smile parted his lips. It was as if someone had just turned on a light bulb.

Eric seized upon the surrounding aliens' attention. "Now, you need to form into four man squads, three men with rifles for every soldier with a rocket launcher. Stagger yourselves along the wall to get the best coverage," he barked into the translator.

The stunned aliens looked first at Geopre, then at Eric, then back to Geopre, wondering who to follow.

"Do as he says," Geopre roared. "To your positions!"

Eric couldn't help but smile as his simple lesson traveled out in both directions along the wall.

Within minutes, the push and pull of the battle had turned, the warriors clearly beginning to gain the upper hand.

Geopre stopped firing and looked down at the line of soldiers happily blasting away. He turned to Eric, who had taken a step back and was watching the scene as well, and smiled.

"Thanks be to you! Eric friend!" he shouted, the elation showing in his voice.

Altare, who had been mending one of the fallen soldiers, smiled up at Eric from her work. He saw her admiring gaze, and it sent a shiver down his spine. She made him feel nervous and a little giddy, like an elementary school boy on the playground who has just bumped into his first crush.

"Colorado"

"No way, man, it's definitely broken," John said, examining his friend's trapped leg. A large boulder pinned Chuck's leg from the just below his knee down to his ankle.

"Is it a compound break?" Chuck asked, clenching his teeth in pain.

"No, I don't think so, but it looks pretty ugly anyway. It's kinda kinked off to one side," John said, screwing his face up into a rather ugly scowl.

The two had been hiking for three days along one of their favorite routes and were just about to start looping back toward home. Chuck had crawled on top of a large boulder to poke his head above the rim of the shallow ravine they'd been trekking through when the enormous rock suddenly shifted. Chuck lost his footing and slid off the top and down alongside the huge stone as it came to rest against the wall of the ravine. Unfortunately, his leg was between the two as the rock slid into place against the ravine with a solid *thunk*.

John had been only a few feet away on the floor of the ravine when the accident happened. He quickly rushed to his friend's aid only to find him quite stuck, the monolithic stone pinching his leg against the ravine wall. Luckily, the top of the boulder had hit the wall nearly at the same time, keeping Chuck's leg from being crushed flat like a hotdog under a steamroller.

After several futile attempts to move the giant rock, John sat down next to his friend, panting from exertion.

"It's no use, man, that thing's way too huge. I can't even begin to budge it," John said, pausing between words to grab a few breaths of air.

"Shit," Chuck cursed, striking the stone with the palm of his hand. Leaning back against the ravine wall, he was happy that he couldn't see the damaged right leg. It disappeared from view just below his knee where the edge of the rock tapered slightly away from the wall.

"What the hell are we gonna do?" he said disgustedly.

John stepped back around the boulder and faced Chuck.

"Well, I don't know about you, but I'm going home," he said with all seriousness, then turned and picked up his backpack as if making ready to leave. "I mean really; it's starting to get dark. I don't plan on staying in this ravine all night."

Chuck contorted his face into a sneer looking very much like a prune. "You son of a bitch! You think this is funny!" he yelled, his voice echoing along the length of the crevice. But he couldn't help but laugh a little at his friend's jest, and somehow it made the pain a bit easier to handle.

"How far back do you think Eric is?" Chuck asked.

"Can't be too far. Maybe I can get in touch with him on the radio," John said, retrieving the walkie-talkie from his backpack. "Well, send him for help."

"You don't think the two of you can move this thing?" Chuck asked.

"Not a chance. It's gotta weigh like a million pounds. We're gonna need some heavy equipment brought out here to do it. At least something with a winch," John said, pulling the radio up to his mouth. "Eric, you out there, come in Eric."

A moment passed interrupted only by the sound of Chuck's grunts of pain.

"Yo." Eric called back, "What ya need?"

John explained the situation to Eric who was insistent that he should come and try to move the rock himself. But John was finally able to convince him that the best course would be to go for help. They were three days out after all, and Eric was nearly a day behind them, having stopped off at a small cave to do some exploring. He'd planned on hanging around the area until Chuck and John looped back to pick him up.

"O.K. But you guys are gonna be out there for at least another day until I can get within radio range to get in touch with someone. Do you have enough supplies, water, and food?" Eric asked.

"Yeah, I think we'll be O.K. until you can get some help. Now get moving! I don't know how much damage has been done to Chuck's leg. At the very least, it's broken and the longer we wait, the greater chance there is of something bad happening," John said.

"What's that supposed to mean?" Chuck said, wrinkling up his brow.

"Nothing," John said, shaking his head, "I'm sure everything will be fine. I'm gonna hop up top for a second and see where we are."

"OK. But be careful of this boulder. It's been known to move on occasion," Chuck said smugly.

"Don't worry about that. I wouldn't be crazy enough to trust an old rock not roll out from under me," John replied, slapping Chuck on the shoulder.

John was more concerned than he let on. Climbing to the top of the shallow ravine, he found he was exactly where he thought they would be at this point on their journey.

They had always liked this particular route because of its diversity. Starting out, they would travel for about a day through a thickly wooded region. The next day would be mostly grassy plains, and the final day before turning back, would be spent in an arid desert-like environment strung with fissures and ravines; it was much like a miniature Grand Canyon.

John turned slowly, taking in the view in its entirety, scanning the horizon for any sign of life. Perhaps someone was close enough who had a truck or a quad and could go for help much faster than Eric would travel on foot. Unfortunately, John saw no such vehicle anywhere nearby. Actually, he hadn't really expected to. They were quite a way out into the desert at this point, well beyond where most casual travelers would venture.

"You see anything?" Chuck yelled up from within the ravine.

"Nothing," John called back. "Just lots of desert as far as the eye can see."

"Well why don't you come down here and keep me company then," Chuck said, doing his best to sound lonely. "And bring me something to eat."

John leaned over the ravine to a spot where he could see Chuck.

"My, aren't we getting snotty! A little accident and out come the true colors!" John barked back. "You'll get some dinner when I'm damn good and ready."

Chuck's giggle resonated along the ravine walls, making it sound rather ghoulish.

John was continuing his survey of the surrounding landscape when Chuck piped up once more.

"John, I think I have to go to the bathroom," he said in a pained voice.

"You've got to be kidding!" John said, leaning out over the edge of the ravine again.

"Ha! I am!" Chuck laughed.

There he was, in the ravine with his leg broken and pinned between a boulder and the ravine wall, and yet he was still making jokes. You couldn't buy friends like that, John thought.

Heading back down into the ravine, John began to unpack his gear for the rapidly approaching night. He set up his tent a few feet away from Chuck then piled up several sticks and some dry brush and started a small fire. Chuck watched intently, issuing orders and critiques about every move John made while laughing at his own jokes.

John checked his friend's trapped leg several times over the next hour or two. It seemed to be doing as good as was possible considering the conditions. Chuck's leg was warm to the touch, and his foot was a healthy pink color, though a small trickle of blood had seeped from a cut above his ankle. It was nothing serious, but it concerned John nonetheless.

"You sure you're really stuck?" he asked Chuck, sarcastic doubt dripping off each word.

"Hey! I'm the one making the jerky comments and jokes around here, alright?" Chuck shot back. "And what kind of sicko would take pleasure in his friend's pain?"

John bent down and tapped his index finger gently against the kink in Chuck's leg where the bone was obviously broken.

"Ouch! You idiot!" Chuck yelled out in pain. "What are you trying to do?!"

John stood up and smiled at Chuck with mock caring in his

eyes. "Just making sure you still have feeling in your leg."

"Oh, you know someday you're gonna need me for something, something real bad, and I'm gonna remember this," Chuck said, then added, "When you least expect it, expect it!"

John puckered his lips and squinted his eyes half shut. "Isn't that a line from a movie or something? You're not allowed to borrow other people's threats, especially if they're from a movie!"

Suddenly a sound emanated from above the lip of the ravine. The sun was only minutes from setting, and the ravine was only faintly lit by the waning sunlight bouncing off the clouds overhead.

"Hello! Anybody up there?" John called out, stepping back to try to get a better look at the area where the sound had come from.

"You're gonna get it now, man!" Chuck laughed. "Somebody else is here to help me out, and you won't be able to torment me anymore!"

Another sound came from the same direction, a scuffling, clicking sound. The hair on the back of John's neck stood up as the source of the noise stepped up to the lip of the ravine. A pair of unearthly yellow eyes set within a dark, hunched silhouette, peered down at him from a distance of one good leap away. A low guttural growl filled the ravine while the predator sized up his quarry.

"Chuck," John said, "Did we bring a gun with us?"

But before Chuck could answer, the beast leapt down onto John with lightning speed, knocking him back against the wall of the ravine. Chuck heard a sickening crack as John's head smacked into the rock wall. Struggling in vain to free himself, he watched as his friend slumped to the floor of the crevasse.

The huge wolf bit twice at John's exposed arm, pulling ferociously at his undefended flesh. Chuck struggled to move to his friend's aid but was immediately reminded of his own predicament, wincing in pain as the trapped leg twisted against the hard stone.

In the failing light, Chuck could see John's blood spray up

from his arm and splash against the stone wall of the cavern. It looked like black paint in the dim light that remained.

"Hey!" Chuck yelled, the only thing he was capable of doing in his current state. "Get the hell off of him, you bastard!" he screamed frantically, watching his friend being devoured before his eyes.

Then he had a thought. His eyes desperately searched the area around his feet until at last; he spied a good-sized rock. Bending over at the waist, he found the stone to be just out of his reach. He was nearly hanging off his broken, trapped leg, twisting his body to get every inch of extension that was possible with his left arm. At last, his fingers grazed the edge of the rock, scratching at it with his fingernails, a thought flashed through his mind about how the damned remote control always falls just out of reach in this exact same fashion. A final thrust allowed him just enough extension to pinch the stone between his index and middle finger. He pulled it back, twisting himself into an upright position.

Wild-eyed, he transferred the rock to his right hand, then hurled it with as much force as he could muster. It was an awkward throw considering the angle he was trapped at relative to the wolf, but it was the best he could manage. Amazingly, the rock found home just behind the wolf's left ear, ricocheting off his head with a resounding pop, drawing the monster's attention away from his supper.

"Take that, you bastard!" he yelled furiously at the animal. Its large yellow eyes came to rest on Chuck, who until now had gone unnoticed. With a quick turn and another leap, the beast was upon him.

All he could do was flail his arms frantically, batting the wolf's huge head back and forth with closed fists. The wolf was taken aback by the fury of its prey's attack, yipping, and snorting as Chuck pummeled his head repeatedly. The wolf dropped back a pace, snarling at Chuck. For a moment, it seemed as though the beast might actually give up and leave, but it only *seemed* that way. Quick as lightning, it struck again, but much more warily this time. It seemed to sense

Chuck's weakness and immediately went for his left leg, seizing it between its massive jaws just above his ankle. Chuck yelled out in pain as the wolf crunched down. Swinging wildly, he was barely able to reach the creature to defend himself, and then only with his left hand. This time the wolf seemed oblivious to the blows Chuck rained down on his back, only shuddering slightly under each stroke. Within seconds, Chuck's leg gave way, and he sank down, hanging his full weight off his right leg where the boulder had it pinned. He screamed out again as the wolf bit at his left shoulder and midsection. The only thing he could do was cover his face and neck to keep the monster from tearing out his throat.

Chuck's mind raced as he imagined his impending death. How long would it take for the wolf to kill him? Would he be partially eaten while still alive like the animals he'd seen in those national geographic shows on T.V.? He was becoming something else's dinner, and there was nothing he could do about it. Exhausted from his struggle and weak from loss of blood, he could feel himself slipping away. Somehow the gnashing teeth of the wolf didn't hurt as much as they had before. "This must be what it's like to die," he thought as his arms went limp, dropping his guard completely.

A horrible barking howl followed by another brought him back from the edge of consciousness. He opened his eyes and tried to focus. Before him, two dark forms wrestled for supremacy on the ravine floor, backlit by the small fire. A cloud that had been obscuring the moon began to pass, revealing the life and death struggle taking place only a few feet away.

John rolled back and forth with the huge wolf, locked in an awful embrace. It looked as though the wolf had John's left forearm clamped inside of its mouth. Blood poured from the puncture wounds up and down his friend's arm as the beast thrashed back and forth, chomping on the exposed flesh. The wolf almost appeared to be gagging. Chuck squinted hard as the cloud overhead finally cleared the moon, bathing the entire area in a pale white light. The scene was primeval, man against beast in an epic struggle. Chuck's eyes widened as he realized that the wolf didn't have a grip on John, but that John had pressed his arm into the gullet of the beast and was using it to hold the wolf down.

A glint of moonlit steel glimmered in the cool night air as John raised and struck time and again with his hunting knife, the large blade plunging into the animal's unprotected chest and abdomen like a hot knife into butter. The wolf's snarls and growls quickly turned to whimpers, then silence. The only remaining sound was the swish of the blade sinking repeatedly into the beast's lifeless carcass.

The battle was over in moments as John finished his grizzly task, then toppled over to one side, dropping his blade onto the sandy desert floor.

The air was turning colder as both men clung to life. Chuck could see John's breath coming in short gasps, sending small vapor clouds into the air. Even with the dire circumstances, he somehow he knew everything would turn out O.K.

Pushing himself up on his shredded left leg, he leaned back against the cool stone of the ravine wall. Looking over at John, he called out weakly.

"Hey, John."

In response, John slowly rolled over onto his side, squeezing the bleeding wound on his arm. "Yeah?" he croaked.

Chuck coughed twice, clearing his throat, and then offered, "I don't have to go the bathroom anymore."

John rolled once again onto his back, a gurgling chuckle parting his lips.

Moments later, another sound reached Chuck's ears. A buzzing of sorts, a rhythmic, warbling sound that seemed like the ring of a far-off chainsaw. Closing his eyes for a moment, he listened intently, clinging to consciousness as the sound grew louder, then disappeared.

Seconds before blacking out, he heard Eric's voice, followed by the sound of running feet. A weak smile graced Chuck's face as he thought to himself *That bastard's never going to let me forget this one.*

"Waking the Dead"

"Come on, John! Wake up!" Chuck called out while shaking his friend's limp body. "Don't do this, John! I've already had to carry you once, and I'm not gonna do it again!" he yelled only inches from Johns' face.

After a few more shakes, Chuck sat back on his heels. "Damn it!" he said, looking around the room for something that might somehow aid in the situation. Of course, there were only a few desks and chairs to be seen, nothing of any real value. Not even a shred of fabric or a piece of wire he might use to tie off the wound again.

Chuck bent over and listened closely to John's chest. He found a heartbeat, but it was weak and slow.

"Lost too much blood," Chuck said aloud, noticing the small pool that had formed even since John had collapsed. "Gotta stop that bleeding somehow."

Chuck ripped frantically at the blood-soaked fabric covering the wound on his friend's arm, then yanked off what remained of his own shirt and began tearing it into thin strips. He wrapped one very tightly around John's arm just above the wounded area, this time pulling it so tight that he thought he might tear John's skin open, grimacing at the thought of how much damage was being done to the soft flesh beneath the twisting bandage. He then used the second and third piece of T-Shirt material to cover the first, hoping that it would help absorb some of the blood. Finally, satisfied with his work, he stood up and surveyed the room, searching for some idea of what to do next.

"O.K., let's see. I'm somewhere underground, John's mostly dead, and I'm stuck in this room. O.K., that's the bad stuff," Chuck said, pacing around and tapping his index finger on the tip of his chin as he always did when faced with a difficult situation.

"What's the good stuff, what are my options? They are always options. Right?" he said aloud.

A final sweep of the room brought his attention to the bank of monitors John had found. He raced over and hurriedly scanned each one, their shiny surfaces each showing a scene from a different room.

"Alright, this is going nowhere," he grumbled, looking back toward his friend who lay motionless in the middle of the room. Spying the laser rifle resting on the floor a few paces away, he made his decision. Striding across the room, he picked up the weapon, leveled it at the locking mechanism on the door and fired. The beam cut through the door like butter, sending the keypad and lock up in a puff of smoke.

"Alright then," Chuck said, pushing the door open with the barrel of the gun. He peered inside the brightly lit room, not sure what to expect. Apparently, when the lights came on in the room he and John had happened upon, they also turned on the lights in most of the other rooms in the complex, or at the very least in this one.

Chuck stepped inside and gave a quick look around. This was one of the rooms he'd seen on the monitors. Dozens of long tubes were aligned vertically along the back wall, each one with a small light at its base. Most of the lights were out, but two shone red while one other cast an eerie green color. Nearly all of the vessels were covered with a filmy haze.

Chuck stepped up to the first one and rubbed his hand over the translucent glass covering only to find that the film was on the inside. Looking around the edges of the curved glass, he was able to discern minute fractures spidering out from where the glass met the metal brackets that held each cylinder to the wall. Checking several more, he found the same pattern repeated on each tube. Apparently, an underground tremor or quake had forced a shift against these containers, cracking most of them and breaking their seal.

Stepping back a pace, he surveyed all dozen or so cylinders along the wall. Only one had a green light at its base. Chuck moved to examine the only unbroken tube, only to find that he couldn't see much through the surface. The opaque nature of the material allowed only a tiny amount of light to be reflected back through the glass.

Leaning in closer, his breath left a small ring on the surface of the cylinder. Squinting hard, he was still unable to make out the contents. Finally, he turned his attention to the green light at the bottom of the tube. To him, it looked like a button with a light in its center. Leaning back, he noodled over whether or not to push the button. Anything could be waiting for him in that tube, and so far it was obvious that the inhabitants of this world didn't take kindly to visitors.

The rest of the room contained the same contents as the others, nothing of any use for helping him or his friend. Another door stood sealed in the left corner of the room. Chuck wondered how many more chambers he would have to pass through before he could find something to help John and how many of those rooms might contain not-so-friendly residents.

As if on cue, a groan came from the other room, then another. John was in a bad way, and Chuck knew he was the only hope for his friend's survival. Without another thought, he reached down and pushed the green button, then stepped back, holding the laser rifle at his hip.

The button began to blink intermittently. The flashing increased in speed until at last, the light was shining steadily green once again. Chuck swallowed hard, his eyes growing wide as he waited for the consequences of pushing the button to become evident.

Another groan from John floated eerily through the room. Chuck knew John couldn't last much longer. In fact, he wondered if it might be too late already. But for now, his gaze was fixed upon this one chamber.

Presently, two small holes opened in the metal bracket near the top of the tube. Gas vented into the room for several seconds. The scene transfixed Chuck. Then, the tube itself shifted back an inch, dropping into some hidden recess in the floor, leaving Chuck face to face with a creature that looked very similar to the one he and John had seen on the view screen in the life hutch.

The being was laying in a mold cast to fit its body in a

standing position. The entire thing was reclined slightly for the obvious reason of not allowing the contents of the tube to fall forward.

Chuck marveled at the alien's body. It was tall, easily seven feet, and very lean. An elongated head with large eyes and small features, exactly matching the images he'd seen back on earth of the creatures that were reportedly stored in Area 51.

"Damned if it wasn't true after all," Chuck mumbled.

The sound of Chuck's voice seemed to have an effect on the alien. His eyes sprang open, and his body jerked momentarily as if he had been awakened from a long sleep. As Chuck would soon find out, he had indeed been asleep for an extended period; a nap that had lasted more than a thousand years.

The alien blinked rapidly as one would do after being abruptly awakened and finding yourself in a very brightly lit room. Raising his hand to shade his eyes from the overhead lighting, the creature's gaze eventually came to rest on Chuck. Chuck stood a couple of paces away with the laser rifle aimed directly at the alien's midsection. A look of surprise registered on the being's face, and for an instant, the two just stood there eyeing each other.

Chuck was speechless. He could tell by the look in the alien's eyes that he was just as surprised to see him. *And why wouldn't he be?* Chuck thought. *I wonder if he has any idea how long he's been out?*

The alien leaned forward slightly and spoke. The words meant nothing to Chuck, which became apparent to the alien very quickly. He began to move out of the capsule slowly. Chuck kept the weapon aimed at him the whole time. Raising his hands to show he meant no harm, he began to move toward Chuck, then seeing the look on his face, decided it might be best to wait for the man with the laser rifle to make the next move.

The two stood still, frozen for a moment longer, Chuck hardly breathing, his finger hovering just over the trigger of the rifle.

Another moan from John broke the deadlock between the two. The alien jumped a bit, his eyes moving between Chuck and the hatch leading to the other room. It was then that Chuck noticed that the creature before him looked rather ill. His mouth hung open just a touch, his eyes watery and deeply sunken into their sockets. As if to confirm his thoughts, the alien coughed suddenly. A sharp, biting hack that sounded very painful. It raised one hand to its mouth and coughed again. When it returned its hand to a raised position, Chuck noticed a few spots of bright pink fluid spattered on the creature's fingers, obviously its blood.

"Sao Mak Domalan?" the alien queried while pointing a finger at the open door.

The words took Chuck by surprise.

"I can't understand you!" Chuck said angrily, wondering how to get out of this predicament. His friend was expiring only one room away, but he had no idea what the alien would do should he lower the weapon. He did, however, know that whatever he decided, he was going to have to make a move soon or John would assuredly die.

The alien was having similar thoughts, albeit for a different reason. Pointing at one of the panels just to his left, he spoke another unintelligible sentence then began to move slowly toward a membranous keypad that protruded slightly from the wall, never taking his eyes off Chuck.

Chuck followed his progress with the rifle, trying to decide if he should blast the creature or wait to see what it might be trying to do. After a few steps, the alien reached the panel. Poking a long finger toward it, he spoke again. Though Chuck couldn't understand the words, his tone seemed conciliatory. The alien paused, finger poised over a particular button as if waiting for an O.K. from Chuck.

John moaned a third time and then called out in a thin, weak voice, "Chuuuck."

That was all Chuck needed to hear. If there was any hope of saving his friend, it lay with the creature standing before him. Taking a step back, Chuck lowered the gun and nodded sharply.

The alien pressed a series of buttons. An entire section of the wall slid open, revealing shelves covered with dozens of instruments and devices unrecognizable to Chuck. He reached for one that looked something like a gun and pulled it out of the large cabinet. Before Chuck could raise the rifle, the alien placed it against his own neck and pulled the trigger. The device let out a hiss as the alien twitched slightly from its contact. He squeezed his eyes shut tight and stood still for a moment, then after several seconds, released his breath, reopening his eyes. He looked somehow healthier than he had before, more relaxed.

The creature grabbed several other items off the shelf and turned back to Chuck.

"Sao Mak Domalan?" the alien said again, pointing at the doorway.

Chuck understood what he meant and nodded his head.

"My friend is hurt. Can you help?" he asked.

The alien smiled thinly and stepped through the door, still keeping an eye on Chuck and the rifle.

The two found John in a terrible state. He lay sprawled out on the ground, a large pool of blood spreading out like spilled paint across a garage floor. His left arm was blue from the elbow down. Dark purple veins ran down to his wrist.

Chuck was terrified by the sight and dropped down next to his friend, the rifle slipping unnoticed from his grip as he cradled John's head with both hands. John's eyes rolled about in their sockets, unable to focus, his mouth hanging slack.

"John! John!" Chuck yelled. "Stay with me, man! Stay with me!"

Chuck turned to the alien, now standing over both of them, a desperate, pleading look marring his face.

The alien dropped to his knees and placed the same unit he had used on himself against John's neck. Using his other hand, he rotated a small dial at the back of the device then squeezed the trigger. The unit hissed, and John's body gave a weak jerk. After only a moment, his condition visibly improved. He blinked several times, swallowed hard then finally looked up at Chuck.

"Chuck? Chuck?" John said, his eyes first recognizing his friend, then widening a little as they came to rest on the alien.

"I'm here, buddy," Chuck said, trying to control his emotions.

"Chuck, I can't believe you let an alien work on me!" John said, his voice still sounding weak, but getting stronger with each passing second. "And I don't even know him!"

Chuck held John's head with trembling hands and laughed through clenched teeth.

"You're a smartass, you know that?" he said, hoping his friend didn't notice the tear finding its way down his cheek.

"Outlander"

Word of Eric's knowledge of warfare traveled through the city. He was accosted several times on his way back to his room by admiring aliens, each one stopping him and thanking him profusely. The whole thing made him feel a little strange. He wasn't used to anyone taking note of his actions, let alone treating him like a hero. But here he was, a million miles from home, playing teacher to a bunch of aliens who didn't know how to use their own equipment.

The trip back to his quarters couldn't have been over quickly enough, and the swoosh of the chamber door closing behind him was a welcome sound. He just wanted to be alone with his thoughts.

Having already decided that he needed to search for his friends, he was faced with a difficult challenge. First off, how to get outside the city's walls without anyone knowing he was gone. Secondly, how to travel into the desert without being killed by those nasty creatures that were constantly lurking about, he was quite sure they'd take note of him wandering alone across the sandy planes. Who knows, with his newfound stardom, they might even recognize him. The thought brought a smile to his face. At least he hadn't lost his sense of humor. But he had to try something. There had to be some way of getting out of here to search for his friends.

Then an idea came to him, and it was in the form of Altare. She knew more than she was telling about what resources were available to get him beyond the walls. There must be vehicles somewhere, tucked away neatly in some chamber or some forgotten storehouse. He'd have to try to find them. He could use the rail car to explore the city, but how could he ever travel incognito when he was so different from everyone else? He'd have to think of something, and quick. Time was a precious resource, and he'd already wasted too much.

Eric lay back on the bed and bit into another piece of fruit that Altare had left in the room for him. This particular item was green and tasted very sweet. Its texture was like a banana, but the flavor was more like a grapefruit. While he pondered the snack, a light knock came at the door.

"Come in," Eric called out over a mouthful of fruit.

The door slid open, and Altare stepped in wearing her usual smile.

"Are you well?" She asked.

"Yes, quite well," he said, sitting up and smiling back at her.

"I see you have learned how to run the rail car," Altare said. "We're all very surprised at how quickly you master new technologies."

Eric frowned slightly at her comment. "I don't understand why you would be so surprised. Do you find humans to be so ignorant that they can't learn?" he said, sounding a bit harsher than he intended.

Altare lowered her head, obviously hurt by his words. "No, but it has been a long time since anyone has ventured to your world. I presume your kind was much less advanced at that time than you are today. You must remember, the last time we visited your people was over two thousand of your years ago."

Eric tipped his head back and closed his eyes. "I'm sorry, I just have a lot on my mind. You've done nothing wrong."

Altare relaxed a bit and stepped farther into the room. "I understand, you are concerned about your comrades' safety and how you might help them," she said.

"Yes, I am," Eric said. "It makes me feel helpless to be trapped here while they are in danger."

"You would like me to help you travel beyond the city?" Altare asked. But it was somehow more than asking. Something in her voice made the phrase sound more like an answer than a question. It seemed strange that she had guessed his thoughts almost exactly.

"You know that?" he asked, looking directly at her this time, a suspicious look in his eye.

Altare met his gaze. "There is much you do not know of us, Eric. We may not be versed in the ways of battle as you are, but we do carry in us the evolution of our ancestors."

"What does that mean?" Eric asked.

"It simply means that we can share more of ourselves than you might at first imagine," Altare said.

"Share?" Eric asked, his interest now piqued.

Altare paced about the room for a moment, finally stopping by the large glass window, her back now to Eric.

"Did you notice how quickly the soldiers picked up your training? How each one seemed to learn the lesson a bit faster than the last?" she asked.

Eric thought about it for a moment then answered. "Yes, I suppose they did."

"That is because we have a common link. There is a collective consciousness that we can share when we wish. It allows us to offer the things we learn to others so that they may prosper from it. When you first taught Geopre to use the weapon properly, he shared the information with the next soldier, and he did the same with the next and so on down the line, each one benefiting from the previous warrior's experience."

Eric could barely believe what he was hearing. "So you can read minds?" he asked.

"In a way," Altare said. "Only when we allow it to happen can we share our thoughts. No one can force their way into the mind of another."

Eric got up from his chair and walked over to Altare. "So how did you know I was thinking about leaving the city?" he asked. "Have you been reading my mind? I thought you said you could only read minds if the person was actively sharing their thoughts?"

Altare turned toward him and smiled. "You are sharing your thoughts, Eric. You don't know that, because you don't know how to control it. It's as if you are broadcasting everything you are thinking all the time. Others here besides myself and Arcos do not understand your thoughts because you are actively thinking in your own language, which they do not understand."

Eric was dumbfounded and terrified at the same time.

"So, you have *heard* all of my thoughts since I've been here?"

he asked, his voice going up and octave.

"Not everything," Altare said, sensing Eric's fear. "When I am some distance away, I do not *hear* them."

Eric was incredulous. "And how far away do you have to be before you stop hearing my personal thoughts?" he asked, the anger starting to show in his voice.

"Please do not be upset, Eric." Altare said, then paused for a moment before adding, "I find your attraction to me – appealing."

Stepping back a pace, then another, Eric's eyes grew wide as he tried to remember everything he'd ever thought about Altare. Dozens of instances came to mind. He felt sick. It was as if someone had just opened the top of his head and taken a look inside. It was an awful place for him to be, having been so closed off to everyone but those who knew him best, those he could trust implicitly. He'd always kept everyone at arm's length only now to find out that this alien, who he'd begun to have feelings for, knew his every thought.

His eyes darted around the room as if looking for some escape route. He was suddenly aware that everything that had passed through his mind in the last few moments had been transmitted directly to Altare.

He turned toward her only to find her watching him intently. She was biting her bottom lip and wearing a pained expression, obviously having already *heard* everything.

The whole idea was unbearable to him. He'd spent his life keeping his distance from those around him, and now when he was making contact with someone who it seemed he might just be able to care about, however odd and unlikely the situation might be, this had happened. There would be no hiding any of his faults, any of his feelings, or any of his deepest fears from this person, the only soul he'd ever begun to feel romantically close to.

All of these thoughts shot through his head while he gritted his teeth, desperately trying to stop them, but it was no use. Finally, he buried his face in his hands in a vain attempt to disappear. But he knew he couldn't, and he knew Altare was still standing there, only inches away. He could feel her presence.

She reached out her hand and gently ran it down the side of his cheek. Then Eric heard her voice, not spoken aloud, but whispered ever so quietly within his mind say, "I like you too."

John lay still while the alien worked on him with a dizzying array of tools, feeling like a wood shop project. The alien injected him with several different serums, then turned to examine his damaged arm. He first removed the bandage then used a tool that sealed the wound nearly shut. Finally, he retrieved a bag of what Chuck assumed to be some type of blood plasma and injected it into John with an apparatus resembling a caulking gun.

"Damn, you think he oughta be pushing that stuff into me so darn fast?" John asked Chuck while the fluid coursed into his arm. Within seconds, the entire tube was emptied, and John had to admit that he felt much better. The color in his arm returned swiftly as well, but he still had little feeling in his hand or fingers.

The alien had to stop several times during the process to choke his way through several coughing spells, each one seeming worse than the last. Chuck watched the creature grew weaker with each session.

Finally, with his work on John finished, the alien got unsteadily to his feet and staggered back to the chamber from where he'd come. Chuck followed a few paces behind and watched as the being pressed another series of the buttons on the wall located just below the set he'd used to open the first cabinet. The button turned from red to green then back to red again under his touch. The alien pressed the button repeatedly, each time having the same effect. Finally, he banged on the panel with a balled up fist, causing the light to turn green and the cabinet to spring open. He rifled through the contents quickly, having to stop in the middle of his search to endure yet another coughing fit. To Chuck, this one appeared much worse than the others, the poor creature even having to support himself on the edge of the cabinet to keep his footing. Chuck wanted to reach out to help him but was unsure of what he could do.

John staggered to his feet and stepped into the doorway just in time to see the alien digging crazily through the last cabinet.

"What's he after?" John asked, his voice still sounding weak.

"I don't know," Chuck said without looking back, "But I'm guessing it's some kind of medicine."

At last, the being found what he was looking for. Retrieving a small item from the back of one of the shelves, he turned and held it aloft, a thin smile parting his quivering lips.

What color there was had drained from his visage, and a small trickle of blood seeped from the edge of his mouth. Pulling the cap from the syringe was enough to send the creature into another bout of extreme hacking. This time blood sprayed from his mouth with each cough, and a gurgling sound accompanied each wheezing snatch of air that he struggled for in between hacks.

Covering his mouth with both hands, he coughed again, soaking both his hands and the syringe with blood. Finally, he gained control of himself and with shaking hands readied the device. Holding it in his blood covered right hand, he raised the instrument to his neck, placing it firmly against his ever-whitening skin. Suddenly another cough burst from his chest, causing him to lose his grip on the slippery syringe. It popped from his blood-covered hand, sailing into the air, tumbling over and over again.

The creature's eyes widened in horror as the device started its descent. Grabbing wildly at the unit as it plummeted earthward, the alien found himself holding nothing but fistfuls of air.

The syringe hit the floor broadside and shattered like a bottle of soda. The being stood over it, his unbelieving eyes traveling back and forth from the broken syringe to Chuck, then back again.

Chuck stood still, his mouth hanging open in disbelief at the irony of the situation. To be woken up from a thousand-year sleep, only to die minutes later by dropping your medicine.

The alien swayed on his feet like a tree in a windstorm. Chuck grabbed him just in time to keep him from collapsing entirely. The alien looked up slowly and met Chuck's gaze, obviously only moments from death. The two stared into each other's eyes. Quick as lightning, the creature slapped both of his hands against either side of Chuck's head, covering his face with bright pink blood. John stepped from the doorway to aid his friend, but Chuck waved him away, sure that whatever the alien was up to was somehow very important.

An instant later, Chuck felt a searing pain coursing through his temples. It felt like someone had connected an electrical circuit through his head. His mouth snapped shut involuntarily, and to John, it appeared that he was being electrocuted. Even in his weakened state, he thrust himself into motion covering the distance to his friend in a few lurching steps. But he was too late. The act was over as quickly as it had begun. The alien dropped like a sack of lead to the floor, leaving Chuck standing stiff as a board, his hands still jutting out in front of him where they'd been touching the alien's body. John grabbed his friend's arms to steady him only to find his muscles rigid, his body feeling distinctly like a dime store mannequin.

"Chuck!" John yelled, shaking his friend by the shoulders. "Can you hear me?"

Chuck stared forward through unseeing eyes, his body trembling. At last, he came to, almost as if he'd just come out of a hypnotic state, his eyes blinking rapidly as he looked about the room.

"Well, say something!" John yelled again. "Are you alright?"

Chuck waited for a moment then answered. "Yeah, I think I am," was all he would say, still looking around as if he'd never seen this place before.

"Well, what the hell did he do to you?" John said excitedly, not sure why his friend was acting so calm after the scene that had just taken place.

Looking down, it was obvious that the alien was dead. It lay flat on its back with its eyes wide open, staring sightlessly toward the rooms white ceiling.

"What happened?" John said again, quizzing his friend, this time enunciating each word while holding Chuck by the shoulders.

"I don't know," Chuck said at last. "But I think Nevak may have connected to my mind somehow."

John let go of Chuck's shoulders and stepped back a pace, eyeing him warily.

"Nevak?" he asked, turning his head slightly to one side and raising his eyebrows. "Just who the hell is that supposed to be?"

Chuck didn't answer immediately but instead knelt down next to the dead alien, checking the being for what appeared to John to be its vital signs. Letting out his breath slowly, Chuck folded the alien's arms across his chest and closed his unseeing eyes.

"What are you doing?" John asked, a bit worried about the whole thing. "Tell me again what he did to you?"

Chuck stood up and faced his friend. "I don't know, man. I just seem to have a lot of extra thoughts in my head right now."

"Such as?" John asked, folding his arms across his chest.

"Well, I seem to know a lot about this city. And the more I think about it, I know a lot about our alien friend here," Chuck said.

John's mouth fell open, then just as quickly his face turned into a sneer. Shaking his head up and down, he said. "O.K. Smartass! You've had your little joke. Now, let's figure out what we need to do next. I don't want to stay down here forever."

"There's a Plain Walker just a few rooms away in the bunker if you want to take that out of here," Chuck said. "I'm pretty sure I can pilot it."

John had known Chuck his entire life and pretty much knew when he was joking.

"So, what exactly do you know?" John asked. "Did that alien transfer his knowledge to you somehow?"

"Yeah, I think he did," Chuck said, then smiled suddenly. "Hey, listen to this."

He then spoke a string of words that meant absolutely nothing to John.

"O.K., so that's alien tongue right? I'm so sure!" John laughed.

"Well, watch this," Chuck said, starting to get into this newfound knowledge. "You see that panel over there?" He said while pointing toward one of the open cabinets.

"Yeah, what about it?" John said.

"It says" Chuck started to say, but John cut him off mid-sentence.

"Alright, alright. I get the point. Now really, do you have anything useful to add to our little expedition here or not?"

"Well, I feel like I didn't get everything Nevak wanted to share before he died. I think he had a lot more to transfer but didn't get a chance. I guess we'll have to make do with what I got," Chuck said, heading toward the cabinets in the back corner of the room, picking up the laser rifle as he went.

"Yes, we'll just have to make do," John said sarcastically, still not sure if Chuck was just being a jerk or if something strange had really happened to him.

A few minutes passed while Chuck sorted through several more cabinets, collecting items that John was unable to identify. John, for his part, had found a chair and sat down, still weak from the whole ordeal, though he'd made a surprisingly quick recovery thanks to the alien medications. Chuck found a rather large bag and handed it to John, saying, "Here, hold this open," as he began to pile his pillaged loot into the sack.

John was quite content to watch as Chuck grabbed an item from a shelf, examined it, then either discarded it, or brought it to pack into the bag. The interesting part was that as he would look at the labels, he would sometimes say the alien words out loud. The whole idea of it seemed comical to John. He watched his friend collect things that only moments before he had known nothing about.

"O.K. That's it," Chuck said, placing the last item in the sack and cinching its top closed. "You ready to go? I know the Gwakon extract can make you a bit tired until it's fully assimilated into your body."

"Yeah, I think I can make it," John said, eyeing Chuck. "And stop that, will ya? It's kind of creeping me out."

"Sorry," Chuck said, smiling. "But it just seems so natural. It's almost like the knowledge has been there all the time. I mean, I've even got memories about this place."

"Well, keep them to yourself for now if you can," John said as he got up and faced his greatly altered friend.

Chuck threw the sack over his shoulder and headed back into the room where John had nearly died. Stepping over to the bank of monitors on the wall, he scanned each one then said, "Good, we should be alright from here on out. Another few rooms and we'll be in the hanger. We need to be careful though, some of the sentries are still active, and they won't let us pass without trouble."

"Sentries?" John asked as the two headed back into the chamber that contained the damaged cylinders.

"Yup, they've been hanging out here for a thousand years, just waiting to kick someone's ass! That's what we ran into earlier," Chuck said, a goofy smile breaking across his face.

John let out a relieved sigh. At last, his friend was starting to sound more like himself, albeit a more intelligent, multilingual, alien version.

Chuck stepped to the door and examined the panel. John moved back a little and said, "Guess we have to blast this one open too, right?"

"Nah," Chuck said as his fingers flew over the keypad, striking a half dozen keys in rapid succession. The red keys turned to green under his touch, and finally, the door slid open with a hiss. At this point, John was totally convinced, and a flood of questions came to mind.

"Do you know where Eric is? How are we going to get back home? Can you fix the teleporter?" he asked quickly, barely getting one question out before asking the next.

Chuck turned around in the doorway and gave him a silly look.

"No, I don't know where Eric is, but I have a good guess. I'm not sure how we'll get back home, and no, I probably can't fix the teleporter, but I do have a better idea of how it's supposed to work," he said. "But first things first. We need to get out of here, and there's one other thing, that's even more important than that."

John hung on every word as Chuck turned around and stepped back into the room with him. "What's that?" he said, expecting something monumental to come out of Chuck's mouth.

"Well, I'm very hungry," he said. "We need to find something to eat."

"Escape"

Eric and Altare snuck through the long hallway toward the rail car. Eric couldn't believe that Altare was helping him make good on his escape from the city to look for his friends.

"So, you can read my every thought, huh?" Eric said, whispering each word in the dimly lit glass tunnel.

"Yes. But I never really meant to because I know it's impolite, especially when you didn't know I was doing it. But when I heard you thinking about me, I couldn't help myself," Altare said, looking up at the star-dotted sky through the thick glass walls.

"That's alright," Eric said, stopping suddenly and turning toward her. "I probably wouldn't have had the nerve to say anything otherwise."

Altare smiled in response. She seemed to glow when she smiled, and Eric loved to watch it. There was an innocence in her that he had rarely found in the opposite sex of his own kind. He knew the whole thing was crazy, but he didn't care. And right now, he had a job to do, and as anyone who knew him would tell you, once he'd locked on to something, it was very hard to shake his determination.

The rail car slid along the tracks, heading toward an older, unused part of the city. Large areas of the city had been abandoned as the population had slowly shrunk over the last millennium. At one point, there had been barely enough room for everyone, but now everything had changed. The increasing number of attacks by the planet's mutated life forms had taken their toll, and it was becoming ever harder to keep them from totally overrunning the city. Eric knew that without intervention of some kind, the entire civilization would eventually disappear. Somehow they had to break the secret code of the ancient alien technologies. This would allow them not only to repair their damaged defenses and better use other existing systems but also to move ahead with newer technologies that might help rebuild their civilization.

Passing by dozens of empty buildings, Eric wondered how

many other alien outposts still existed.

"Altare, are there many other cities left?"

Altare thought for a moment then answered, "We really don't know anymore. Most of our ability to communicate across the planet has been lost. Much of our infrastructure was based on orbiting communication systems that would transfer our data from one point on the planet to another."

"Have they just broken down over time?" Eric asked.

"No, most were destroyed in the great wars. At least that is what we can surmise. And now that it is so difficult to travel outside of the city, we have lost all contact with our brethren. In fact, no one has been beyond the walls in over a dozen of your years." Altare said.

"What about your colonies on other planets? Haven't you heard anything from them?"

"Again, to the best of our knowledge, those bases were all closed down, and their inhabitants called home to fight in the wars," Altare informed Eric. "Perhaps you've wondered why some of the peoples of your planet have suddenly disappeared without a trace?" she said, raising one of her delicate eyebrows.

"No way," Eric said, amazed by the revelation. "So all those old ruins scattered around the globe are yours?"

"Well, not all of them, of course. But have you ever wondered why you find pyramids on every continent of your planet? Even when they appear to have belonged to different races who supposedly never knew of each other?"

Eric was dumbfounded. "I just can't believe that with everything you've got going for your people, they still ended up nearly wiping themselves out of existence."

"Yes, it is hard to believe," Altare said sadly. "However, have the differing cultures of your own world never warred with each other? Of course, they have. But only imagine now that those battles took place with unbelievably powerful weapons."

Eric thought in silence then said somberly, "Oh, I can believe it. Back home, we are on the verge of such wars every day."

"Your technology has advanced much since the last of our

brethren returned home. I believe when the last of them left Earth, your people were still fighting with sharpened metal weapons."

"Yes, we've come a long way since then," Eric said sarcastically, shaking his head in disbelief. "We can kill millions with the push of a button now."

"I see, then you understand," Altare said.

"All too well," Eric answered. "All too well."

Their conversation finished just as the rail car began to slow. Altare looked over at Eric, a worried look crossing her pretty face.

"We are here," she said as the vehicle came to a complete stop, its single headlight illuminating only the area directly in front of them.

They had passed into an underground section of the city, traveling at a steep downward angle for at least the last ten or fifteen seconds. Eric estimated that they had to be roughly fifty feet underground.

Altare gripped a laser pistol as she pressed the release button for the rail car's hatch. It slid open with a hiss, and for a moment, the two sat in silence, soaking in the eerie feeling of visiting a ghost town. Eric's hand tightened on his laser pistol as he stepped slowly from the rail car.

"Where are the lights?" he asked, barely able to see his hand in front of his face, and then only because of the pale light emanating from their transport's headlight.

Altare reached into a compartment within the rail car and retrieved two flashlights.

Handing one to Eric, she said, "Use this," while flipping the unit on. "Most of the power for this region has been redirected to other, more needy sections of the city."

Eric panned around with the flashlight. It was very bright and cast a broad beam onto the surroundings, illuminating everything for quite some distance.

"How long do the batteries last?" he asked.

"Forever." Altare said, then seeing Eric's inquisitive look, added, "Essentially forever. Remember, these units are very old, along with everything else you will see within these walls. The flashlights, as you call them, have a renewable energy source. Once again, we do not understand the science behind them, only that they seem to be able to run continuously without dimming."

Altare pointed off to the right with her flashlight. "We need to go that way," she said, sounding a bit nervous. "I've not been here in quite a long time."

"Do we really need the lasers?" Eric asked.

"Perhaps not, but seeing as we are the only ones to venture here in many years, I thought it would be best to err on the side of caution," Altare said, turning on her own flashlight.

Eric instinctively moved a little closer to her, assuming a more protective stance, his eyes sweeping the area around and behind them, looking for any sign of a possible impending threat. Altare stepped along very quietly, keeping her eyes peeled as well.

The two passed down a long, wide corridor, their footfalls ringing off the walls no matter how gently they placed each step.

"Guess if anything is here, it's going to know we're coming," Eric said, tagging a mock chuckle onto the end of his sentence.

Altare pressed in a little closer to him in response. She was a bit shaken by the whole idea of even being there. Eric was moved that she was willing to help him, even though it obviously filled her with fear.

"Why is this tunnel so large?" Eric asked. "It's big enough to drive a tank through."

Altare just kept walking, "You'll see."

At one point, they passed over a huge metallic plate in the floor. Altare stopped to examine a control panel off to one side of the tunnel.

"It looks dead," Eric said. "No power getting to it."

Altare smiled as she turned her flashlight over and unscrewed its back end, exposing three metallic prongs. She pushed the prongs into an outlet of sorts that was located just below the panel, and the lights on the membrane keypad glowed to life.

"Well, you've just got a whole bag of surprises, don't you?" Eric asked, smiling at Altare.

She smiled back broadly. "Just a few. Now let me borrow your flashlight."

Eric dutifully handed the device over to her.

After she pushed several of the buttons, the metal plate in the floor began to shift.

"Now be ready," she said, stepping back and pointing both the laser pistol and the flashlight down toward the moving plate. Eric gripped his laser, watching intently and half expecting some kind of monster to come crawling out of the darkness into which the lift was quickly disappearing. Within seconds, the lift had completed its descent and landed with a solid *thunk*. Altare shone the flashlight in and around the gaping hole left by the plate's movement.

"You see anything?" Eric asked, getting to his knees in order to get a better look into the underground tunnel.

"No," Altare said, leaning back and quickly pressing another series of buttons on the panel. The lift began to ascend slowly, and within seconds, it stopped flush, covering the tunnel once again.

"What was that all about?" Eric asked, having assumed that they were going to be heading down through the hatch.

"Just follow me," Altare said, turning to head even farther into the concrete tunnel they'd started down in the first place.

"Alright, you're the boss," Eric said, catching up with her. He knew she was scared, but he was trying not to let his own fear show. "But what about your flashlight?" he asked, pointing back toward the panel.

"Leave it," Altare said without turning around.

A few more minutes of walking brought them to the end of the tunnel. A huge set of plates resembling the gates of a medieval castle stood closed in front of them.

"O.K., what's your next trick?" Eric asked. "I don't suppose that flashlight will open this one too."

"In fact, it will," Altare said, performing the same action with Eric's flashlight that she had done on the previous control panel with the same results.

The giant metal doors began to groan open slowly. A deep rumbling sound rolled through the tunnel as the foot-thick doors slid on giant tracks. It took a full thirty seconds for the doors to open completely.

Eric stepped inside, holding his pistol out warily in front of himself as he made his way into the chamber. Until now, he thought he'd been joking about the tunnel being large enough to drive a tank through, but he found that that was the exact purpose of the tunnel.

Before him stood dozens of heavily armored vehicles that could only be described as main battle tanks, each hunk of metal sprouted two barrels from a thick, low slung turret, and several smaller weapons jutted from the sides of the behemoth. The largest of the barrels was two dozen feet in length and easily three feet in diameter.

Eric tried to imagine what kind of projectile would require this much iron to master it. A smaller gun only five or six feet in length was mounted on top of the turret on a swiveling pod. The treads were massive, four or five feet across in width, and they ran the entire forty-foot length of the tank

The machines were easily fifteen feet high and double that in width. They made the tanks he'd seen on earth look like playthings in comparison.

Eric stood in the doorway with his mouth hanging open, unable to believe what he was seeing. Altare stepped up beside him.

"Did you think that all of the old weapons were gone?" she asked. "When the biotoxin that killed off the populace was used, it did nothing to damage these machines. That was supposed to be its strong point. One dose could destroy an entire population without damaging any of their infrastructures. Of course, as I've told you, the plan backfired, killing essentially all of the adults on the planet, leaving only the very young. It was such a shame since it was shortly before the catastrophe that all of the remote colonies had been called home to join in the war effort. We effectively smote our entire way of life as the toxin spread out across the planet in the course of just a few short days."

Altare lowered her head, disheartened by the retelling of the story that had so adversely affected her entire race for the last thousand years.

Eric reached out and put his hand gently on her shoulder. She looked at him, questioningly. "Do you think less of my people for the foolishness of our actions?" she asked.

"Never," Eric said. "I can only imagine that we're not far away from destroying ourselves back on Earth. There's a lot of hate wherever you go. I suppose it all comes from fear. Fear of anything that seems different from us."

Altare watched Eric as he spoke. She paused for a moment before speaking.

"You're not at all like other men I've known," she said suddenly.

Eric smiled at this. "Well, I should hope not," he said, half laughing. "But I guess that would depend on how many humans you've run into lately."

Altare laughed out loud at his jest, then just as quickly the smile disappeared from her face, replaced by a look of pained seriousness. Eric saw the look and became concerned.

"What's wrong?" he asked, grabbing hold of Altare by both shoulders. "Altare, what's wrong?"

"Nothing." she said, "nothing at all." Then suddenly she leaned forward and kissed him full on the lips.

Eric barely knew how to respond. A tremor raced through him as if electricity was being applied all over his body at once, the moment literally taking his breath away.

Altare stepped back a pace, smiling. It was obvious to her that Eric had enjoyed the kiss. And it was clear to him that she had found the sensation agreeable as well.

"Uhm," Eric stumbled over his words. "Thank you?" he said at last.

This made Altare's smile grow even wider.

"We should find your friends," she said, pointing toward the battle tanks with her flashlight, the whole time not taking her eyes off of Eric's.

"Yes," Eric said finally then turned toward the tanks, his face positively glowing now. "Shall we?" he asked.

"Into the Frey"

Chuck began rummaging through another cabinet until surfacing at last with a thin foil bag.

"Ah-ha!" he said, holding the bag by its edge out toward John. "Found one!"

"Found one what?" John asked.

"A sack of food," Chuck said. "What else?"

He proceeded to tear the bag open. It made a crinkly hissing sound as its airtight seal popped open. Chuck peered inside, reached in, and pulled out a handful of what appeared to be trail mix – small pieces of dried fruit mixed with nuts of some sort. He threw a handful into his mouth and chewed noisily. John watched from across the room, wearing a rather disgusted look on his face.

"Do you know how old that stuff must be?" he asked, screwing his face up into a nasty looking scowl.

"Who cares? It was still sealed," Chuck said rather haughtily. "As long as it's sealed, it won't hurt you. Just like Twinkies back on Earth."

"Just like Twinkies, huh?" John said, stepping over and grabbing a fistful of the mix for himself. Tossing the salty, sweet mixture into his mouth reminded him of how hungry he had become through this whole ordeal.

Seeing the look on his face, Chuck piped up, "Not bad, is it, Big Man?"

John just smiled and shook his head, then grabbed for another handful.

The two quickly pounded down the entire bag. After finishing, Chuck returned to one of the cabinets and found a bottle of water. He cracked it open for the two of them to share.

They finished up their small meal, and Chuck hopped to his feet. "O.K., let's hit it!" he said, picking up the laser rifle and the sack of items he'd salvaged from the cabinets. "Time's a wasting."

John got to his feet as well, letting out a big sigh from the effort. "I'm actually feeling a lot better," he said, looking forlornly down at the dead alien. "Too bad about him, though."

"Yeah, but I think I've got a pretty big piece of him tucked away in here," Chuck said, pointing at his own head.

"Well, at least there was plenty of room!" John laughed. "So just where are we headed?"

"Just a few minutes walk, and we'll be riding in style, John Boy," Chuck said, stepping through the open hatch and into the room beyond. John followed closely, only a step or two behind. "You might want to hang onto this," he added, handing John a laser pistol he retrieved from one of the cabinets. John accepted it gladly.

They passed through the next several rooms with no events, considering that Chuck now seemed like he was on his home turf. Each locked door or cabinet yielded to him as if he had opened them a thousand times before. Occasionally they would step into a room only to have Chuck say, "Nothing in here," even though to John it looked like there could be any numbers of places where something they could use might be stored. But he quickly realized that Chuck had indeed been given something by the alien, his knowledge of this facility being the very least.

Finally, they arrived at a large door resembling something you might see guarding the national treasure at Fort Knox. Another glowing keypad was anchored in the thick metal. Chuck approached it, paused for a second as if to think, then rapidly keyed in the security code. Sure enough, he got it right on the first try. The heavy door began to rumble as unseen locking bars slid slowly out of place. The seal around the edges of the portal broke loose from a thousand years of closure. At last, the door began to swing inward with a hiss of air pushing its way through the widening gap.

John and Chuck moved back to allow the huge door to complete its movement. The room beyond was very dark, and the air wafting in through the open portal seemed fresher somehow.

"You don't suppose it's open to the outside somehow, do

you?" John asked, squinting his eyes into the darkness just beyond the doorway.

"I don't know, but" was all Chuck got out before he was knocked off his feet by one of the Kalwaers as it leapt through the door and straight onto him. The force of the blow lifted him off his feet and carried him and the beast a dozen feet into the room before the two came crashing down. Chuck skittered across the smooth flooring, the bare skin on his chest and back, making squeaking sounds as he slid.

John, though startled by the attack, responded instantly. Leveling the pistol at the back of the creature's head, he squeezed off a single shot. The beam leapt from the pistol with every bit as much ferocity as one of the larger laser rifles, cutting a hole through the monster's skull. Chuck managed to roll out of the way just in time to avoid the creature's collapse.

Like an acrobat, he spun twice then vaulted to his feet without using his hands. John was amazed but quickly found himself too busy with the next Kalwaer to stop and applaud his friend's newly acquired abilities.

The second creature stepped through the doorway a little more warily than the first. This would be its undoing. Chuck scooped up the laser rifle and fired a volley at the same time that John launched several shots of his own. The beast was pummeled in the crossfire and was rent limb from limb within a split second.

Chuck stormed into the darkened doorway, yelling out something in an alien tongue. A moment later, the lights in the chamber came to life, illuminating the entire area. The room was huge and loaded with vehicles the likes of which John had never imagined. He glanced around, eyeing towering robot-like machines along with fantastic tanks and other tracked vehicles. An entire arsenal was laid out before them, one that had been locked away in this storage chamber for a millennium.

Chuck dispatched another Kalwaer as it sprinted at them from between two of the tanks.

"There!" he yelled, pointing at one of the enormous robot-like vehicles. "Head for that Walker!" He barked, taking off at a dead sprint. John followed as quickly as he could just a few paces behind, the whole time wondering what a *Walker* was. From the corner of his eye, he could see Kalwaers rushing toward them.

Chuck moved like lightning, reaching the Walker well ahead of John. Scrambling up the first dozen foot pegs, he turned and began to fire at the Kalwaers as they closed the distance between themselves and John. Chuck dropped two of the lead creatures, giving John just enough time to leap onto the bottom rungs and begin his ascent. Chuck moved up the pegs in spurts, stopping every half dozen to fire deadly accurate shots at the closest Kalwaers, allowing John to climb to safety.

Seconds later they had scaled the entire height of the Walker. John spun around, gripping a rung in one hand while blasting away at the creatures with the pistol.

"Chuck, whatever you're gonna do, you better do it fast!" he yelled up to his friend while squeezing the trigger so fast it made his finger ache. "Lots of critters here!"

Chuck got the message and swung open a hatch on the side of the behemoth's head. Crawling inside, he called back to John, "Come on! Get in!" then disappeared into the vehicle.

John pounded up the last few rungs and made to squirm his way into the hatch himself when an earth-shattering rumble shook the ground. John whipped his head about, searching for the source of the commotion. From this vantage point, he could see all the way across the giant chamber. In the far corner, a huge section of wall had just collapsed, exposing a towering monster unlike anything he had seen on this planet before. The bug-like creatures were bad enough, but this thing must have been sixty or seventy feet tall. In fact, it was tall enough to tower over the Walker he and Chuck were now scrambling into. The huge animal came straight for them, crushing tanks and smaller vehicles under its massive talon shod feet. All John could imagine was that it looked like one of the monsters Godzilla had fought in one of those cheesy monster flicks.

The beast roared as it came, charging with surprising speed at their position. For a second, John considered taking some pot shots at it with the pistol but immediately thought better of it.

A handful of spikes clanked against the Walker's metal skin, bringing his attention back to the Kalwaers now swarming around the vehicle's armored feet.

"Damn!" John yelled, leaping through the hatch into the relative safety of the Walker's interior. Scrambling through a small tube, he found Chuck buckling himself into a seat located inside the head of the giant machine.

"Glad you could join me!" Chuck yelled, seeing John's head appear at the front of the access tube. "Get your ass in here and get strapped in!" he yelled again, poking at keys and flipping switches on a control panel just in front of him.

John leapt into the seat while behind him, he heard the access door slam shut. He'd no more than got seated when Chuck called out again, "Hang on!" His words were followed by an enormous jolt. The whole Walker lurched to the left, sending John to the floor of the compartment. A moment of weightlessness followed, accompanied by a terrible feeling of tipping over on a very tall ladder. There was another bone-jarring jolt as the entire Walker crashed to the ground.

The two large view screens in front of the pilot's seat sprung to life, showing the scene outside. A terrifying site greeted them on the monitors. The huge monster was standing directly over them, raising its arms to deliver another blow.

"Get strapped in!" Chuck bellowed. "We have to get on our feet."

John pulled himself into the seat and locked in the belts just as the creature slammed its huge fists down against the Walker's armored chest. A hollow ringing sound reverberated through the compartment, shaking John's vision.

Chuck grabbed the control sticks and pulled back hard while pressing one of the many buttons lining either side of the control yoke. An explosive roar reached John's ears as the rockets mounted to the Walker's back fired, dragging the vehicle backward across the floor of the chamber and knocking smaller vehicles aside as it went.

Chuck jammed his feet into two stirrups on the floor and began moving all four of his limbs. The Walker skidded to a halt and bent forward at the waist. Chuck pushed the rocket button again, this time moving both of the control sticks and the controls attached to his feet at the same time. The Walker rose off the floor of the huge chamber just high enough to get its legs under it. Chuck cut the thrusters, allowing them to drop back onto their feet once again.

The monster strode toward them again, but this time, Chuck was ready. Moving all of his limbs independently, he sent the Walker charging toward the looming threat.

"What the hell are you doing?" John sputtered as they raced at their target.

Looking over, John could have sworn that Chuck was wearing a smile; his eyes fixated on the monster like a hawk eyeing a small mouse in a cornfield.

John braced for the tremendous impact that he knew would result from their current course of action, but it never came. At the last second, Chuck gyrated in the pilot's seat, sending the Walker into a sudden dip, followed immediately by a huge leap. Mashing the thruster button at the same time, Chuck sent them launching skyward.

John felt his stomach drop into his feet from the force of the jump. The monitors spun wildly as the Walker turned in midair, pivoting around the charging beast, sidestepping it completely. Chuck cut the jets, and the Walker landed with unbelievable agility, both arms thrust out at the enemy. John looked on in amazement as bright green laser beams blasted from either arm, searing the air on their way to meet the creature. The beast was only now beginning to understand what was happening, but it was too late for it to act, and the lasers cut through its thick flesh, slicing into its unprotected hindquarters.

The whole show was over as quickly as it had started, leaving John breathlessly watching the creature sink to the floor of the chamber, its lifeblood flooding out around the Walker's metal feet.

Chuck looked smugly over in his friend's direction. "You don't have any more of that trail mix, do ya?" he asked.

John could only stare out through the viewscreen, unable even to speak, and for once Chuck got the last word.

"Hitched"

"I can't believe you're getting married, man!" Eric said, clamping a hand down onto John's shoulder. "I just never thought you'd have the guts to do it."

John pulled on the long jacket to his tuxedo and adjusted his cummerbund.

"Well, I guess we all have to take the plunge sometime," he said. "Sarah certainly had to wait long enough, and I don't think her opinion of you two *confirmed* bachelors has gone up any either."

"Now wait a minute!" Chuck said, feeling the need to protect himself from this obvious slander. "I never said a word about getting married, and now you're lumping me in with this toadstool?" he added, pointing a finger at Eric, who raised his eyebrows in shock.

"Toadstool? Chuck, I really expected more somehow, but I guess I should have known better," Eric said, blanketing each word with mock sadness. "And on a day when we should all forget our differences and be happy for our soon-to-be-wed friend John."

It was all Chuck and John could do to keep from throttling Eric. And as usual, he would have deserved it.

His friend's silliness made John feel a little less nervous. He was struggling with the huge commitment as it was, but the way Chuck and Eric were acting made the whole thing seem like a walk in the park. Even though they were acting up, they weren't acting like it was a big deal, and that made John feel much better.

"You 'bout ready, man?" Chuck said, catching John in a moment of thoughtfulness. "I think they're ready for us."

John looked up at the two people he'd known the longest in his life, other than his parents of course. Both of them wore smiles. They weren't the kind the two usually had either, where they'd done something mischievous or the type where they'd just finished an entire pizza by themselves, but a smile that comes from knowing someone you care about is happy.

"Yeah, I think I am," John said, smiling back while slowly nodding his head, offering a small bow to his two closest friends. "Let's do this."

All three stood up and headed out to their places. Eric and Chuck collecting their bridesmaids on the way. John followed behind, taking his place next to them.

It had been hard to decide who was going to be the best man since he'd been so close both of them. Finally, they had flipped a coin to decide, and that had kept everyone happy.

John waited for Sarah to appear, and after several more minutes, she came into view, looking even more beautiful than he had imagined she would.

Sarah had been very careful to keep him from catching a glimpse of her in the wedding dress. She loved the ceremony of the whole thing and had taken each little tradition to heart. The whole "something old, something new, something borrowed, something blue" saying had been strictly observed. John had found that it was best to stay out of the mix and let Sarah and her girlfriends do all the planning and make all the decisions. And seeing how things were turning out, it had obviously been for the best.

John watched as Sarah strode slowly down the aisle, her father walking alongside her while one of their favorite YES tunes "You and I" rang out. He struggled to hold back his tears. Of course, he knew that his friends would never let him live it down if he were to start crying.

Sarah was a vision, and as she stepped up next to him and smiled, he knew that with this wonderful woman by his side, he would feel complete.

"Battle Lines"

Altare walked to the closest of the huge tanks, a dozen or so of which lined the enormous room. As far as Eric could tell, they were all the same.

"How long have these been here?" Eric said, stopping in his tracks to take note of the monstrous machines. Then seeing the look on Altares face, he added, "You're not going to tell me these have been here all along, and that you guys haven't ever gotten the idea of going out and running around in them."

"I'm afraid that's correct, although father has allowed me to pilot one on occasion," Altare said, holding her head up in pride at the last part of her statement. "Only around this room, of course," she added quickly.

Eric stepped up next to her as she examined the giant tank. Its metal skin shone as brightly as the day it had rolled off the assembly line.

"So you're telling me that everyone's been scared to venture out into the desert when these have been sitting here all along?" Eric said, waving his arms to indicate the entire fleet of tanks arrayed before him. "I mean, how could any of those critters out there ever penetrate one of these?"

Altare looked down at her feet. "Please do not belittle us, Eric. My people are no longer prone to violence. We are very peaceful now and care little for our ancestors' warring ways. As you have seen, their acts have brought us near to total destruction. We have a legitimate fear of this technology," Altare said without looking up, her voice barely above a whisper.

Eric felt like an overzealous fool. He'd hurt her feelings and had put down her people all within a single breath. Reaching out, he took hold of her hand.

"I'm very sorry, Altare," Eric said, gently. "I have no business speaking of your people's motives or their initiative. I was not here to live through the difficult times you have endured, nor do I have any right to question their strength. I am very sure they have had a good reason to keep these vehicles contained."

Altare looked up and smiled thinly. "Thank you, Eric," she said. "Believe me when I say we have no desire to be vanquished by the creatures that roam our planet, but we also have a great fear of our history and what may become of us should we return to our old ways."

"I understand," Eric said. "And I thank you for the courage it took to bring me here and show me these things."

Altare smiled again, this time with much more warmth, then turned toward the tank.

"Come with me. We should hurry," she said, climbing up onto the giant chariot.

Reaching the top of the turret, she swung around the hatch to open it and descended into the bowels of the machine. Eric started down just behind her, closing the hatch as he went.

The inside of the tank was quite spacious. Altare moved hastily to the pilot's station, and upon reaching her destination, she plopped down into a sparsely padded seat and buckled herself in.

"I will need you to man the weapon systems," she said, looking at Eric worriedly, the idea of what she was doing finally sinking in. Eric could see it in her eyes.

"We don't have to do this. I mean, maybe you can show me how to pilot the tank, and I can go out myself," he said.

Altare looked over at Eric. "I cannot leave you," she said in a commanding voice. Then she smiled a broad grin and added, "After all, you are mine now."

Eric smiled as well and planted himself firmly into the seat next to Altare. "O.K., how does this work?" he asked.

Altare gave him a crash course in firing the main gun and using the joystick to control the smaller laser turret. It looked simple enough. The main weapon was self-loading, and the laser turret had an unending supply of energy, at least as long as the tank was functional.

"Are you ready?" Altare asked, reaching for a large red button on one of the many control panels.

"Ready as I'm gonna be," Eric returned.

Altare pressed the button, and the tank hummed to life. There was less noise than Eric had anticipated. A single, panoramic view screen lit up in front of them, showing the long tunnel they'd passed through to get into the armory.

Dozens of other gauges and symbols flashed across the screen, their meaning lost on Eric. Altare, however, watched them intently for a moment, then said, "Everything looks ready. Let's go."

Altare pressed on the two foot pedals, and the machine glided into motion. Eric was amazed at how many similarities there were between this vehicle and the tanks back on earth.

Pushing one of the buttons Altare had shown him brought another small view screen to life. Grabbing one of the control yokes that rose from the floor between his legs, Eric found that the viewscreen was showing the outside world as seen from a camera mounted to the laser turret. Pushing another button changed the viewpoint to that of the main gun, a large targeting crosshair taking up a portion of the screen.

Altare watched as Eric became familiar with the controls, then pushed more firmly on the two foot pedals, causing the tank to pick up speed.

They rolled down the tunnel at quite a pace, covering the distance in seconds while it had taken them minutes to get through it on foot. Within moments, they were approaching the large metal lift that Altare had tested before. Rolling to a stop atop it, she pushed a series of buttons while watching the lift's control panel.

"Oh, I see," Eric said. "That's why you left the flashlight plugged in there."

Altare smiled as if she'd done something extremely clever.

The light on the panel turned green, and the lift began its slow descent into the underground passage. Eric's heart raced as he realized the position he was putting Altare and himself in by venturing out in search of his friends. He'd seen what the creatures that roamed the desert were capable of and was fearful of what else might be waiting for them in the sandy expanse. But he was even more worried that he was flying blind, having no idea of where to begin to look for them.

"We'll head for the outpost where your friends were last seen," Altare said as the lift touched down onto the floor of the dark tunnel.

"Were you reading my mind again?" Eric asked, not nearly as upset by the fact this time as he had been when he first found out.

"No," Altare said in response. "But it is hard not to listen in. It's like having someone talking in the same room and trying not to hear their words."

"Sorry about that. I'll try not to think so much," Eric said in a silly sarcastic voice.

"That would be helpful," Altare said without looking over.

Eric liked her sense of humor and loved the idea that she might actually like his as well.

A few quick presses on the console sent bright beams of light out in front of the tank, illuminating the area around them. This tunnel appeared much like the one they had just passed through, only longer, the lights trailing off into darkness some distance along the way.

"This should bring us out under the wall," Altare said as the tank began to creep forward. "We should be able to activate the door at the other end remotely, just like we did on this end. The flashlight's power source will drive both of the lifts."

The tank's speed leveled off as it slid smoothly along the concrete-lined tunnel, rising gradually up to the desert floor.

The two spent the next minutes in silence, each contemplating the consequences of their actions. For Altare, it meant the possibility of death by the claws and teeth of the Kalwaers. For Eric, it meant taking the chance not only of losing his own life but the life of his newfound love in the search for two friends who might already be long dead.

He knew he had to try, though. John and Chuck would have done nothing less for him. While there was any hope of their continued survival, he had to try.

The tank rolled to a stop at the end of the underground shaft at a spot where it ramped suddenly up toward a large hatch in the ceiling of the passage. Two metal plates came together, keeping the outside world cut off from the city.

"This is it," Altare said. "Are you ready?" she asked, her delicate fingers poised over the control panel, waiting for the go-ahead to open the hatch.

Eric nodded sharply. "Let's go."

Altare pushed several buttons, and the hatch sprang open with surprising speed. Within seconds the plates had recessed to either side, allowing the bright desert sun to pour into the tunnel. Eric squinted into the blinding light, trying to adjust his eyes to the glare.

Altare stomped on the foot pedals, causing the tank to leap forward up the slope and it headed straight for the opening. In the short distance to the top of the ramp, they had acquired enough speed that the tank left the ground while exiting, like a whale breaching the surface of the ocean, only to slam back down onto the desert floor at a dead run.

"Wow!" Eric yelled, hanging on to the arms of the chair as the tank bounced once, then lurched forward, its tracks digging into the soft sand. "Where'd you get your license?"

Altare smiled while tapping away at the control panel, sending the command to close the portal behind them.

The tank shot across the sand at a very quick pace. Eric estimated their speed to be in excess of eighty miles per hour, and even at that rate, it seemed to float on its suspension, totally composed.

Within seconds, the Kalwaers began to appear from the large mounds dotting the sandy expanse. They poured like bugs from a hive and headed straight for them, but the first many creatures were much too slow, and the vehicle blew by them untouched. But within moments, Eric and Altare found themselves surrounded on all sides.

"Man the laser turret!" Altare yelled as she plowed headlong into a huge group of the creatures.

Eric grabbed the control yoke and began firing indiscriminately into the crowd of Kalwaers directly in their path. The laser spewed ruby beams as it cut a swath through the horde. The tank jostled and pitched as Altare drove it over the living and dead alike in a desperate attempt to keep moving. The horrible crunch of carapaces being smashed and limbs being crushed could be heard even through the tank's thick armored walls.

Altare was all but standing on the foot pedals now, but even with the tank's tremendous power, it began to slow as the bodies of their adversaries piled up before them.

"How far to the outpost?" Eric yelled, whipping the laser turret about, blasting away as quick as he could pull the trigger.

Altare pressed a button on the panel, and a small map popped up in the corner of the large view screen. "About twenty miles," she said. "If we can make it."

The tank continued to slow until it seemed that the crush of Kalwaers would ultimately bring them to stop.

In desperation, Eric flipped the small view screen over to the main gun, leveled the crosshairs some distance out, and squeezed the trigger. A tremendous jolt shook the battle tank. It delivered its ordinance in a split second, the shell smacking into the ground two hundred yards in front of the tank and exploding like a tiny atomic bomb. The force of the blast completely stopped their advance. Eric and Altare lurched forward in their seats, their restraints the only thing saving them from splatting against the view screens.

Outside, hundreds of Kalwaers were vaporized instantly while thousands more were sent hurtling skyward or laid flat by the force of the blast. Altare lost no time in mashing the foot pedals again, pushing the tank back up to full speed as she veered right to avoid the huge crater left by the shell.

"Probably ought not do that again, Eric," she said in a stern voice. But as Eric looked over, he found her wearing a wide grin. "Yes, very bad," she added for effect.

The explosion had given them just the edge they needed as the tank sped past the last of the mounds and out into the open desert. The remaining Kalwaers raced after them but were unable to keep pace.

Once they were out of immediate danger, Eric turned again to

Altare and asked, "So, exactly where did the Kalwaers come from?"

"They were similar in size to the ants on your planet, and they lived in a similar type of colony. They have grown exponentially over time due to the toxins we introduced into our biosphere. They were always very aggressive, but as tiny creatures, they couldn't hurt anyone. Now they pose an enormous threat, as each generation seems larger and more dangerous than the last. They are very territorial and have come to see us as interlopers in their world. That is why they attack the city almost constantly. Many have taken up residence just beyond our walls, as you've already seen."

Eric scratched his head. "I guess I don't clearly understand why you don't use all of the defenses you have against them. Perhaps you could even eliminate or at least subdue them and stop them from spreading even more."

Altare thought for a moment then said, "Most do not feel as you do, Eric. Most are afraid of things from our past. They believe that we will not be able to control them and will destroy what remains of our civilization."

"I see," Eric said, at last, still feeling unsatisfied with the answers he was receiving. "Many seem hungry for knowledge to me. The warriors were very pleased with the lesson I taught them. I can't imagine that they would not desire the use of machines like this one."

"Perhaps they would," Altare said. "But our elders are fearful, and in actuality, no one but the elders, my father, and I know about the underground stockpile of weapons."

"Oh," Eric said, leaning his head back. "That's why they're not being used."

He looked over at Altare then, a sly look crossing his face. "I bet you could get in lots of trouble for stealing this tank, couldn't you?" he said while chuckling an evil little laugh.

Altare was taken aback. "I did not *steal* this vehicle!" she said, letting off the pedals then stomping on two others, causing the tank to skid to a halt. "I merely borrowed it," she fumed. "And might I add that I did it all for you and your friends!" she added, her voice rising higher with each word.

Eric was thoroughly amused, and it showed on his face.

"What?' Altare said, turning toward him with her arms folded tightly across her chest, her chin jutting out while she raised her nose up into the air.

Eric's grin widened at her display of emotion, but he could say nothing. He just sat there thinking, *We've only been a couple for a few hours and have already had our first fight.*

Chuck turned the massive armored walker toward the hole in the wall left by the monster's entrance. The bright desert sun shone in through the massive gap, which provided an easy exit from the huge underground chamber.

Kalwaers poured in by the hundreds. The audio sensors in the Walker relayed the clacking sound of their talons on the metal flooring and the chirps they used as rudimentary communication.

"Shall we?" Chuck asked, gesturing toward the gap with an outstretched hand.

John crawled back into his seat and began pulling the seatbelt harnesses tight about him. "Yeah, just give me a second," he said, still dazed by the events of the last few minutes. Shaking his head in disbelief, he began to repeat one short sentence over and over again. "Damn it."

Chuck manipulated the controls as though he'd done it a thousand times before, propelling the Walker forward, Kalwaers crunching under its massive feet.

John watched the view screen as they made their way to the gap, totally unfazed by the hundreds of bug-like creatures swarming around the Walker. The Kalwaers launched spiny quills from their tails in a desperate but vain attempt to bring down the metallic giant, and John couldn't help but smile at the futility of their efforts. It seemed to show a general lack of intelligence on their part. These beasts seemed to be nothing more than overgrown cockroaches, incapable of understanding when they were outmatched, just as a spider will square off against a sparrow who's about to eat it.

The Walker reached the hole in a handful of strides, and under Chuck's newly found expertise began a short ascent to the desert floor. Within moments they were free from the underground world that had nearly claimed John's life. Much had changed in the hours spent in that frightening place. John looked over at his friend wondering just how deep the transformation he'd seen in him went, and he wondered if

Chuck would he ever be the same again.

"O.K., I think we need to head that way," Chuck said, pointing out across the desert, its flat expanse broken here and there by what they now knew to be Kalwaer mounds. Streams of the insect creatures still poured out, racing across the desert to attack them.

"How do you know that?" John asked, then raised his hand dismissing the inquiry before Chuck could answer. "Never mind. I forgot. We now have with us the all-knowing and great Oz."

Chuck just smiled at his display. "You know, John, I might have taken offense at that if I weren't so damn smart."

John grinned back at his friend. At least he knew the old Chuck was still in there somewhere. He had just turned into a new and improved version.

"Actually," Chuck continued, "that's the way to the nearest city that I'm guessing is still inhabited. The robot from the life hutch was about three hundred years older than Nevak, so its databases were off by at least that much. Now that's not to say that Nevak's information was much better, but at least it's three hundred years newer. Should be interesting – this path will take us right back past the life hutch." Chuck said. Then he added, "Did you leave anything there that you need to pick up? Or maybe we could stop just in case you need to take a potty break."

John couldn't help but laugh out loud. Yes, Chuck was definitely still in there. And perhaps even a bit wittier than before, John thought. He would have to be on guard.

"The Meeting"

Eric and Altare raced across the plain headed for the life hutch. Here and there Kalwaers sprang from their dome-shaped mounds to sprint after them, only to be left in the dust as the tank blazed past.

"How much farther?" Eric asked.

"It should only be a few minutes now," Altare said. "Assuming nothing else gets in our way."

Her words turned out to be prophetic as the desert floor off to their left suddenly erupted. Sand burst into the air as a giant creature pushed its way to the surface.

"Hang on!" Altare yelled, swinging the tank wildly to the right to avoid dropping into the sinkhole. The tank slid sideways, churning the desert into a plume of dust that billowed out behind them.

Eric swung the turret around and began firing at the thing. It looked like a giant insect, somewhat akin to the Kalwaers, only much, much larger, easily topping seventy or eighty feet in height. Moving with amazing speed for something so large, it shot from the hole, launching itself after them.

The red laser beams struck against the creature's hard shell, dotting it with black scorch marks, but having little if any effect.

"This is bad!" Eric yelled to Altare. "Drive faster; it's catching us!"

"I'm going as fast as I can!" Altare called back, mashing the already depressed foot pedals even harder.

The beast loped along with its long spiny tail curling over its back like a scorpion. Giving it a quick shake, the creature shot out huge quills at the tank as it desperately wove its way toward the life hutch. Altare managed to avoid them by yanking the controls hard to one side, narrowly missing one of the Kalwaer mounds as she did so. The quills landed all about the tank, stabbing into the desert like giant steak knives.

"Use the main gun!" Altare yelled over at Eric, who was still futilely plugging away at the beast with the smaller laser turret.

"Hurry!"

Just then, one of the quills struck home, piercing the metal hide of the tank with a terrible screeching sound. The tank slowed immediately as though some part of its power supply had been hit. Altare screamed out in fear, wrestling to maintain control of the vehicle. Eric slapped the switch to arm the main gun and yanked the control yoke to target the beast, only to be greeted by an awful grinding sound and the realization that there was no movement at all from the turret.

"What the hell!" he yelled only seconds before the monster was upon them. A quick slap from one of its oversized legs sent the tank skittering sideways. Eric and Altare were left dazed by the assault. It was like being shaken inside a giant can.

Eric regained his senses just in time to see the thing raise an arm and bring it crashing down on top of the stalled tank. The ceiling of the vehicle collapsed under the weight of the blow, compressing the thick metal pilot's compartment by several feet, bringing the roof to within inches of the passengers' heads. The impact split the side of the tank open like a tin can, leaving Eric facing one of the monster's oversized feet.

"Altare!" Eric yelled, looking back over his shoulder. "We have to get out of here!" But his words fell on deaf ears. Altare had been knocked unconscious during the scuffle.

Eric crawled through the cockpit and began to wrestle with Altare's seat belt harness as the beast struck a second blow, this time squashing the compartment down to only a few feet in height. Luckily, Eric had managed to pull Altare part way out of her seat before the impact.

Dragging her across the subfloor toward the crack in the hull of the tank, Eric spied one of the view screens only moments before it flickered and went out completely. The screen showed another lumbering giant heading toward them. Eric's jaw hung slack in disbelief. He'd seen one of these monsters before, on top of the wall of the city. It had taken all of the city's combined strength to finally bring it down.

The giant robot strode toward their position at a full run, the ground shaking under its very approach.

"Oh no," Eric whispered while trying to shield Altare with his body. It was the last thing he had to offer his love for protection, and it would be over his dead body that these monsters would take her.

"Desert Dealings"

"What the hell's going on up there?" John asked, eyeing a huge dust cloud marring the otherwise tranquil desert horizon. Straining his eyes, he could see some large object protruding from the ground. Dozens of smaller dust plumes sped back and forth some distance away from the fray.

Chuck pushed several buttons. The view screen image scaled up several times, allowing them to make out the cause of the ruckus.

"Oh shit!" Chuck cursed. "Looks like another Bowarq."

"Bowarq?" John said back sneering at the sound of the word without taking his eyes off the monitor. "Now you're just making up names!"

Chuck didn't stop to respond to his friend's quip. Instead, he pushed the Walker into a sprint.

"Whoa there!" John yelled, grabbing hold of the seat arms. "What's the rush? Shouldn't we be going away from that thing, not right at it?"

Then he saw the object of the Bowarq's brutal attention. A battered tank lay at its feet, smoke billowing from its hindquarters while its turret was bent askew.

"Send some fire its way, John!" Chuck yelled. "We have to pull its attention off that tank!"

John grabbed the joystick as Chuck reached over and pushed several buttons on his control panel. Another view screen came to life and depicted a small targeting reticule.

"Alright, this is more like it!" John laughed, placing the targeting cursor on the midsection of the Bowarq who was raising his gnarled arm to strike the vehicle again. "Here goes nothing," John said as he pressed the red trigger.

Several rockets streaked toward the monster, twisting and spiraling as they went. Two struck home an instant before the creature completed its stroke. The explosion took the Bowarq by surprise, knocking it off balance and buying Chuck the few precious moments he needed to close the distance between themselves and the beast. But when he arrived, he found the

Bowarq quite ready for his attack, the rockets having only stunned the creature, leaving two large charred sections across its chest.

Leaping across the tank, Chuck plowed directly into the monster like a linebacker. Given that the Walker was roughly half the size of the Bowarq, this was no small undertaking. Luckily for Chuck and John, they carried enough inertia to send both themselves and the Bowarq to the ground.

John clung to the seat as they pitched into a shoulder roll, spinning several times before coming to a halt. Watching his view screen, he could see that the Bowarq had already righted itself and was roaring toward them.

Chuck pushed the Walker onto its arms just in time to receive a kick in the midsection. This beast was obviously much more intelligent than the Kalwaers who would only have leapt on top of Walker, biting and scratching in an attempt to get at the soft flesh of the passengers inside. No, this creature had evolved from a different line, one that had fighting instincts.

The kick lifted the Walker off the ground and sent it crashing down fifty feet away, jostling the pilots. They found themselves in nearly the same position as before, lying on their side with the Bowarq bum rushing them once again. John watched as it quickly filled his entire view screen.

Chuck cursed and wrestled with the controls. "What the hell's wrong with this thing!" he yelled, yanking on the control stick and slapping at various buttons on the control panel.

At the last possible second, with the Bowarq all but on top of them, John somehow found the presence of mind to press the fire button once again.

Three more rockets shot out, striking the creature at point blank range. Two rockets slammed into its chest while one struck its head. The concussion sent it sailing backward, landing flat on its back on the desert floor, smoke rolling from its midsection and head.

"What's the problem?" Chuck yelled, oblivious to the action that had just taken place. "The damn thing won't respond!"

Yanking the control sticks again and moving the foot pedals, he managed to roll the Walker onto its back and up into a seated position. He then fired the lift rockets, and in a moment, they were back on their feet, and not a moment too soon as the Bowarq had also gotten back to its feet, albeit much more slowly this time. A gaping hole marred its armored chest, bluish blood running freely from the wound. Apparently, the first set of rockets had cracked its armor while the second had actually penetrated it.

One of its three bug-like eyes had been damaged by the last attack and its head now tilted oddly to one side. It waited for a moment as if reevaluating its opponent, then made ready to charge.

The momentary pause in the Bowarq's battle plan proved to be its undoing as John launched a third and final volley from the rocket pod. In the same instant, Chuck cut loose a bright green beam from the arm-mounted lasers. The beam struck the creature in the already damaged chest, cutting clean through and passing out of its back. Only a split second later, the rockets crashed into nearly the same area. The Bowarq dropped where it stood, dead before it hit the ground.

The Kalwaers, who had been circling the area during the fight, some instinctual intelligence telling them to keep their distance while the Bowarq was alive, now started to move in. They seemed to have no such fear of the Walker.

Chuck reached over and tapped a single button on John's console, causing his view screen to change perspective to a viewpoint just above the top of the Walker's head.

"Try to keep them off the tank till we can see what's going on," Chuck said, propelling the Walker back into motion.

John spun back and forth, firing green beams in every direction from the head-mounted laser turret, popping Kalwaers like grapes as they approached from all sides.

Chuck brought the Walker to a stop next to the mangled and smoking battle tank. A large split ran down the side of the vehicle where the Bowarq had pummeled it.

"I'm going in," Chuck said, un-strapping himself and grabbing a laser rifle from the wall behind him. He then leapt into the access tube.

"Hey, wait a minute! You don't know what's out there!" John shouted after him.

"Keep those damn bugs off me!" Chuck called back as the outside hatch swooshed open.

"Shit!" John yelled, returning his attention to the view screen. In the time they'd taken to have their short exchange, several Kalwaers had approached to within a hundred feet. John began blasting away at them at a feverish pace.

"Just get your ass back here quick!" he yelled even though he knew Chuck was probably out of earshot already.

"You're on your own now, buddy," he said to himself as more Kalwaers began to appear from every direction.

Chuck scrambled down several rungs and leapt to the ground and into a roll. Hopping to his feet, he headed for the tank at a run. Glancing back over his shoulder, he quickly found why the Walker had been so hesitant to respond when trying to stand up during the battle. The left arm was totally missing from the shoulder down. When the creature had attacked them, its kick had been forceful enough to remove the limb entirely.

Reaching the incapacitated tank, Chuck peered inside warily.

"Wao canei sa lomaeat?" he yelled into the smoky interior. No answer came from inside.

"Wao canei sa lomaeat?" he called again more urgently. And this time a response came, though it was not quite the one he had expected. A laser pistol sprung from the dark interior of the tank, poking into his ribs.

"Shit!" Chuck said, lowering his own weapon.

"What? What did you say?" a voice called from within the tank.

Chuck lowered himself down and looked inside the damaged vehicle again, waving his hands to clear the smoke away. What he saw both took his breath away and somehow made him gasp at the same time. Eric was lying atop an alien form, nearly pressed flat by the crushed roof of the tank, a laser pistol dangling from his shaking hand.

Eric squinted and blinked through the smoke, poking his head toward Chuck while trying to hang on to consciousness.

"Well, you son a bitch," he croaked. "Who the hell taught you how to speak alien?"

Chuck reached into the mangled tank, grabbed Eric by the arm, and began to pull.

"Wait!" Eric moaned. "Get the girl first!"

Shocked by Eric's outburst, Chuck let go of him and began dragging the limp alien's form out from the tank's wreckage. She was a bit beaten up, but would certainly live, assuming he could get her to the Walker before the approaching Kalwaers managed to slip past John's barrage of lasers.

As soon as she was free from the tank, she came to and began coughing violently, expelling a lungful of smoke that she'd drawn in from the tank's smoldering interior.

"It's O.K.! You're going to be O.K.!" Chuck said in his newly acquired alien tongue. But to his surprise, the alien didn't seem remotely impressed by his mastery of her language. Instead, she began thrashing around, calling out "Eric! Eric!" while desperately trying to squirm from his grip and return to the tank.

"Well, that's gratitude for ya!" Chuck said, letting go of the skinny, wiggling alien girl.

He then grabbed hold of Eric and hauled him from the tank as well. Eric sputtered and coughed, his eyes rolling about in his head while the alien girl crouched close by, a worried look in her eyes.

"Eric!" she yelled again as Chuck plopped him down solidly onto the desert floor.

"He'll be fine," Chuck said to the Altare. "I think he's faking anyway." This time he didn't bother speaking in alien, as it was obvious that the creature before him could speak English.

"O.K., let's get moving!" Chuck said, standing up while retrieving the laser pistol that Eric had dropped while being pulled from the tank.

"Come on, guys, we need to move!" he yelled again, taking a couple of pot shots at the Kalwaers that had gotten a bit too close for comfort.

"Geez!" Eric barked, rolling onto his hands and knees. "Give me a damn minute, will ya! I'm mostly dead here!"

Chuck was about to say something smart-alecky when he looked down and saw tears streaming from Altare's eyes as she helped Eric up off the ground.

"Alright, alright," he said, easing up his tone a bit. "But we need to get moving, or we're all going to be dead."

Eric and Altare turned and began staggering toward the Walker. Upon seeing it, they both reeled in fear.

"Shoot it, Chuck!" Eric yelled, grabbing Altare and shoving her behind him. "Blast that thing before it kills us!"

Chuck watched the antics for a moment before speaking.

"What the hell are you doing?" he said sarcastically then pointed to the Walker. "Now get the hell in there before I have to shoot you myself."

Eric looked back and forth between the robot and Chuck. Altare didn't have any idea what to do.

"Move!" Chuck said finally, shoving his finger toward the Walker commandingly.

When Eric and Altare still hesitated, he leaned in a little closer and spoke through his teeth, "Move it, Sissy Boy!

This seemed to snap Eric out of his momentary dementia. He grabbed Altare by the hand and took off toward the Walker. Chuck followed along a few paces behind, firing laser blasts at Kalwaers all along the way.

Upon reaching the vehicle, Eric helped Altare onto the first rung. She climbed quickly, her slight form allowing her to move quite fast when she wanted to.

"That's it, help your girlfriend up," Chuck said, slapping Eric on the back as he began his ascent to the cockpit. Eric turned and gave Chuck a quick smile, surprising him.

"Wait a minute," Chuck said, stepping onto the first rung himself. "What's going on with you and that alien girl, Eric? I think you better start talking!"

"Just shut it, Chuck," Eric said, the smile showing easily in his voice. "You never did know when to keep quiet!"

Chuck just laughed and called one last time after his friend. "You just wait till I tell John!"

Eric didn't even turn around at the last comment, but Chuck knew he had heard him. And the whole idea made him quite happy. He'd found his old friend, rescued him and his girlfriend, and been able to *diss* him all in within the span of about two minutes.

Climbing into the cockpit, Chuck hopped into the driver's seat while John continued his grizzly task of blasting the attacking Kalwaers.

"They just keep coming, don't they?" he asked rhetorically, squeezing off burst after burst before adding, "What'd ya find, Chuck?"

"They reproduce very quickly," Altare said, taking John by surprise. He hadn't even noticed that she and Eric had entered the cabin. Turning around in his seat, he saw both of them standing there for the first time.

"Eric!" he yelled, his eyes wide with surprise, and upon seeing Altare, he added, "And a girl alien!" his voice going up and octave.

"Wow, that sounded really stupid, John," Chuck said, laughing. "You act like you thought you'd never see Eric boy again." Then he pointed at Altare. "Oh, and this is Altare, Eric's girlfriend."

John was stunned, a huge grin cutting across his face in the same instant that both Eric and Altare's faces turned a nice shade of red. "Girlfriend?" he said.

Altare and Eric just stood there looking uncomfortable until Chuck broke the awkward silence. "Hey, laser boy! Those critters out there are getting awfully close. And if enough of them hop on us, they may just be able to pull us down!"

Chuck knew he was telling a lie. The Kaelwars had no chance of toppling the huge Walker no matter how many of them bothered to pile on. But his ruse drew John's shocked stare back to the viewscreen, allowing Eric and Altare to relax a little. Chuck shot a quick wink at Eric who just shook his head and exhaled loudly.

Chuck sent the Walker forward at a quick pace, heading toward the city Altare and Eric had come from.

"How do you know our language?" Altare asked after several minutes of travel, and it had become obvious that they were relatively safe.

Chuck thought for a moment then spoke.

"Well, I had a little run-in with one of your people back there in Numaraq." Chuck said, pointing over his shoulder with his thumb. "And, well, to make a long story short, a character from your past history 'shared' a bit of himself with me."

Altare was stunned. "You spoke with someone from another city?"

"Well, not really spoke with, more like melded with," Chuck said while turning around in his seat. "You see, we found him in some kind of cryogenic suspension or something. And when we brought him out, he was in pretty bad shape. He managed to fix John up, but then things went downhill, and he ended up dying on us."

Eric and Altare were awestruck.

"You say he *melded* with you?" Eric asked. "What's that supposed to mean?"

Chuck shifted in his seat. "Well, just before he died, he put his hands on either side of my head and put some of himself, or his knowledge at least, into my head. So now I know lots of stuff about your people," Chuck said, looking over at Altare, then he added, "Or at least about how they used to be roughly a thousand years ago."

Altare's jaw dropped open as she mouthed the last few words Chuck had just spoken.

"What do you know?" she asked, accidentally slipping back into her native language.

Chuck smiled at her. "I know much about your technology and how it works. I know that your people nearly destroyed themselves a very short time before my friend Nevak was frozen. I know that when he came out of that suspension, the reason he died was that he was infected with the same plague that killed your ancestors. And I know that he was put there to act as a time capsule for future generations to teach you and your people about who they are and where they come from," he said, watching her intently. "And I know that he was meant to transfer this knowledge to one of your people, but unfortunately I was the only vessel that was available," Chuck finished, a gentle smile softening his face.

Altare sat silently, eyes wide with her hands pressed tightly together between her knees, a tear streaking down her face.

The rest of the journey back to the city was uneventful. No more Bowarqs were encountered along the way, and the Kalwaers that bothered to attack were quickly brushed aside as well. The group stayed pretty quiet, each one lost in his or her own thoughts. Eric chatted a little with John about what had happened with him, and John offered up some of the details of his and Chuck's adventure. But for the most part, everyone was just glad to be safe, at least for now.

"So, the teleporter's broken then?" Eric asked Chuck, breaking the silence.

"Yeah, I think so. But I think I may be able to fix it," Chuck returned. "Actually I think it will be pretty simple to repair."

John perked up at the exchange. "I thought you said you couldn't fix it!" he exclaimed, the words tumbling out of his mouth so fast that the entire sentence sounded like one long slurred word.

"Well, I seem to be remembering more as we go along. Kind of like the stuff is just now really starting to soak in," Chuck said.

"How so?" John asked.

"Well," Chuck started. "I think I know another couple of languages now, or at least some different dialects." He said, turning back to Altare. "Tell me if this means anything to you."

Chuck spoke a complete sentence that sounded very foreign to John and Eric, though totally different from the way Altare spoke when using her native tongue.

"I don't know much of what you just said, but pieces of it sound like one of our ancient languages," Altare said amazedly.

"Yeah, that's what I figured," Chuck said. "I've got lots to share with you and your people. There's so much you've missed because of the great wars."

"Yes!" Altare said, extremely excited by the idea. "I'm sure my father would love to speak with you. For that matter, everyone would love to hear what you know."

John looked up suddenly. "Just how long will all this take?" he asked, looking back and forth between Chuck and Altare. "I mean, aren't we going to be heading back home ASAP? I'm sure there's lots to share, but what about fixing the teleporter?"

Chuck laughed. "Well, I'm sure there will be plenty of time for fixing the teleporter. But there's so much to do now. These people are on the brink of an enormous disaster," he said and looked again at Altare. "I don't think you know this, but your city is really the only one left, and it's in grave danger of being overrun, as you already know."

"Yes, I know this," Altare said. "Perhaps with your help, we could rebuild our civilization. You could teach us about our technology and help us to develop new ones."

Altare glowed at the idea. Her people had been in decline for so long that any hope of a better future nearly brought her to tears.

Eric just smiled at their exchange, watching Altare as she conversed with Chuck. The way her eyes flashed in the light when she was excited, the way she had befriended him and helped him to find his friends even under the threat of great peril to herself. The fact that she accepted him for who he was. And finally and most importantly, the idea that she might love him, regardless of his history or his shortcomings. She knew who he was inside in a way no one else before ever had.

In an instant, he made a decision that would mark the rest of his life. Only a second later, he smiled at the thought of it.

A word from John broke into Chuck and Altare's excited conversation.

"Hey, I think I see something on the horizon." He said.

"Looks like your city," he added, turning back to Altare.

"Yes, indeed it is," Altare said, a bit of worry coming through in her voice.

"What's the problem?" Eric asked, sensing that something was wrong.

"I fear that my people will misjudge us as an enemy and will fire upon us," Altare said. "And the city's defensive turrets will also attempt to repel us."

"I think I can take care of the defenses," Chuck said while punching a series of buttons on a nearby control panel. Several cryptic codes flashed across the view screen in bright red colors. A handful of keystrokes later, the codes turned green.

"That should do it for the turrets," he said. "But we're going to need to let them know that we're not bad guys somehow," he added, pushing several more buttons causing the view screen image to magnify several times, showing dozens of alien soldiers streaming from access tunnels and taking positions along the wall. "Or those boys on top of the wall are going to light us up. Any ideas?" he asked, slowing the Walker to crawl.

"I have an idea," Altare offered, stepping up next to Chuck. She began punching away at the control panel herself, then after completing a particular sequence she leaned back. The view screen showed a blinking antenna-like symbol that looked to Chuck and John just like the symbol they'd seen in the life hutch. The beacon flashed for a handful of seconds until suddenly, the screen was filled with Dr. Arcos's visage. He was half clad in armor and was obviously preparing to go into battle.

"Father!" Altare yelled out in her native tongue.

Arcos's face registered first surprise, then wonder as he spotted not only one human, but two others clustered closely around his daughter.

"Where are you?" he called to her. "I have been sick with worry." He added, shaking his head. "You took a battle tank!" he sputtered, overcome by the knowledge that his daughter was still alive. Lowering his head as he wept as he spoke again. "We thought you had been lost to the desert creatures."

Altare was moved by her father's show of emotion.

"I am sorry, Father," she said. "But I am well. Eric and I

have the other humans with us. We are in the robot that even now approaches the city."

Arcos collected himself quickly, a wrinkle creasing his brow as he digested the information Altare was imparting to him. "You say you are in the robot?"

"Yes, Father," Altare said. "Tell the warriors there is no need to attack us."

"But what about the automatic turrets?" Arcos asked.

Chuck leaned toward the view screen. "I've taken care of those, sir."

Arcos shot a bewildered look at this as yet unknown human. "What?" he asked befuddled.

"Just have your men stand down," Chuck said, this time using Arcos's own language, just to be extra clear. This made Arcos's eyes and mouth both open wide.

"So be it," he said as he turned away from the view screen and began barking orders toward an unseen lieutenant.

"O.K., then," Chuck said. "Let's go before we attract any more attention out here. Wouldn't want to have anything big come by while those turrets are offline."

Luckily, they had reached the city at one of the rare times when a Kalwaer attack was not underway. The Kalwaers usually began their assaults in the early morning, attacking all day until nightfall, but there were rare occasions when they would go to ground and showed no signs of activity for days at a time.

Approaching the wall, the soldiers stood with laser rifles leveled at them, watching for any false move. Arcos had spread the word, but the city's defenders were very suspicious of letting a giant robot Walker stomp its way to within kicking distance of their wall.

Luckily, their advance on the city went smoothly, bringing them to a spot where the head of the Walker was nearly level with the top of the wall.

"Here goes nothin'," Chuck spouted as he hopped up from his seat and slithered into the small access tube. The rest of the group followed close behind, each one popping through the tube and stepping out on the massive armored shoulders of the Walker.

A great number of soldiers stood with rifles at the ready as the small crew faced them. A moment of silence passed while the soldiers waited for a sign that everything was O.K.

"Here comes Arcos," Eric whispered to Altare as he saw the doctor running toward the wall through one of the many clear access passages. But before Arcos could reach the wall and address the soldiers, Chuck stepped forward, raising his arms like a prophet addressing his people from atop a mountain.

"Gawi, Jan, Gawi," he began. "Kiljuop thawn grano. Kiljuop wo tosap!" he called out, shaking his hands in the air.

A pivotal moment passed as Chuck stood there, arms still raised, his head bobbing atop his neck, as he looked up and down the line of soldiers.

Eric shot an inquiring glance at John as if to ask what the hell their friend had just said. But his question was answered quickly enough as a bark-like giggle burst from one of the soldiers standing close by a laser turret. Another chortle discharged from a soldier some distance down the line on the other side. Then the entire wall erupted in laughter, and howling guffaws brought some of the soldiers almost to their knees while others just shook their heads, smiles washing the grim looks from their faces.

John and Eric looked on in awe, while Altare rolled her eyes.

"What the hell did you say?" John said, at last, watching as the laughing soldiers lowered their weapons, some of them clapping or pumping closed fists into the air.

In response, Chuck grabbed his two best friends, each one by a shoulder and said. "Who would have known it! I guess our old friend Nevak was a comedian!"

Then just as quickly, he turned and headed back into the access portal on the side of the Walker's head.

"Come on, they're waiting for us!" he called just before disappearing into the tube.

John looked over at Eric. "What just happened?" he asked as the soldiers began funneling their way down from the wall and into the city once again.

"I don't know," Eric returned. "But it looks like we can go in," he said, grabbing Altare by the elbow and turning toward the hatch as well.

John followed, feeling somewhat befuddled by the slew of events and revelations that had taken place within the last hour. He began to wonder what all this meant for his chances of heading back home anytime soon.

Once they were firmly seated back in the cockpit of the Walker, Chuck fired the rear-mounted lifter rockets and performed a short hop over the wall, landing firmly in the center of a courtyard on the other side. Dozens of aliens had already amassed as hundreds more made their way there upon getting word of the strange events taking place.

Chuck was all too happy to exit the Walker. Climbing down the rungs one at a time, he stopped every now and then to turn and wave at the gathering crowd. John, Eric, and Altare followed, swept along by the tide of events.

Upon reaching the ground, Chuck began talking to the aliens in their native tongue. Grabbing the first one he saw and hugging him close. The alien wore a startled look as Chuck nearly squeezed the air out of him, then moved on to the next in line, offering greetings as he went. The whole scene seemed like that of a war hero returning home after an extended stay in another country.

Arcos appeared in the crowd and hurriedly made his way to the group. Altare clenched her jaw tightly at the sight of him, anticipating the trouble she was in for making off with the tank. But Arcos was far too interested in this new alien-speaking human to bother chastising her at this time. He simply gave her a quick hug and an accusing wag of his finger before moving on to Chuck.

Within minutes of getting there, all four of them were spirited off to a secure building where they could be debriefed. The crowd quickly dispersed, all of them excitedly talking about the "outlanders" in their midst and what that might mean for them. They also puzzled over how the one human, in particular, seemed to know so much about them and their history.

The next few days were spent shuttling back and forth to various meetings with high-ranking officials and VIPs. Chuck did all of the talking essentially since John didn't really have anything to offer other than his own story of survival in the desert. Of course, how could he rate against the likes of Chuck? His friend was exploding with information about the people of this planet. He knew about their technologies, their history, and was even beginning to be able to selectively read minds just as they could. It was very apparent that John wouldn't really have a place in this society, at least not in the same capacity as Chuck.

Eric and Altare visited with him when they could, but Altare was also very interested in learning what she could from Chuck and his stories of the past. Training sessions were set up to allow Chuck to pass some of his inherited knowledge to the scientists and inventors in the city. His mastery of their technology was nearly absolute. He began disassembling complex machinery and reprogramming items to better serve the current needs of the city dwellers, all to the amazement of the aliens. They stood around him in tight circles, taking notes, mental and otherwise, trying to absorb as much of the information as they could.

Chuck shared everything with them, freely giving whatever knowledge he had to anyone who was interested. It rapidly became clear that he was an invaluable asset to them, and that it would be years before anyone would even come close to mastering the knowledge that he had accumulated in those few short moments with Nevak. Unfortunately for the aliens, he was unable to fully understand what had transpired between himself and Nevak well enough to offer the same experience to them.

In the meantime, Eric and Altare were joined at the hip. Eric had started giving military training sessions to the soldiers under the watchful eye of Geopre. Altare would help out with translations that the "Squawk box" translator (as Eric had come to call it) would have difficulties with.

Even more important than the training was the blossoming love between them. John had never in his life seen Eric so happy. The pained expression he had worn for so many years was long gone, replaced by an easy smile born of the overriding happiness he had with Altare. That was something Eric had never had back on Earth, and John could tell from his friend's sidelong glances that he had no intention of ever leaving this place for home. In fact, it seemed that this alien planet offered more solace to him than his life on Earth ever had.

John asked about using one of the few remaining teleporters to return home but was told that the prospect was entirely too dangerous as so little was known about how to use them properly. He was also told that sending one out to be lost once again was unthinkable. They had spent too many years watching for and trying to retrieve the handful of units still in existence that letting one go now would be folly. This news did little to lighten John's mood. The last thing he needed was to be told that he would be a captive here forever.

There was much to see and learn, but John had to do most of it alone. He'd been given one of the speech translators, but after the first couple of days, few individuals wished to speak with him. One or two would stop him as he passed by to ask a question, but their smiling faces would quickly turn somber when they found that they'd gotten the "wrong" human. John would just smile and tell them where Chuck could be found and that he was sure he would love to answer their questions.

He became more of an oddity to them, rambling about in a culture he couldn't understand, wishing only to go home and see Runt again. But the idea of returning to his previous life just made things worse. If he went back now, he would lose the two people in the world who he needed the most right now. Eric and Chuck had been his friends since childhood, and the thought of leaving them here for a cold empty house back in Jackson made his shoulders slump in sorrow. He'd already lost Sarah, the one person who really made him feel complete, and if he went home now, he wouldn't even have a shoulder to cry on.

Thoughts of Sarah sent him heading back to his chamber at a quick pace, passing by dozens of silent, staring aliens. He was still very new to them, much like an animal at the zoo, something to be examined and scrutinized.

Reaching his apartment, John entered quickly then closed the door behind him. He was spending more time than ever cooped up between these four walls. He even began longing for the time he'd spent with Chuck in the ancient underground city.

Perhaps if he'd given it a bit more time, he would have found a way to deal with his new condition, but instead, he fell into a deep depression. Days would pass without him ever leaving his room. Someone would always come by to bring him food, but his appetite was gone. Eric and Chuck stopped by when they could, but they were both incredibly busy elsewhere, and by the time they'd taken note of John's condition, it was too late.

Eric, Altare, and Chuck did what they could, but it seemed that John had given up. The one-two punch of first losing his wife and now his friends was more than he could take. He grew thin and pale within weeks, eating only enough to barely stay alive. His will to live had been broken.

Chuck met with Arcos and the Elder Council to try to convince them to give up a teleporter to allow his friend to return home but to no avail. They would not be budged. Their fear of one of the units falling into the wrong hands once on Earth overrode any sympathy they had for John's condition. Chuck understood their concern. The teleporters were the most powerful devices the alien race had ever constructed. And as Chuck now knew, they were far more powerful than even the Elders understood.

Eric sat with John when he could, telling stories about their time together as children, recalling events both happy and sad in an attempt to draw John back from the bleak edge on which he teetered. Altare would stand at the back of the room while Eric talked to his friend, wondering what she might do to help.

John's thoughts seeped from his troubled head and into hers. Many times she would have to leave the room for fear of crying, an event she imagined would only make matters worse.

Eric even resorted to trying to steal one of the teleporters for John but found that they were kept under heavy guard at all times. Stealing the tank had been child's play compared to what it would take to get one of the units. And in the meantime, John continued his self-induced downward spiral.

"Sarah"

"Wake up, John," Sarah called out in her playful voice. "Where are you? Come out, come out wherever you are," she spoke again, each word sliding off her tongue like honey.

John awoke to find a vision before him. Sarah floated inches off the ground, clad in a white robe, white light dancing around her like a halo. John pinched himself hard, trying to wake up from the dream, but still, she remained. Squeezing his eyes shut hard, he began rubbing them with the backs of his hands. But upon opening them again, he found her there, just as before, watching him.

"Are you done trying to get rid of me, my love?" she asked gently.

John sat up in bed, looking around the room. His eyes registered that he was still in the alien city, still in the chamber he'd been holed up in for the last few weeks.

"I don't want to get rid of you," he whispered, pulling the blankets up under his chin, his lower lip beginning to quiver uncontrollably. "I don't know how to live without you."

"You have your friends," she said. "They are here for you, John. They've always been here for you," she added, tipping her head forward slightly as she spoke.

"It's not the same, Sarah," John said, tears running down his face as he spoke her name. "They've got other lives now. Lives that I'm not a part of."

Sarah furrowed her brow questioningly as if to ask, "How so?"

"Chuck is different, and Eric has a lover. They've got some purpose here. And all I can think of is how much I miss you," John said, grinding his teeth together all through his last sentence.

"Oh, I see," Sarah said slowly, looking down at the ground. After a few moments' pause, she looked up and met John's gaze, a gentle smile breaking across her face like a new morning sun. "Then perhaps you should come home to me."

John's eyes went wide as tears streamed down both cheeks.

He let slip the cover from under his chin, allowing the thick blanket to slide down into his lap. She could see how the many weeks without food or sleep had left him emaciated and weak.

"I'm trying to, Sarah," he whispered out through clenched teeth. "I'm trying to come to you."

"Your Wish"

For John, the next day dawned with a knock on his chamber door. Stirring himself up from his troubled sleep, he wrestled with whether or not even to answer.

"Yes?" he called out, pushing himself up in bed and wrapping his blanket tightly around his midsection.

"Can we come in?" Chuck called from the other side of the door. John really wanted no visitors, but even in his current state, he couldn't bring himself to deny the two people who had known him the longest.

"Come in," he croaked, reaching for a glass of water sitting on his bed stand and taking a small sip.

The chamber door slid open, revealing Chuck, Eric, and Altare. The three stepped quickly into the room, allowing the hatch to snap shut behind them. Chuck and Eric walked over to John's bed, surveying his condition.

"What?" John half barked at them. "You don't look so great either."

"Well now," Chuck said, smoothing his hair back with one hand. "We both know that's not true."

John couldn't help but grin at Chuck's little joke.

"What's up?" he asked, tipping his head back while poking his nose toward his two best friends. "You guys need something or just coming by to make me feel worse?"

"Let's beat the hell out him," Eric said, punching a balled up fist repeatedly into his other hand. "I think he really deserves it."

John grinned openly now as he looked back and forth between the two men. It was a weak smile, considering his condition, but it warmed his heart a little nonetheless.

"Alright, alright," Chuck said, placing a hand on Eric's wrist. "We probably don't need to kick his ass just yet."

Sitting down on the edge of the bed, John could see that Chuck's eyes had gone a bit watery.

"You O.K.?" John asked.

Chuck shook his head back and forth, and John thought he

saw a tear squeeze out from the corner of his friend's eye.

"Yeah, I'm doing great," Chuck said, this time nodding his head up and down. "But you know, I've got this friend who's in trouble."

"Who's that?" John said with all honesty, wondering who Chuck could be talking about.

Chuck reached out suddenly and grabbed hold of John's forearm.

"I think you know who I'm talking about, buddy," he said, the tears flowing freely now.

Eric sat down on the other side of the bed, his face pale and his jaw muscles squeezed tight.

John looked back and forth between the two of them, his own resolve beginning to crumble.

"You know," he said at last. "I just want to go home to Sarah."

Eric choked back tears, wiping at his eyes with one hand.

"You know what I'm talking about, don't you, man?" John said, looking over at his friend.

Eric looked up at John, then over at Altare who stood against the wall by the door, tears staining her delicate features.

"Yeah, man, I know," he said. "I know." He looked over at Chuck and nodded.

Chuck leaned back and drew in a deep breath. John noticed the unspoken exchange.

"What's up?" he asked, watching as Chuck reached into his pocket. "You gonna shoot me or something?"

Chuck drew a familiar object out from under his jacket, and John eyed the device that had brought him to where he was today. The teleporter glinted in the morning sunlight as Chuck turned it over and over again in his hands.

"You know," Chuck began. "These things aren't really all that hard to fix," he said, holding the unit up and examining it closely.

John watched him closely, touched by the idea that his friends would give him the chance to return to Earth.

"That's great," John said at last. "But you know what? I don't know what I'd have to go home to," he added, wiping at his running nose with the blanket, his eyes red ringed from crying by this point.

"Well, just think about it," Chuck said, laying the teleporter in John's lap.

He stood up and turned toward the door, followed closely by Eric.

Just before reaching the portal, Chuck turned back to John.

"Oh, by the way, there's a little more to those things than anyone of us really knew," he said. "See that little button with the wavy lines on it?"

"Yeah?" John said, looking at the unit.

"Well, if you push that, you'll find its set to a particular date that might have some meaning for you. You see, that thing doesn't just send you to the location you pick, it also sends you to *when*," Chuck said, chewing on his lower lip.

John pushed the button Chuck had indicated and read the date at the base of the small view screen. It did indeed have special meaning to John, who immediately looked up at his friends, nodding vigorously. "Yeah, that's a biggy," he said, not even trying to wipe his tears away.

"Yup, thought you might think so. That's a little tidbit that I got from Nevak. The folks here don't have any idea that the teleporters can do that. And I think it might just stay our little secret," Chuck said through his own tears before turning toward the door once again. "We're gonna go now, man. We'll see you later, alright?"

John was beyond speaking. All he could do was nod as his friends left the room. Just as the hatch was sliding shut, Eric turned back around, holding out a clenched fist to his good friend. It was the only way he knew how to say goodbye.

"Dinner"

John looked down at his watch. It read 5:38 p.m.

"Why do you keep looking at your watch?" Sarah asked. "You expecting company or something?"

"No, nothing like that," John said, "Just thinking about old friends."

"Oh," Sarah said, turning in her seat. "Hey, I heard this great joke today at work, you're gonna love this one. You'll be telling everyone in the office tomorrow, and you better give me credit!" she said while unbuckling her seat belt and shifting onto one hip to get a better look at Johns' face.

She couldn't wait to tell him and wanted to see his expression when she did. She began to tell the joke when she noticed that John seemed preoccupied.

"What's up?" she asked. "You're acting very strange tonight, my little man. Are you up to something?" she added, leaning in close and whispering the last few words into John's ear.

"No, not at all," John said as they approached a fork in the road. "Just keeping my eyes on my driving."

"Oh," Sarah said, plopping back down into her seat, forgetting about her joke for the moment. "Well, that's probably not a bad idea. It's pretty icy out here."

The road began to slope off to the right a short distance in front of them.

John checked his watch again.

"What's up with you and that watch?" Sarah asked again, grabbing at his arm and reading the numbers off the timepiece.

"Is 5:42 a big deal somewhere? If you thought we were going to be late for the movie then we should've gone to my parents for dinner like I wanted in the first place," she said, turning the corner of her mouth up into a little sneer.

John smiled as they approached the turnoff that headed into town.

"You know what?" he said guiding the car to the left and onto the road that led to Sarah's parents' house, avoiding the icy curve winding its way off to the right and into the city. "Why don't we go to your parents for dinner tonight instead of seeing a movie? I bet they'd just love to see us."

"You jerk!" Sarah barked. "You've been planning this all along, haven't you?" she yelled while slapping John on the leg playfully.

"For a while now," John said, "I've been planning it for a quite a while."

The End

63201533R00155

Made in the USA
Middletown, DE
25 August 2019